Michael Simpson is married to Ellen and lives in Cambridgeshire with his children, Evelyn, Rory and Max. He only started writing during lockdown and *The Devil's Ferryman* is his debut novel.

Michael has been a secondary school teacher for over sixteen years and he teaches physical education, history and sociology.

In his spare time, Michael enjoys keeping fit, playing football and spending time with his family.

Michael Simpson

THE DEVIL'S FERRYMAN

AUSTIN MACAULEY PUBLISHERS™

LONDON * CAMBRIDGE * NEW YORK * SHARJAH

A CIP catalogue record for this title is available from the British Library.

ISBN 9781398493896 (Paperback)
ISBN 9781398493902 (ePub e-book)

www.austinmacauley.com

First Published 2022
Austin Macauley Publishers Ltd®
1 Canada Square
Canary Wharf
London
E14 5AA

Thank you to Stewart Simpson for inspiring me to love reading.

Chapter 1
Prey

Night was closing in. The flickering courtyard light was fighting a losing battle against the shadows that grew menacingly on the concrete walls of the old tenement. The faint glow illuminated the decaying building that stood like an empty shell against the horizon. Tentacles of graffiti were sprawled across the walls like a fluorescent foliage that had suffocated all life from within. A dog barked but aside from that, it was eerily quiet. The people inside the building did not want to draw the attention of the devils that inhabited the courtyard below.

The pack leader looked up as if sensing movement. He had chosen his vantage point with the experience of a seasoned hunter. From here he could survey the dilapidated urban jungle that he considered his territory. He was perched imperiously on the highest concrete step before the crumbling stairs twisted into the innards of the estate. He reached out and drained the last dregs from his beer can. The bitter taste reacted with the bile in his stomach, and he paused momentarily as it surged up his throat, before regaining his composure and hurling the empty can into the courtyard below. He was only in his early forties, but years of alcohol and substance abuse had ravaged his body and aged him prematurely. He wiped his mouth fastidiously, rubbing his fingers over the decaying stumps of his front teeth until his hand clasped at the rubbery skin at the base of his neck. The euphoric effects of his last hit were wearing off and he was beginning to feel paranoid and agitated. It annoyed him that he was always short of money. That no good whore of a girlfriend seemed to spend his money like it was going out of fashion. Perhaps it was time to get rid of her.

There was a faint crunching sound in the distance, as if someone had stepped on a broken bottle. There was definitely someone out there. He stared intently in the direction of the sound, but it was too dark. He looked down at his three acolytes, who were sprawled out in a drug fuelled stupor in the courtyard below.

Batkin with his long greasy hair swept back, was focussed on tying a grubby tourniquet round his bicep in an effort to raise blood veins to the surface of the skin, which would make it easier to inject a needle. He clearly was oblivious. Randall and Taylor, still teenagers were both in a vegetated state, each clutching a bottle and propped up only by an old mattress. They too had heard nothing.

The pack leader was called Baldock. Once upon a lifetime ago, he had been a rugby player. He had very nearly been offered a professional contract but his penchant for fast booze, drugs and promiscuous women had put paid to that profession. His face, he knew, was terrifying, but he was still physically impressive and the neighbourhood cowed in his presence. It gave him a thrill to bully others. If people didn't do what he wanted, he would pulverise them into submission.

"Wake up, fuckers," he hissed impatiently. All three of his subordinates heard and responded in an instant. Batkin dropped the tourniquet and the two teenagers jerked upwards and sat bolt upright, anxious not to disappoint their alpha. "There's someone out there."

Baldock pointed over in the direction of the sound. No-one in their right mind would be out on their own at night in this part of the city. It was a soulless place. The few remaining businesses had been closed hours earlier and their premises would have been reinforced by stainless steel security screens and iron bars. There was an illegal betting shop a few streets away but that was owned by the McGovern crime family and patrons were off limits to the street gangs.

The pack did not try to hide as the sound grew louder. The barbed wire fence that enclosed the estate meant people could not see in, particularly at night while anyone in the courtyard had a perfect viewpoint to watch intruders.

It was definitely a person. A human shape stumbled into view. They were wearing a black hood pulled tightly over their head and seemed to be inebriated. Baldock smiled wickedly. Easy pickings.

With a deft flick of his hand, he instructed Randall and Taylor to sweep around the tenement and come round the back of the intruder. He gestured for Batkin to come with him. They would cut him off down the main street and force him to take one of the narrow alleyways with no exit. From there it would be easy. The four men would easily overpower the stranger and then it would be a simple matter of slitting his throat and taking whatever riches he had on him.

The intruder picked up his pace as if he sensed the danger. Baldock vaulted over the concrete fence with the power and agility of an athlete, to land

8

impressively on the adjoining pavement. Batkin carried on up the street in a classic pincer movement. Black hood looked up. There was an instant when there seemed to be a resigned acceptance to the situation, before he sharply turned and sprinted for safety. Baldock grinned. He followed at a leisurely pace behind, conserving his energy for the coup de grace. Batkin jumped out of a gateway to surprise the intruder, who turned agilely into the nearest alleyway.

"We've got the bastard now," growled Baldock to no-one in particular. Black hood ran down the alley but there was no escape. A huge brick wall blocked the way. He paused to catch a breath and was about to turn before Taylor crashed into him, propelling him backwards into a collection of bins. Black hood, his body crumpled on the floor, instinctively clutched his hands to his face and began to sob.

The pack closed in with Baldock taking the dominant position in the centre. "You must have a death wish," he said his voice dripping with contempt. "This is my estate. No-one comes here at night unless I say so. Your life is mine scum, unless you give up everything you've got."

Black hood's sobbing became louder and more guttural. Baldock shook his head in disgust. "Did you hear me, punk? Wallet first then jewellery and phones. Don't make out like you ain't got nothing." He kicked the intruder's outstretched leg angrily.

Batkin pulled on Baldock's shirt. His face was illuminated by the dim glow of a solitary street light to reveal grotesque liver spots that covered his entire face. "Let me deal with him," he pleaded, drawing Baldock's attention to the dirty serrated knife in his pocket.

Baldock was about to answer when his attention was caught by black hood who was still on the floor. His guttural screams had intensified and were seemingly sending convulsions throughout his entire body. He was about to unleash another kick to quieten him up, when black hood sat up drawing his legs into his midriff and rocked back and forwards, still emitting his high-pitched shrieks. Baldock paused and then suddenly, the slow realisation began to dawn on him. Black hood was not crying, he was laughing. It was a laugh that he, nor any of his pack had heard before, but it was definitely a laugh, and it was clearly at their expense.

The pack instinctively stepped backwards. There was something unnatural about this person, convulsing in a fit of shrieking hysterics on the floor. Batkin stepped nervously forward, uncertain how to proceed. He looked at Baldock for guidance, but Baldock had nothing to offer. Batkin waved his knife tentatively at black hood but there was no authority in the gesture. "Shut the fuck up you freak," he hissed uncertainly, but this only seemed to intensify black hood's amusement at the situation.

"Who are you?" said Baldock, making a conscious effort to make his voice sound decisive. "You'd better answer me, or I'll cut out your eyes."

The threat lingered in the atmosphere like a dirty fog that enveloped black hood. He stopped laughing and took a deep breath, before bringing both hands to the top of his forehead and pulling down his hood. His face was covered by his pale hands and cloaked in shadow.

"I am the devil's ferryman, Baldock, you son of a bitch and it's time for you to answer for your sins." His voice was shrill and sinister.

Baldock felt a very palpable chill descend down his spine at mention of his name. He was uncharacteristically speechless, and his obvious fear infected the others. Randall and Taylor contorted their faces in bewilderment at the bizarre response. Batkin took another step forward, but his gaze was still glued on Baldock, pleading desperately for a decision. It was then that black hood made his move.

With the athleticism and savagery of a starving feral dog, he sprang forward and kicked Batkin to the ground. He reached into his pocket and whipped out a huge knife that glinted in the feeble streetlight. Batkin was winded by the power of the blow and barely had time to raise his arms, before black hood's hands flashed, and the blade severed his carotid artery. For a second no-one reacted and time seemed to stand still. Batkin's eyes widened in amazement and he groped frantically to plug the wound, but it was no use. A crimson torrent of bright red blood cascaded down his neck and saturated his clothes in an instant. Batkin jerked momentarily like a fish out of water before his body went still in an expanding dark pool.

Baldock stepped forward instinctively, but black hood sensed the movement. His mouth stretched ominously into a cavernous smile in anticipation, but the rest of his face was still concealed by the darkness. Baldock felt defenceless against this dark energy that black hood emitted. He glanced at Randall and Taylor who were frozen motionless in terror. He fumbled desperately for the knife in his pocket, but black hood was on him in an instant. Baldock swung a colossal punch at his target, but black hood stepped nimbly inside and drew his weapon back. Time seemed to stand still and Baldock was astonished to see his petrified face reflected in the blade as it arched towards his face and plunged into the cavity of his right eye. For a split second there was nothing. Then the pain came and it was like a molten explosion that ripped through his entire face. Baldock reached up to cradle the ruined remnants of his eye and felt his legs give way. He stumbled in a foul smelling pool that reeked of urine. His senses had taken leave and he pawed desperately at a brick wall in the hope it would open up to salvation. He heard two intermittent screams that must have been from Randall and Taylor but nothing in his mind would compute and the view from his good eye was obscured by the blood that covered his face. He slipped and fell head first into the rancid puddle. He heard footsteps behind him, and he stumbled to his feet, raising both hands in supplication.

"Please," he wailed incoherently. "Take my wallet. You can have anything. Don't kill me." The footsteps were almost upon him and Baldock braced himself for the pain. How had it come to this?

Black hood leaned down and pulled Baldock up towards his face. Baldock was a big man, but the action was effortless. Baldock squinted from his good eye. He didn't want to see his assailant. That would surely be his death warrant.

"Look at me," demanded black hood. Baldock tried to shake his head but the force of the dynamic presence in front of him was enough for him to tentatively prise open his good eye.

Batkin shuddered. The eyes in front of him did not look like they belonged to any creature on this planet. They were quite dead in every sense.

Black hood laughed and dropped Baldock unceremoniously in the reeking puddle. He drew his blood soaked knife slowly towards his face and grinned wickedly. "Now is the time for you to pay your dues."

The bloodcurdling screams that Baldock made could be heard from the tenements.

Detective Inspector Jimmy Nicholls drained the dregs of his latte and took a long final puff of his last cigarette, before exhaling a grey plume of smoke out of the small gap in the driver side window. He popped off the lid of his roadside cup and extinguished the dying embers of the cigarette in the foam that had accumulated in the bottom. It was his ritual, caffeine and nicotine before submerging himself in the decaying corpses of London's murder victims. He was twenty-six years old and already the darling of the media due to a string of murder cases that he had solved almost single-handedly the last year. "Nickem Nicholls" was the nickname that had been emblazoned in the one of the local papers, after he had successfully caught a man who had killed and then raped a young lady in a city park. Nicholls was a shy man. He didn't particularly enjoy being in the spotlight, but he was ruthlessly determined to catch killers and protect the public. It was his calling, his unique purpose in life.

He had parked his silver BMW a stone's throw from the alleyway where the murders had taken place the previous evening. The road had been closed off and there was a banner of translucent crime scene tape across the entrance that was resolutely protected by two well-built police constables.

"Are you ready for, this old man?" he grinned sardonically at his passenger. "I heard the killers did a real number on Baldock and his cronies. Might be a bit too much for your sensitive stomach."

His passenger Kevin Page took an overexaggerated breath of exasperation at his younger partner. "Easy sir," he laughed raising both hands in a gesture of supplication. "I've seen things that would make your blood curdle. Don't worry about me."

"But I do worry, Kev," joked Nicholls. "You're getting on a bit now and with your dodgy ticker…" He left the last sentence unfinished to see if Page would rise to the bait.

Detective Sergeant Kevin Page sighed and turned away. He was forty-eight years old. He had been Nicholls' partner for the last few years and the pair had developed a close bond. He was short and rotund with two cheeks like heavy bags of cement. His complexion was similar to that of boiled ham and he had crow's feet wrinkles that rippled out from the corner of both eyes. His wispy grey hair was heavily receding and combed over in an unflattering attempt to conceal the prominent bald spots on the top of his head.

Jimmy Nicholls on the other hand was well-built and handsome. He had a sharp, distinguished nose and chiselled good looks. His chestnut black hair was slicked back and shone imperiously when it caught the light. He also had the confidence of a young man in the prime of life who had sped up the ranks of the police force at lightning speed and was seemingly destined for a great future ahead of him.

They were both part of murder team seven in the Metropolitan Police's Homicide and Serious Crime Command Unit. Page had arrived shortly into Nicholls' first year as a detective. He had been transferred from a department in Yorkshire after splitting with his wife and requesting a move away. It was a subject that Page did not seem to want to talk about so Nicholls left it well alone.

The pair had been assigned to work together and Page had instinctively seemed to take an almost paternal duty of care towards Nicholls. It was probably a combination of natural ability and Page's tutelage that helped Nicholls to learn his trade and flourish as a young detective. Nicholls had shown a real aptitude for detective work from the start. He had a sharp, analytical mind, insatiable energy levels and a gut instinct that was nearly always right. Page was quiet and dogmatic with a wicked sense of humour. They complimented each other well and the pair quickly developed a reputation as formidable detectives. However, whereas Nicholls was young and ambitious, Page seemed quite content to stay on the same rung of the career ladder and it wasn't long before Nicholls outranked him. There were eight murder teams in total although murder team seven had gained a reputation for a calculated methodological approach and always seemed to be assigned the more complex cases.

The murder teams were led by detective superintendent Daniel Bircham. It had been Bircham's decision to promote Nicholls and make him the lead detective, despite his youth and inexperience. It had proved to have been a very pragmatic decision as Nicholls has marshalled his colleagues with all the expertise of a senior detective and his leadership had been instrumental in galvanising the unit into one of the top performing murder investigations teams in the entire city of London.

They had received a call at precisely eight-fifteen in the morning about the murders and the Met's specialist homicide assessment team (HAT) had arrived earlier to secure the scene. It was now ten past nine and after a brief delay in the capital's tumultuous traffic, Jimmy was anxious to get stuck in.

"Seriously are you ready Kev?" he enquired meekly in a gesture of conciliation after his earlier jibes. "This could be a drug war." It was well known that Baldock was a petty drug runner in the area. "We need to be all over this from the start, or more people could die on our watch."

"I'm with you Sir. Lead the way" responded Page sarcastically.

The two men stepped out of the car and walked towards the crime scene. To causal observers they looked an odd pair. Page with his overweight, diminutive stature, struggled to keep up with the confident strides of the powerfully built Nicholls and looked almost comical as he tried desperately to stay with him. The two police constables nodded grimly at the detectives and one of them removed the yellow tape so they could enter the alleyway.

The alleyway was set between two abandoned factories and was approximately five metres wide. Nicholls looked up. The adjoining buildings rose high into the sky with overhanging tiled roofs that starved the ground level of much needed light. There was a solitary streetlight standing impotently beneath a bricked up window, that Nicholls presumed used to be the entrance of a factory workshop. Much of the brickwork was crumbling and dilapidated and the few windows that he could see were elevated and punctuated by formidable iron bars. It was an unremarkable setting for a truly horrific crime.

The scale of the murders meant that two teams of Crime Scene Investigators were present at the scene preserving the evidence. Page and Nicholls were very conspicuous in their causal jackets and corduroy trousers, amidst the plethora of figures wearing bone white hooded jump suits, purple gloves and masks, hovering like bees around four grey tents that sheltered the dead. It was like a scene from a different world.

Nicholls felt drops of light rain prick his face and hoped it wouldn't get any heavier and wash away potential evidence. He rubbed his face and caught the attention of a hooded figure who walked over briskly to the two men. The hooded figure tugged at her mask and smiled ominously.

"Good morning, inspectors," she said quietly. "I hope you're ready for this. I've seen some sights in my time, but this is up there with the worst of them"

"Morning Ellen," nodded Nicholls respectively. "Why don't you lead the way?"

Ellen Simpson was the Crime Scene Manager and the most senior forensic investigator present. Nicholls and Page had worked with her on numerous occasions, and they had always been impressed with her calm, efficient manner. She seemed an unlikely candidate for this role judging by her appearance. Simpson was thirty-nine but looked years younger. She was small in stature and stick thin. It looked like the merest gust of wind would blow her away and she spoke in a quiet, emotionless manner. Simpson though was an expert at her job. She had investigated some of the most gruesome murders the capital had seen in recent years, and she had always remained unfazed by the unpalatable scenes, even when more senior male police detectives had gone green and made hasty exits. Simpson's job was to preserve the evidence and she coordinated her team like an expert orchestral conductor. If there was a shred of evidence, be it blood, clothes fibres, skin flakes or hairs then she would find it.

She stopped at a patch of mud by a broken window and pointed down at an imprint in the soil. "We've found a number of footprints along the alleyway," she said grimly. "We've matched them all to the deceased, all that is except this one." Nicholls and Page glanced down at the footprint and hexagonal pattern cut into the mud. They didn't need to be forensic experts to deduce that the owner of the footprint was huge. "The same footprint is evident in a couple of other spots but there are no different ones anywhere."

Nicholls understood Simpson's suggestion immediately. "Are you saying this is the work of a lone killer?" She nodded her head in confirmation. "Jesus Christ!" gasped Nicholls in disbelief. "What kind of killer can dispatch four men in their prime with such ease?" It was not a question but a statement, so nobody felt the need to answer him. He stood with his hands on his hips and gazed at the scene of carnage before him. There were dark puddles of blood on the pavement and splashes of red rivulets all along the brick wall. He felt a nauseating fear biting at his innards. This was no ordinary killer.

Simpson led the men to the nearest tent. She walked through without pause but Nicholls and even Page had to stoop to duck through the narrow flap at the front. Nicholls and Page recognised Liam Batkin immediately. His entire front was patterned with spatters and rivulets of blood that drenched his jacket and spilled onto his jeans. His eyes were glazed wide open with dilated pupils in an expression of shock, and his discoloured tongue protruded through an open jaw. The gaping wound in his neck almost stretched from ear to ear and had nearly decapitated his head. It was only skin and a few chords of sinew that kept it attached.

"Jesus Christ," muttered Page bringing a grubby handkerchief to his mouth.

"Yep, that's our friend Liam Batkin," confirmed Nicholls to no-one in particular. He glanced at the notes that Simpson had made on her clipboard. "Twenty years old. A deep, oblique, long incised injury at the front of the neck is the likely cause of death." He paused and nodded his assent to Simpson.

Simpson's face was neutral. "The force of the blow must have been phenomenal to inflict such trauma," she said quietly. She turned to face the detectives and aimed a slashing blow at Nicholls that looked oddly comical coming from her diminutive figure against his powerful frame.

"What are you saying, Ellen?" asked Nicholls. "Do you think this is a professional hit? We know about his links to McGovern. He was a drug addict who would sell out his own mother for a hit. Perhaps McGovern felt he was a liability and wanted him out the picture."

Simpson paused and considered the question momentarily. She shook her head. "I don't think so Jimmy. Wait till you see the state of Baldock. There was something sadistic about it. It doesn't fit at all into the picture of a professional killer."

Nicholls nodded. "Have you managed to find anything?"

"Not yet. But if there's anything that can identify the killer, my team will find it."

"Do you at least have a time of death that we can use?" he asked.

Simpson pursed her lips. "It's a difficult one. Rigor mortis has taken hold in his arms and neck and his body temperature is twenty-four degrees."

"What does that mean?" Nicholls knew that rigor mortis was the stiffness that occurred in the body when someone died and their heart stopped beating, depriving muscle cells of the oxygen they need to generate energy. This stiffness was normally quite visible within the first thirty-six to forty-eight hours after death, before it left the body, and the muscles became flaccid again. He had seen many photographs of deceased bodies with their faces contorted into a fearsome grimace because the facial muscles had contracted as the energy molecule adenosine-tri-phosphate drained from them.

"I would say that he died somewhere between seven and ten last night, but it's still early spring and it was a cold evening, so even that time frame could be extended. I know," she said quizzically. "I took the dog for a walk at nine last night and the wind was really bitter."

"Can't you give a narrower timeline?"

"I'm afraid not," she said defiantly. "Rigor mortis is extremely temperamental. It can be affected by a whole number of variables; the outside temperature, the age of the deceased, even their muscle girth. Was the deceased running at the time of death? If they were, then lactic acid will build up very quickly during high intensity exercise and even that can speed up the process. There's no way anyone can give a more accurate time of death than that. If they do, they're lying."

"Ok Ellen," said Nicholls quickly, raising his palms awkwardly in deference to Simpson's authority. "Show me what else you've got?"

Nicholls and Page were escorted methodically to see the corpses of Randall and Taylor. Nicholls felt a twinge of sympathy pull at his heart strings at the young ages of the victims. They were barely men. Impressionable stupid boys who had been indoctrinated into the criminal fraternity by their gang master Baldock. Nicholls had tried to arrest Baldock on a few occasions, but he seemed to have an uncanny ability to evade justice, like he was protected by some kind of celestial force.

Page took one look at Baldock and spluttered out of the tent, before vomiting in a nearby gutter.

Nicholls grimaced but just managed to check the churning of his stomach before it disgorged its contents.

He turned quickly to face Simpson. "Well, Baldock's definitely looked better, hasn't he?"

As ever, Simpson offered no comment, and her expression was emotionless.

Nicholls took a deep breath to prepare himself, before bringing the corpse back into focus. Baldock's corpse was grotesque. His right eye was a ruined mess of putrefied jelly that was coated in congealed yellow puss. His face was deathly pale, and the underneath of his skin had begun to turn a purple pink colour as damaged blood cells had begun to spill out of broken vessels, and aided by gravity had pooled in the lowest parts of his body. Baldock's ears for whatever reason had been hacked off and there were dark puddles of blood underneath the jagged flesh. Even though Baldock was wearing a dirty hoodie, Nicholls could see the frenzied stab wounds that Simpson had mentioned in her report. He quickly counted twelve separate stab wounds that punctuated Baldock's upper body and abdomen, suggesting that the murderer had attacked Baldock in a feral rage. The ferocity of the murder confirmed Ellen's suspicions that this wasn't the work of a professional killer. Professional killers rarely wasted unnecessary energy on their targets and dispatched victims clinically and efficiently. This had all the hallmarks of something personal and contract killings were never personal. They were just business. Nicholls had seen domestic murders where husbands and wives had murdered their partners in fits of jealously and had inflicted multiple injuries as they unleashed their rageful vengeance on the victim. But this didn't make sense. It was almost as if the killer had taken perverse pleasure in killing Baldock. He imagined Baldock's terrified face as the killer had gone to work and the sadistic grin on their face as they butchered the drug dealer.

Nicholls turned to Page, who had just returned into the makeshift tent, his cheeks pale and his handkerchief firmly pressed against his mouth. "Whoever did this Kev must have been covered in blood by the end," he said assertively. "Someone must have seen or heard something. I can't believe Baldock would have gone quietly."

Page nodded affirmatively. "We'll get started on the door to door enquiries then. But don't hold your breath Jimmy," he warned. "This neighbourhood doesn't like the police. I doubt we'll get anything."

Page wiped a speck of vomit from the corner of his mouth and stumbled out the tent. It was his job to debrief the rest of the team when they arrived on the scene and to allocate them roles for the forthcoming investigation. Murder team seven consisted of fifteen detectives, two police officers and four police staff. They all needed to be brought up to speed about the facts of the case and assigned duties. That was Page's job. The first steps would be to conduct door to door enquiries and review CCTV footage of the local area. The Crime Scene Investigators would continue to swab for evidence before the bodies were brought to the mortuary for the post mortem.

"Kev," called out Nicholls. Page turned, his face still grey and stony. "I want to see everyone in the Stratford office at five sharp."

"Where are you going?"

"I'm going with the bodies to the mortuary," he replied grimly. "Something doesn't sit right here."

St Martin's mortuary was a modern building tucked neatly between two recreational parks. It was quite common for football players to turn into the courtyard looking for the changing facilities, before heading tentatively into the building for directions. Nicholls had stopped off for another coffee and to make a few phone calls before he reached the mortuary at around eleven thirty that morning. He parked his car under a vibrant looking ash tree and briskly made his through the majestic double doors into the main waiting room. The pretty receptionist on the front desk must have seen him pull up because there was a small crowd of people waiting for him when he got there.

As well as the senior pathologist, Gerry Schofield, there were five mortuary assistants, a scenes of crime officer, Scott Johnson, a detective from murder team seven and a police photographer. It was a policy of the unit that at least two detectives be present at every autopsy to compare notes and ensure nothing had been missed.

Gerry Schofield was a bullish man with broad shoulders, unnaturally dark hair and a mischievous grin. He had been a pathologist for over thirty years and was close to retirement, although you wouldn't have thought that with his boundless energy and raucous laugh, that made him appear years younger. He was one of the few people who could stand shoulder to shoulder with Nicholls, but he was fighting a losing battle against the bulk that protruded from his belly and hips.

"Jimmy," he said in a gravelly voice. "It's good to see you." Schofield's mouth stretched into a cavernous smile, and he enveloped Jimmy's right hand in a vice like grip.

"It's good to see you too Gerry," replied Nicholls enthusiastically. He always enjoyed meeting up with Schofield. The man had an infectious personality and an aura about him that seemed to captivate everyone around him. Nicholls and Page had spent many an afternoon with Schofield down the Black Swan after an autopsy, sinking pint after pint of Guinness and listening to Schofield entertain the locals with his wicked sense of humour.

"We didn't want to start without you," he said mockingly. "Besides we've had lots of fun breaking the rigor mortis." He tensed his muscles and smiled wickedly. "It's about the only exercise I get these days." Schofield began to laugh and as he laughed his sagging jowls began to shake which sent a vibration throughout his entire body, reminding Nicholls of a percussion instrument. It was impossible not to like Gerry Schofield.

The small party headed into the mortuary where the four bodies of the victims were lying on parallel tables covered by paper shrouds. The powerful pickle like odour of formalin assaulted the nostrils. Detective Scott Johnson approached Nicholls and opened a notebook. He was a slight man in his forties with bone white hair and a sharp, cunning mind. "We've had the toxicology reports in from forensics Sir," he said glancing at his notes. Nicholls nodded encouraging him to continue. "They were all drunk as skunks and had been using heroin and cocaine."

"That doesn't surprise me Scott," said Nicholls. He remembered the stale stench of alcohol from the crime scene that morning. "They were all addicts."

Schofield headed to the first table and motioned for the nearest mortuary assistant to remove the paper shroud that had already been stained with blood. Nicholls could see it was Randall. He almost looked alive although his lower body where most of his injuries were concentrated, was a mass of angry blueish purple blotches as blood cells continued to leak from the damaged blood vessels. He was naked apart from plastic bags around his hands secured with a cable tie.

"What are they for, Gerry?" said Nicholls inquisitively as he had never seen them before.

Schofield was busying himself with the nearest trolley and didn't even look up to see what Nicholls was pointing at. "Simpson rang me before you got here," he said nonchalantly. "She thinks there may be some skin under Randall's fingernails. It may have been that he scratched the attacker as he tried to fight him off. She put them there to preserve the evidence. We may be able to get something identifiable."

Schofield was already wearing some deathly white scrubs, a pair of mortuary wellies and a pale yellow apron. He disinfected his hands and then skilfully put on some rubber gloves and moved swiftly to Randall's head and felt his jaw and lower neck. "The body is cold and with slowly declining rigor," he said grimly. One of the mortuary assistants began to scribble furiously on a gleaming iPad. "The skull is symmetric, and the victim appears to be wearing contact lenses," he continued slowly and methodically. "The victim has a broken nose and several abrasions to his face that are consistent with someone falling and hitting the ground heavily." He paused briefly to allow a photographer to take several photos of the injuries he had described. Schofield removed the plastic bags and grabbed Randall's wrist with his thumb and index figure. "There is one incised wound on the palmar surface of the right hand at the base of the index finger. The wound is approximately 2cm in length and is consistent with a defence wound." Two of the mortuary assistants pulled Randall so he lay on his side whilst Schofield traced his hands down the spine, searching with probing hands for any injuries. Satisfied that there was nothing of note here, he moved around to the other side of the table. "There are six deep wounds, four in the medial abdomen and two in the umbilical region" He fiddled with his fingers into the wound. "The wounds are slit like and range in depth from thirty millimetres to forty-eight millimetres. There is significant damage to the internal organs. I won't know for sure how much till I've done a thorough internal examination." He glanced at his watch. "How are you doing for time Jimmy? Do you want me to give the others a once over? I doubt you need to stay for the internal. I can email you the full report later."

"That would be helpful Gerry. Thank you"

"It's a shame Detective Page isn't here. I'm sure he would have relished the chance to help me inspect the organs." Schofield laughed again fully aware of the elderly detective's sensitive stomach. He turned back to Randall and his brow furrowed as he concentrated on the task ahead. "In my opinion these would all have been fatal injuries. It is likely that the victim would have bled to death in about ten minutes."

"What kind of knife are we looking for Doc?" said Johnson.

Schofield looked at him intensely, as if he was pondering an answer to the question. Nicholls was fairly confident his mind would already have formulated an answer some time ago. "Assuming the knife didn't penetrate the victim at an oblique angle, I would say you're looking for a razor sharp blade that's approximately three and a half to three and three quarter inches long, with a clip point." He stared at the ceiling momentarily as if collecting his thoughts. "It's no ordinary kitchen knife that's for sure. This is a custom made weapon." He turned to face Nicholls. "I've got a website I can look on later and send you images over with the official report." Nicholls nodded in gratitude.

Schofield turned abruptly towards two of his mortuary assistants. "Pete, Steve," he called impatiently. "While we move on to the others, can you get some hair samples and nail clippings from the deceased and send them straight to forensics?" He didn't wait for an answer and moved swiftly over to the next victim.

Nicholls tried to pay attention, but he felt his mind wandering and he began to daydream. It was sometimes a battle to wrestle his thoughts back to where they needed to be. The other two autopsies were conducted relatively quickly. The fatal injuries were pretty obvious to anyone. He glanced at Johnson who was enthusiastically listening to Schofield and making notes. After finishing with Batkin, Schofield stood and looked solemn. "The same weapon killed all these men," he said quietly. "I agree with Simpson. We are looking for a solitary killer."

A mist of incredulity descended upon the room. It was hard to believe that a single person had the strength or tenacity to be responsible for all these murders. Schofield broke the silence. "I am glad that it is not my job to find this killer," he said turning to Nicholls. "I fear you are going to be searching in the depths of hell, my friend. This is certainly no ordinary human being."

The final victim was Baldock. Schofield seemed to have been drained of energy by his last admission, and he laboriously pulled the paper shroud off the deceased like an exhausted marathon runner in the final stages of a race. Baldock's injuries were still as horrific as Nicholls remembered and his stomach churned. "Well, they certainly went to town on this one," he said with a grimace. "And he still has hell to look forward to by all accounts, from what I've heard about his lifestyle?"

Schofield set to work examining the corpse, probing the wounds and pausing every so often to allow the photographer to take pictures of the injuries. When Baldock was propped on his side, Nicholls could see that unlike the other victims, he had a number of stab wounds on his upper and lower back and that there was extensive bruising along the upper leg and buttocks. All of a sudden Schofield must have seen something unusual because his nostrils flared, and he bent down to stare at Baldock's bottom.

"I don't believe it," he stammered. "Get me my scalpel quickly." The entire party seemed to hold their breath. Nicholls instinctively knew something was wrong as he had never seen Schofield so flustered.

"What is it, Gerry?" he asked.

"His arsehole has been stitched up. I don't fucking believe it," he squealed in a high-pitched tone.

"Are you kidding me?"

Schofield ignored the question and slashed at the stitching with his scalpel. There was a moment of silence before Schofield screamed, took two backward steps and crashed into the trolley sending a stainless steel maelstrom of needles, scissors and other surgical tools flying through the air.

Nicholls protectively stepped over the pathologist who was collapsed on a heap in the floor.

"What is it, Gerry?" someone barked.

Schofield was trying to speak but was spluttering saliva drenched nonsense that no-one could understand. His face had turned a beetroot red, and he was pointing a quivering finger at Baldock. "Gerry, for Christ's sake!" Nicholls bellowed.

"It's a fucking snake, Jimmy," stuttered Gerry. "Look for yourself; a fucking snake."

Nicholls turned and saw that Schofield was absolutely right. Squeezing out of Baldock's anus was a snake, its flickering tongue darting nervously from side to side as it surveyed the room.

Chapter 2
Dangerous Alliances

Redmead police station had previously been an old jail and was perched precariously astride a stone bridge overlooking the Thames. Officers working the night shift often claimed to hear ghostly noises and the sounds of door opening and closing in empty rooms. If there were angry spirits occupying the building, Jimmy Nicholls had certainly never seen them.

Murder Team seven were based on the second floor and the Trafford office was their designated meeting room. Jimmy Nicholls glanced impatiently at his watch. It was half past four. He was sitting on the black leather chair at the head of the Trafford office where he would soon meet with the rest of murder team seven to discuss the early stages of the investigation. He had just finished another coffee and could feel the euphoric rush as the caffeine hijacked his brain and made him feel temporarily more alert. There would be no sleep tonight that was for sure. But even without the coffee, Nicholls doubted he would sleep. The day had been traumatising from the offset and his mind was bubbling over with theories.

The Trafford office used to be one of the old holding cells in the jail and Nicholls often wondered about all the people who had occupied this room in the past. Many undoubtedly would've been poor, destitute people who guilty or not, were unlikely to escape the gallows. Like much of the building, the room had been largely gutted but the old timber frames still clung resolutely to the north and south facing walls, guarding a pair of tinted double windows which allowed people in the office to look out but not be seen.

He switched on the computer and projector and opened his emails. He was relieved that Page had sent him a Smartboard file containing information about the case to share with his colleagues. He busied himself by going through each slide, adding little anecdotes where appropriate and copying pictures from

Schofield's report. Occupying most of the room was a huge eight barrel walnut table which allowed the entire unit to sit comfortably while facing the huge projection screen at the front. Nicholls just needed a clicker for the presentation. He opened a drawer in the small oak side cabinet next to him and saw the beaded eyes of a toy snake staring back at him. News of the autopsy had evidently already reached the station. He picked up the snake and threw it out the window before nonchalantly resuming with his work. This was no time to stew on childish pranks.

Detective superintendent Daniel Bircham did not look at all like a policeman. He was in his early fifties, heavily overweight and had ringlets of dark, wavy hair tinged with splashes of grey. His health had been deteriorating steadily for years due to a penchant for whisky and cigarettes and many of his colleagues thought it would not be long before he took early retirement. "Ah there you are Jimmy," he wheezed as he opened the door of the office and saw Nicholls. "I've been looking all over you."

"Afternoon sir," responded Nicholls respectfully. "Did you get my messages?" He had rung Bircham up several times during the day to keep him up to date with Baldock's murder. Bircham often kept murder team seven under tighter reigns than the other murder teams, which didn't overly trouble the pragmatic Nicholls. He was fully aware that it was extremely rare for someone so young and inexperienced to be the lead detective for a murder team, so greater supervision on him was nothing unusual.

"I did, Jimmy," he said slowly, still catching his breath after the exertions of climbing the stairs. "Are you serious, a snake up his arse?" His brow furrowed and his forehead glistened with sweat.

"As I live and breathe, sir. I thought Schofield was going to have a heart attack."

"What happened to the snake, Jimmy? Was it poisonous?" Nicholls was well known in the force for his love of animals and nature.

"It was a grass snake, sir. A juvenile one. The poor thing was terrified, as you can imagine." Bircham's puzzled look illustrated his ignorance on the subject and Nicholls stifled a chuckle of amusement. "Not venomous, sir. It's in the back on my car at the moment in a box. If it survives, I'll release it into the wild tomorrow," he said with a hint of condescension.

"Was it a message do you think?" Bircham said quickly, ignoring Nicholls's admirable conversation efforts.

"Honestly sir, I don't know," responded Nicholls. "Nothing makes sense at all about this case. It seems personal. Perhaps the killer wanted vengeance for some past transaction and the snake was a way to degrade Baldock even further."

"What does your gut tell you?"

Nicholls shook his head in exasperation. "The murders were brutal sir. They were committed by a formidable killer in the backyard of the most notorious crime boss in London. We know that Baldock had links with him in the past. It makes sense to start with McGovern."

Bircham's nostrils flared, and he puffed out his chest. "We don't speculate in homicide Jimmy. You'd better have something pretty fucking concrete if you want to go after Patrick McGovern. Flack will have your balls skinned if you don't, even if you are shacked up with his daughter."

Nicholls was momentarily shocked by the vehement defence of the notorious gangster. He was temporarily lost for words and was relieved when three detectives in the team interrupted the conversation by walking into the room.

Bircham frowned, muttered a few words of greetings as more colleagues spilled through the door, before taking a seat on the angled corner of the table. He crossed his legs and folded his arms, indicating that he was going to be mainly an observer in today's meeting and let Nicholls take the lead.

Nicholls waited five more minutes and the room filled up. He did a quick head count and it looked like the entire unit had made it. Many of the detectives broke into small groups and cliques and there were animated pockets of conversation. Nicholls was sure that he heard stifled fits of laughter that seemed to be aimed in his direction. He moved cautiously towards the front of the room and felt a palpable glare of intense scrutiny settle upon him.

As the room fell silent in anticipation, Nicholls took a deep breath and paused to collect his thoughts. He felt the suspense in the room build until the tension was almost suffocating and then he spoke in a calm and assured voice.

"Mickey Baldock was a nasty son of a bitch. No-one here is going to deny that. He was a human parasite that sucked the life out of everyone and everything he met. By all rights he should have been locked away a long, long time ago and we should have thrown away the key. That is a failure on our part. Mine and yours." He pressed his hand slowly on to his chest and then extended the arm outwards in a chopping motion to emphasise his point.

"Now is not the time to dwell on our failures." He pressed a button on the clicker and Baldock's grotesque corpse appeared on the main screen. "Whatever our feelings on the man, he was brutally murdered along with three others in his gang. Some of us might be privately glad that he is dead, one less scumbag to deal with, but that is not the attitude I expect to see from anyone involved in this investigation. It is our job to catch the killer and we must do that using all of the skills and expertise that we have honed throughout our years in the force. Whoever did this is a danger to society and there is little doubt more people will die unless we catch them." Nicholls walked towards the door as if he was deep in thought and then turned sharply back to face the table. "We are searching for a solitary killer. There is no evidence that anyone else was involved. It was the same knife that killed Liam Batkin, Lee Taylor and Kane Randall." Another click and Baldock's acolytes were projected onto the screen.

"We must remember that all of these men were in the prime of life. Baldock was an ex-professional rugby player for Christ's sake. They were all butchered like animals, and the coup de grace was reserved for him alone. I don't need to tell you all about the scene from animal planet we had to deal with at the end of the autopsy. Someone was kind enough to leave a reminder." He motioned to the side cabinet at the front of the room and there were a few murmured snorts of laughter that Bircham silenced with a swish of his hand. "The others were dispatched quickly, yet the killer wanted Baldock alone to suffer and be degraded even in death." A handful of detectives recoiled in disgust as the screen shot to close ups of Baldock's ravaged flesh and ears. "There are no pictures of the snake but if anyone wants to see it, then it is in the back of my car." The room was silent, unsure how to respond. It wasn't clear whether Nicholls was joking or not. The man wasn't known for his sense of humour.

"We are without doubt looking for a powerful man, probably with special forces training and a grudge against Baldock." Nicholls was about to continue, when the door slowly swung over and in walked the Met Commissioner Daniel Flack.

There was a collective gasp from the room at the surprise visitor and out the corner of his eye, Nicholls saw several detectives stiffen in their seats in deference to Flack as if he was the pope himself. Nicholls smiled wryly. He was engaged to Flack's daughter, Jennifer and was on good terms with the Met commissioner. He had known him most of his life. Redmead was also only a stone's throw away from where Flack lived, so he often liked to pop in when he had a moment.

He still remembered the day when Flack had turned up at his school, a rundown comprehensive in Hackney when Nicholls was an acne ridden, gangly outcast. The police were running an anti-drug programme in partnership with all the schools in the local area and Flack was the face of the campaign. He had only been a senior detective at the time, but the event had generated lots of media publicity and Nicholls had been mesmerised by the charismatic policeman as he spoke to the students in the school's assembly hall. After that, the day had been broken up by smaller activities led by other police officers and Nicholls has participated in each activity with insatiable zeal and enthusiasm. Nonetheless it still came as a massive surprise when Flack had sought him out at the end of the day to tell him how impressed he was with Nicholls and to encourage him to join the police when he left school. He had even given Nicholls his number and from then on, the gangly youth had been sold. He was going to be a police officer. Nothing else mattered. I was his calling in life.

Flack always seemed to have time for him, even though his star had begun its meteoric rise towards the heavens. When Nicholls qualified as a police officer, it had been Flack who had come to celebrate with him at his passing out parade. Whenever Nicholls needed advice or support, Flack was there, either on the end of a telephone line or over a pint of real ale. Nicholls even suspected that Flack had pulled some strings in order to help him secure his dream move to homicide, even though he always flatly denied it. It was Flack who had introduced Nicholls to his daughter Jennifer and the old man had seemed really happy when the two of them had begun dating.

He and Flack were close. That was why he was upbeat and unperturbed at his entrance, while everyone else in the room was panicking.

Flack was in late fifties, with neatly cropped silvery-grey hair and a kindly, affable face that was heavily creased with wrinkles. He had a white beard that jutted out from his chin like a rock face and piercing blue eyes that reminded Nicholls of a hunting dog. The entire unit instinctively made to stand to attention, but Flack motioned for them to sit and beckoned Nicholls to keep speaking. He pulled out a spare chair from a table by the wall and sat incongruously in the background, wearing his pristine uniform, with one leg crossed and his arms folded.

"Now as yet," he paused to emphasise the words, "the forensic investigation hasn't yielded much. A solitary foot print that confirms the assailant was a big man." Another click and the screen changed again. "Gerry Schofield sent us a picture of what he believes is a good representation of the murder weapon."

Nicholls look up at the fearsome blade that was emboldened on the screen and shuddered at the thought of it being used with such deadly force against the victims. "This file will be emailed out to you all after the presentation so make sure you read everything carefully and get an imprint of the weapon in your heads. Note the distinctive clipped point at the end." He motioned to Page who was sitting obediently next to him.

Page stood up and without taking his eyes off a grubby looking notebook that he gripped tightly in his right hand, slipped on a pair of olive brown spectacles. He shuffled to the front of the room. "Afternoon gentleman," he said nervously. "As most of you know we spent a large part of the day checking CCTV footage and making door to door enquiries in the Whitehill estates. As you can imagine, many of the residents were quite unhelpful and antagonistic towards us. As well as the usual abuse, we had to deal with threats and several soiled nappies that were hurled at us from windows in the estate." He paused to take a drink of water. "CCTV yielded nothing but one of the residents claimed to have seen Baldock and the other victims chasing after someone at around eight-ish. They can't remember exactly what time it was, but they can remember X-factor being on TV at the time. So, this gives us a window between eight and nine when the victims were killed and ties in with Ellen Simpson's estimated time of death."

He turned to Nicholls and gestured for him to move on the next slide. A young, beautiful twenty-something woman appeared on the screen. Nicholls could see out the corner of his eye that several of his detectives had jolted upright in their seats to get a better look at the attractive lady. She had pretty, symmetrical features and beguiling hazel brown eyes that were almost hypnotic. Her hair was raven black and flowed over her shoulders. "This is Holly Maxwell," said Page grimly. "She was Baldock's girlfriend. At the moment, she is the only living connection we've got with Baldock and his past. His other family members are either dead or estranged. She has gone missing. We need to find her and bring her in for questioning. She may have the knowledge that will identify the killer. That is the priority for tomorrow."

"Jesus Christ," said a detective sitting at the front. "How did a piece of shit like Baldock get a girlfriend like that?"

Nicholls patently ignored the comment. "Has anyone got any questions?"

A young detective at the back of the room raised his hand. "What about Baldock's links to Patrick McGovern?" It was well known that Baldock had worked for McGovern in the past.

There was a silence. The Commissioner Daniel Flack stood up slowly and implacably. "That is not a line of inquiry that is open to us at the moment," he said firmly. Flack had an aura about him that commanded obedience and his words hung in the air like an executioner's axe. He sat down and beckoned for Page to continue with a wave of his hand. Any lines of inquiry that involved McGovern had been declared off limits by the head of the Met.

Detective Chief Inspector Bircham stood up hurriedly, perhaps to show everyone that he was still the senior policeman in the room. He spoke to the entire unit but clearly had one eye on Flack. "Tomorrow you will all be split into units and given assignments for this investigation. As DI Nicholls said at the start, we need to catch this person quickly before more people die. Go home tonight and get a good night's sleep. We will meet back here at seven tomorrow morning ready to go."

Within a few minutes, the room was nearly empty as people spilled out the door, anxious to get home for the evening. Only Page, Nicholls, Bircham and Flack remained. It was Page who usually assigned the team responsibilities for investigations so he hovered impatiently around his senior partner, waiting for Flack to conclude his business with them.

Flack pointedly ignored Bircham and Page and motioned to Nicholls. "Jimmy, a word please if you can spare a few minutes."

"Of course, sir," said Nicholls obediently. He followed Flack out the room. Flack turned and scratched his beard ponderously. His face was always a mask of geniality and his lips curled into a good-natured smile that was betrayed only by sharp, penetrating blue eyes. "How is Jenny?" he said disingenuously. Flack rarely spoke about his daughter at work and Nicholls could tell by the tone of his voice there was something more pressing he wanted to discuss.

"She's good sir. She is very busy what with work and her studying but she's happy and looking forward to the future." Nicholls lied. His relationship with the Commissioner's daughter was beginning to show signs of strain. His demanding work schedule and her desire to become a lawyer had led to cracks and fissures forming in their relationship.

"Good, good," nodded Flack with little enthusiasm. "You must come over soon to me. It's been a while since we had some time together. I can try and butcher a Sunday roast and if that fails, we can open that bottle of cognac you got me last Christmas."

"Of course, sir. Name a date and we can pencil it in. That would be most welcome."

"Now unfortunately we must talk about work." His smile vanished abruptly, and he pursed his lips together and took a deep breath. "I can't believe what I heard about Baldock," he said incredulously. "Never in all my years have I heard anything like it. It beggars belief that anyone could even conceive of doing that to another human being. As Bircham says, we must do everything in our power to catch this individual and quickly. I have every faith in you and your team Jimmy." He pressed his hand firmly on Nicholls' bicep. "You must though steer your men away from McGovern. He is not on our menu, for the moment at least. I want to go into more detail with you but I'm afraid I can't Jimmy. You're just going to have to trust me. Do you understand?"

"That's crystal clear, Sir. I trust your judgement."

"Thank you, Jimmy. It is much appreciated." Flack patted Nicholls on the shoulder like a dog owner would stroke a well behaved pet. "Tell Jenny that I will be in contact soon."

"I will Sir. Thank you." Flack smiled only this time the smile engaged the muscles around the eyes and the skin at his temples crumpled into crows' feet wrinkles. He nodded and headed back down the corridor.

Nicholls frowned. He had just been warned off the most notorious crime boss in London, not once but twice by the most senior police officer in the Met. Something didn't sit right.

Jack Marsden twitched with excitement as adrenaline seeped into his blood stream and energised his nervous system. He could feel his heart racing and his chest tightening as the primal animal survival instinct gripped his entire body. He was about to embark on his first operation for the Special Command Firearms unit of the Met. It didn't seem real, a drugs sting. He could almost see the faces of his old friends at school. They wouldn't believe it. This operation had been three years in the making; the culmination of a rigorous selection process that had taken him to the limits of his physical and mental endurance.

He was sitting on one of the two fitted wooden benches that had been installed on the insides of a lorry trailer. The rest of his team were all sat at one metre intervals alongside him. Above them was a metal rail that had been rivetted to the ends of the trailer and was draped with plastic straps that the officers could hold to stop them falling forward as the lorry jolted and jerked in the traffic. The last month had been like a whirlwind for Marsden since he had finished training and been plunged headfirst into the high octane environment of the firearms unit.

He had been quite perturbed by the frosty reception he had been given by his new colleagues, but this was now an opportunity to ingratiate himself. Surely all new recruits were shunned by the unit until they had proved themselves. Once they had seen him perform when it mattered, the ice would thaw, and he would be welcomed as an equal. Of that, he was sure. There was no going back now. He would not let anyone down today.

He glanced to his right. Gary Darnell the commander of the unit was sitting next to him. His granite like jaw muscles were pumping away like pistons in an engine as they pulverised a piece of chewing gum that had long since lost its flavour. Darnell was a grizzled old veteran. He looked like something had chewed him up but didn't like the taste, so had spat him out. Marsden had noted from his first day that Darnell had a hold on the men that was difficult to explain. He didn't talk much but when he did, men listened and followed his orders implicitly.

"Have you done anything like this before sir?" It was a stupid question. Marsden silently cursed himself as he said it. He knew he was nervous but needed some form of reassurance.

Darnell turned his head, his face as implacable as a stone cliff. He had a wrinkled scar that ran from the temple to the tip of his mouth. "I've done everything you can imagine son and even more that you can't," he growled. "You don't need to worry about today. It will be over quick. Once they see our guns, they will shit themselves."

Operation Odysseus was the code name for the operation that had been running for the best part of four months to try and take down the ruthless new drug lord Pavel Kornilov. Kornilov had been a secret policeman in the Russian Security Service but had decided that crime was a more profitable enterprise. He had "made his bones" as a soldier in the Moscow mafia and had risen to the rank of Pakhan or boss, where he coordinated a vast drug smuggling and human trafficking operation across Europe. It was during this period that Kornilov had fallen foul of the boss of bosses Sergei Ivankov and been lucky to escape with his life. He had wisely decided to leave Moscow and had used his criminal smuggling contacts to establish a minor criminal enclave in East London. Kornilov had used a potent mixture of brutal savagery and dexterous planning to tighten his grip on the area, but he was young and ambitious. His lust for power was insatiable. He wanted more. He wanted London itself.

The driver of the lorry that now transported the Firearms unit to Tilbury docks was an undercover police officer, whom Marsden knew only as Stan. He had worked his way into Kornilov's organisation and had won the trust of the boss himself. He had convinced Kornilov that he was the man to transport the latest shipment of heroin from Tilbury to an industrial complex in Chelmsford where it could be distributed around the country. Instead of finding an empty trailer that they could load up with the drugs, Kornilov's men would soon find the lorry was full of armed police officers and they would be caught red handed. That was the plan anyway.

Marsden had sat enthralled like a schoolboy at the detailed team meetings. Darnell had orchestrated the planning for the operation and assigned each member of the team a role. After that, every conceivable eventuality had been discussed and ironed out amongst the team. His role was to provide back up support during the operation to prevent Kornilov's men from outflanking their position. He was determined not to let anyone down today.

He scanned the other officers with a tinge of envy. They were all silently focussed on the task ahead. No-one talked. It was as if they had been born to do this. He fiddled with the straps on his ballistic helmet to dissipate some nervous energy and made sure his body armour was positioned correctly. All of the men had bullet proof vests that were made with the fibre Kevlar. He knew that this fibre was tough and uncompromising. He had seen demonstrations in training that had shown how these vests were capable of stopping most shot gun projectiles and many types of knives, but his mind was not so sure.

A buzzer sounded that nearly made Marsden jump off his seat. Stan the undercover police officer who was driving the bus had flicked a switch on the dashboard. They were nearing Kornilov's gated compound so from here on in there was to be absolute silence. The lorry slowed and came to a halt. He heard muffled talking and raised voices. Darnell ominously raised his Sig Sauer semi-automatic rifle and gave his arms freedom to move. The rest of the team along with Darnell shuffled nervously. The voices calmed down and there was a clinking sound followed by an abrasive dragging noise as a gate was forced open. The engine started again, and the lorry crawled forward.

Kornilov owned two large hangars close to the docks. They were surrounded by a formidable high security stainless steel fence fitted with an anti-climb chain link mesh. At the northern section there was a guard house that was manned twenty-four hours a day. Marsden knew that they had entered the complex. There was no going back now.

After what seemed like an eternity, the lorry came to a halt. Marsden took a deep breath and exhaled slowly. There was a palpable tension in the air. His muscles were so wired they didn't seem to respond to the brain's commands. Darnell's eyes fixed on him with a fierce intensity as if to say, "don't fuck this up now." He had his hand planted on his ear to ensure there were no distractions to the radio conversation that Stan was having outside the lorry. Stan was wearing a wire and would say a code word to initiate the assault, but he had been given strict instructions to wait at least four minutes for the team to move into position. There were two trapdoor exits at the front and at the rear of the trailer. The eastern row made their way to the one at the front and the western row moved backwards slowly.

The plan was for the unit to position themselves at various points behind the wheels and wheel arches until they were ready to move. Engineers had secured extra mud flaps along the edge to help conceal the officers from view. The element of surprise was key. Darnell had insisted that a sudden visceral charge would immobilise the criminals and secure the initiative. Stan estimated there would be no more than ten of Kornilov's crew at the hangars. For them to fight back would surely be tantamount to suicide.

Each member of the unit fastidiously climbed down the small set of steps and moved into their designated positions. They had practiced this manoeuvre repeatedly over the last weeks until Darnell was satisfied they could all do it in their sleep. As Marsden stepped on to the floor, he almost slipped but just managed to regain his balance in time. A few of the experienced veterans shot him angry looks but he didn't see them. Marsden moved into position behind the fifth wheel mud flap. His view was obscured by a large pallet, but he could hear voices.

Stan spoke with a broad Liverpudlian accent and Marsden could hear him quite clearly. Stan's appearance was perfect. It wouldn't take much to convince anyone that he was a criminal based on how he looked. He had wispy brown hair and unkempt stubble that sprouted unevenly in clumps around his chin and cheeks. His eyes were shifty, and he had a rat like nose that conveyed a sense he couldn't be trusted. He spoke quickly and fluently using a mixture of slang and expletives in almost every sentence, that made it difficult for other people to get a word in edgeways. It was almost as if he had been born to play the role of an undercover criminal.

It had been raining quite heavily and the wet tarmac glistened in the late afternoon sun. Marsden could hear Stan getting quite animated about something. A heavily accented voice tried to calm him down. Marsden glanced at Darnell who seemed poised. Darnell was not a tall man, but his shoulders were broad, and he had thick muscular legs like tree trunks. He gave the impression of a tiger stalking a sambar deer in thick leaves, his muscles coiled ready to explode into action in an instant.

Darnell raised his hand so the unit could see that they were ready to strike. "On me now," he roared. The entire unit rose as one and majestically stormed in to position like a pack of wild dogs. They caught Kornilov and his crew by complete surprise. "Armed police," bellowed Darnell again in a thunderous voice pointing his gun resolutely at Kornilov. "Drop your weapons and put your hands on your head."

Pavel Kornilov was thin and lithe with small, delicate features. He had oily brown hair that was immaculately swept back and glinted in the light. His skin was smooth and velvety. He looked like a nervous student about to start his first term at Oxbridge rather than a brutal gangster who had the ability to kill another human being with impunity. He looked first at Darnell and then back at Stan. His eyes shimmered with pure malevolence. Marsden could see his hand twitching for a Tokarev pistol that hung conspicuously in a holster by his waistband. For a second, he was convinced Kornilov was going to go for it. He had six other men in his crew and five huge pallets of drugs that could provide cover. Kornilov quickly assessed the situation and visualised the likely carnage at that course of action. Rationality prevailed. He shrugged his shoulders and looked at his crew.

"Do as he says," he said with surprising joviality. His men followed his orders instantly. He turned to Stan and mockingly gave him a round of applause. He wagged his finger provocatively. "You were good my friend." Stan said nothing. His face was impassive. "It is a shame that I will have to kill you for this betrayal. I really liked you. You're a funny man."

Kornilov looked directly at Darnell, ignoring the fact his weapon was aimed squarely at his head. He stretched out his arms to show Darnell his palms. "So, Mr Police officer," he said patronisingly. "What do we do next?" He pointed towards the pallets. "As you can see, we have a lot of business to do and I do not have time for this nonsense. The ball is in your court, as you English say. If you turn a blind eye to my business, I will make you very rich."

Darnell ignored him and turned and spoke to the man immediately to the left of him, an officer by the name of Peter Clark. Clark nodded and beckoned to two other officers. He gave them some orders and they obediently broke formation and cantered into the first hangar. Two more of Darnell's officers headed off in the direction of the gate.

Kornilov smiled. "I have much wealth hidden back there too." There was a hint of tension in his voice. "I am happy to share. Why let the government keep all of this? You must understand the way the world works. You are a practical man. It makes sense to come to an arrangement."

"I am not interested in coming to an arrangement with you."

"Be careful," warned Kornilov. "I have many powerful friends. You do not want me as an enemy."

For a split second Darnell seemed to hesitate and this seemed to embolden Kornilov. The Russian's eyes flickered like a snake as he sensed a potential weakness. "Come now detective. It does not make sense for us to be enemies. I am good for your city. I get rid of all the low life criminals who prey on the weakness of others. I just provide a service that people want, that's all. If I'm gone someone else will take over. They could be far worse than me." He laughed manically. "I also know how to look after my friends," he said defiantly.

As Kornilov was talking, Clark and the other officers returned. They had two more of Kornilov's crew in tow. "Are there any others?" asked Darnell.

Clark shook his head. "We searched everywhere. There are no more."

"The guard house is also empty." Another officer said. "As expected, they've all legged it like rats leaving a sinking ship."

Darnell absorbed the information and nodded his head. He turned to his second in command, Phil Ward. "Have you disabled the body cams?"

Ward looked insulted. "I sent a jamming signal before we left. All of the body cams stopped filming in the lorry. Nothing will be recorded."

"Are you sure?"

"Positive?"

Kornilov looked apprehensive. "Detective, do we have a deal or not?"

Darnell turned to face him and smiled menacingly. "Yes, Pavel we do have a deal. We will take your drugs and your money."

"Fuck you, arsehole. You don't fuck with me you motherfucker," hissed Kornilov.

Darnell turned to his unit. "Kill them. Kill them all."

For a split second, Marsden thought he had misheard, but then the firearms unit unleashed their weapons. Bullets exploded from their rifles and tore

Kornilov's crew to shreds. The Russian was hit at least five or six times and his body was tossed around like a rag doll as each bullet crushed and shredded his flesh. Marsden couldn't believe what he was seeing. He had heard gunfire before but the sound of ten weapons firing in synchrony was absolutely deafening. It took him a second to adjust and to make sense of what was happening. Had he missed something? Perhaps Kornilov had gone for a hidden firearm and Darnell had fired in self-defence, but then what about the others? They had already dropped their weapons and were defenceless. No, there were no excuses for this atrocity. This was cold-blooded murder, pure and simple. His world had just turned upside down.

Darnell raised his hand and the unit stopped fire. Kornilov and all of his crew were either dead or dying. The destruction was total. Kornilov lay prone on the floor. One of the bullets had disintegrated his spleen and torn his aorta. Blood poured out of his chest cavity. Another bullet had punctured his lung and pulverised several ribs. Blood bubbled out of his mouth as he tried to inhale air into his ruined lungs. He was clearly not long for this world.

Darnell walked over to him. With his last remaining reserves of energy as his life drained away, Kornilov turned to face the police officer. "Who the fuck are you?" he garbled.

Darnell crouched down beside him, so their faces were nearly touching. He whispered softly into his ear. "Patrick McGovern sends his regards Pavel."

Kornilov seemed to laugh but he was coughing and spluttering so much blood it was difficult to tell. He tried to reach for his gun but his body jerked and stopped in mid motion. He exhaled a final gasp of air before his brain switched off and his body sagged lifelessly to the floor. Darnell stooped down even lower and picked up his Tokarev pistol from the floor.

Marsden stood in total bewildered disbelief at what he had just witnessed. His brain couldn't make sense of what had happened. Darnell just stared intently at the Tokarev pistol, as if he didn't have a care in the world. "What have you done?" Marsden finally stammered. "You've just murdered them in cold blood. They were unarmed. You didn't have to do this."

Darnell looked at Marsden and brought his finger to his lips to hush him up. "You don't understand son."

"Then tell me for God's sake," demanded Marsden. All his life he had believed in the virtue of the police and their duty to uphold the law. That sacred belief had been shattered in just a few moments on a rain-soaked spring day. He clawed desperately for something tangible to cling to. "I'm one of you now." He hesitated. "I always wanted to be one of you."

Darnell raised his hand quickly and Marsden felt something powerful thump into his neck and propel him backwards. His body hit the tarmac but there was no pain. He felt his neck and there was a huge hole of ragged flesh. Blood pulsed over his hand. The world dimmed. He couldn't understand what was going on. He heard voices somewhere in the distance, but his vision was consumed by millions of flashing lights that converged into a singular, dazzling glow. He felt a wave of tiredness wash over him and then there was just blackness.

Darnell walked slowly over. "I'm sorry son," he said softly, "but you are not one of us." He looked at his crew. "We have forty-five minutes. You all know what to do."

Jason Kilbride looked at his watch. It was half past seven. He didn't like working this late but with a general election coming up soon, his workload was never ending. The Conservative Party Headquarters was a hive of activity as departments busied themselves with fundraising and campaign planning. As the shadow Home Secretary, he had to finalise his department's priorities and action plan ready for approval by the leader of the Conservative leader, Darren Healey. The cornerstone of his action plan was a mandate for cutting crime. The Labour government was facing huge criticism for the way crime had snowballed in the capital in recent years and the Conservative party fed voraciously on these failures.

Kilbride looked at his phone and smiled. The internet was lauding the anti-crime speech he had made the other day. He had claimed that London and many cities in Britain were in anarchy and that criminals operated with impunity. Ordinary, decent law-abiding citizens were too afraid to venture out at night and that swift decisive action was the only way to combat this crime wave. He advocated for a zero-tolerance policy, similar to the one used by New York in the 1980s, as a way to curb crime. The police needed greater powers and more funding to cut crime. To put it simply the country needed more police officers out on the beat and every facet of the law needed to be enforced strictly and without prejudice. The police could no longer turn a blind eye to minor crimes as this would only encourage more serious crimes later on. He had called it "broken windows" in his speech; a theory pioneered by American sociologists Wilson and Kelling. Little cracks in a window become gaping holes, if they are not dealt with at the earliest opportunity. It was the same with crime. That had been Labour's undoing. They had been too soft, not assertive enough. Money that could have been used to build prisons had been spent on tackling poverty and improving opportunities in deprived areas. Criminals knew the police didn't have the resources to tackle them, so became emboldened and more brazen with their illegal activities.

Kilbride's head swelled as he read some of the headlines in the media. He had been patient all his life. Now was his time to reap the rewards. He was in his late forties and although his hair had turned a silvery grey, he knew that women desired him. Christ, he had four women on the go at the moment, all of them under twenty-five. It was a wonder he had any energy for anything else.

His desk was piled with papers and manifestos. A half-opened box spilled out dozens of campaign badges with the slogan, "Making our streets safe again." It was a slight tweak to a phrase a ten year old boy had used recently on a visit to a primary school. Kilbride had liked it and suggested using it as a slogan, to which Healey had agreed. He opened a drawer in his desk and pulled out a bottle of vintage Glenfiddich whisky. He poured a generous serving into a nearby tumbler and drained it in one go. He refilled the tumbler and looked out the window. The sky was inky black against a myriad of dazzling lights that illuminated the horizon.

All of a sudden there was some commotion outside his office door, and he heard raised voices. His office intercom buzzed. "Mr Kilbride?" said the agitated voice of his secretary.

Kilbride felt a surge of arousal as he pictured the curvaceous body of his beautiful PA and her provocative lips. She would be another one of his conquests, preferably before the end of the summer. Once he had seduced her, he would take her to his villa in Tuscany for a long weekend of sexual indulgence. He imagined her lying in a bikini by the pool with her olive skin ripening in the Mediterranean sun. "Yes Charlotte," he said with a sly grin on his face.

"Mr White is here. He hasn't made an appointment. He says he needs you to see you urgently," she said hurriedly.

Doug White was CEO of the Bister Group construction company, one of the biggest building firms in the UK. White had built up the company himself from humble beginnings through hard work, graft and a fusion of blood, sweat and tears. He was in his late fifties now but still prided himself on his work ethic and old-fashioned values. Even though he was the supreme boss of this multi-billion pound business, he still insisted that all employees, from cleaners to directors had to ring him personally if they were ill and intended to take the day off. It was no coincidence that the Bister Group had the lowest number of staff absences amongst all the other building firms in the country.

The Bister Group was based in Reading but had several substantial sites dotted around London. Kilbride smiled. He didn't particularly like White. He found him coarse and arrogant. It would be good to bring him down a peg or two.

"Let him in Charlotte. It will be alright."

The door buzzed and White marched in. His face, which was usually a beetroot red with enlarged, spidery blood vessels, was the colour of an over ripe tomato. He was clearly incandescent with rage but trying unsuccessfully to keep his temper. Kilbride picked up some forms on his desk and pretended to read them. He held his hand out like a policeman holding up traffic and White stopped a metre away, his anger blazing like a raging inferno.

After a moment, Kilbride put the forms down. "Sorry Doug," he said innocently. "You know how it is. This place is a mad house at the moment. What can I do for you?"

White held up a letter in his left hand. Spittle bubbled out of his mouth. "What do you think you're playing at?" he roared.

Kilbride knew exactly what White was referring to but wanted to provoke him further. "I'm not sure what you mean?"

White was incredulous. "This, this…" he was struggling to find the words and waved the letter vigorously in front of Kilbride's eyes. "This outrage."

"Ah, the proposal," said Kilbride gleefully like a young child who had solved a challenging math problem. He sat back in his chair and offered White some whisky. He shook his head. "That is our vision for the future. We have promised the people that we will protect them from the criminals that are plaguing our country and what better way to do that than to build a supermax prison and lock the scum up."

Supermax prisons had first been developed in America. They were typically harsh and secure prisons designed to incarcerate and isolate some of the most dangerous criminals in American society. Many inmates in Supermax prisons were locked up in tiny cells for twenty-three hours a day with only one hour outside the cell for exercise. Supermax prisons were also often said to be virtually escape proof. If a prisoner did somehow get out of their sound-proof cell, they would still have to contend with massive guard towers, security cameras, ferocious guard dogs and state of the art laser technology with remote controlled door systems, that were all enclosed within an imperious razor sharp metal fence.

"Why you arrogant son of a bitch," growled White. "You haven't even won the election yet."

Kilbride took a slow sip from his tumbler, deliberately trying to antagonise White as much as he could. "That Douglas is just a formality. Labour have done their best to screw up the county for the last four years. We need to sort out their mess. It makes good sense to start planning as early as possible."

"I don't give a fuck what you smug sons of bitches do. That's your business." He waved the letter in Kilbride's face again. "This is my business. How dare you think you can take it away from me."

Kilbride kept a staunch poker face. White's face was turning an even darker shade of beetroot, if that was even possible. "Calm down Doug. That is not what is happening here at all." He pulled out from his drawer an architectural blueprint. "Look see here." He traced a finger down the outline of the design for the new supermax prison. "We feel your site at Reading is the perfect location. That's all. You can easily relocate to any of your other sites round the London orbital. You would be doing a massive service for your country here Doug."

"You intend to ruin me. That's what you're doing," sneered White. "You think I will just give you my site for nothing and then ramrod me into building it for you. You've got a fucking nerve."

"Come on now Doug. Stop being overdramatic. You have a personal fortune of 1.2 billion and your company turnover last year was £853 million. This development will barely scratch the surface." Kilbride raised his eyebrow. "We can also give you exclusive shares in the private security firm that will be running the prison and a contract for all building work in the future. In a few years this will seem like a drop in the ocean."

White clenched his teeth and placed two enormous hands on the desk so he could look Kilbride squarely in the eyes. They were the hands of a man who had toiled all his life and were scarred with many rough callouses that had become as hard as leather. "Now you listen to me Mr Kilbride" he seethed quietly. "You may have me over a barrel at the moment, but it will not always be like this. When your world comes crashing down, I just want you to know that I will be there." He scrunched up Kilbride's letter and left it on the desk, before leaving the room as quickly and as noisily as he had entered.

Chapter 3
Ghosts

Nicholls yawned and looked at his watch as the alarm bleeped. It was half five in the morning. He had barely slept at all. When he got home after work, Jenny had already been in bed. There had been no point in waking her up and risking another explosive argument, so he had ordered a take-away and fallen into a fractured sleep on the sofa. His mind had been ticking like a bomb all night conjuring up different types of theories and avenues to explore in the forthcoming investigation. As a result, he woke up even more tired and irritable than he had been the night before.

He had purposely left his wash bag in the downstairs toilet, so as not to wake up Jenny. Within minutes he had splashed some cold water on his face, brushed his teeth and put on a spare suit that had also been deliberately placed in the cloakroom. He grabbed a slice of leftover pizza and stuffed it into his mouth before grimacing at the taste of the toxic combination of tomato relish and toothpaste.

It only took him ten minutes to make the short drive to a deserted car park in St John's forest. The first job that morning was to deal with that bloody snake. He had briefly considered taking it to an animal rescue shelter, but he knew the best thing he could do for the creature, was to release it back into the wild. As he sat in the car, his focus was suddenly drawn to the morning sun casting a rosy hue across the sky. The dewy grass that stretched before him, glinted in the light like billions of tiny stars in a far-off galaxy. He took a deep breath. There were a couple of people he could see in the distance walking their dogs but asides from that, the woodland looked empty.

St John's forest was a four and a half thousand acre area of ancient woodland nestled incongruously in the middle of an urban housing development. As well as woodland, St Johns also contained areas of grassland, heath, bogs and a large lake that was often used for fishing. It was a ten minute drive from his house and a perfect habitat for the grass snake to be released in.

He had taken the snake after Baldock's post-mortem and placed it in an empty wooden tool box that lived in his car. He had half expected the snake not to survive after the trauma of being rammed up a man's rectum, but to his amazement, when he opened the box this morning, the snake was staring back at him quite calmly with its tongue flickering inquisitively.

Nicholls triumphantly coaxed the snake into a canvas grocery bag that he had found in a cupboard that morning and started to make his way over to the lake. There was secluded spot on the eastern bank of the lake with overhanging reeds that he had chosen as the perfect spot. As he walked, he took a deep breath of fresh air. There was something about the woods that reinvigorated his soul. It was as if there was some kind of welcoming spirit in the rich sights, sound and smells of the green and brown canopy that stretched before him. As he approached the corner of the lake, a flock of starlings took flight and soared into the air in a whirling pattern that resembled some kind of giant organism. It was as if the organism had one just mind as the birds' movements all seemed to be synchronised together with precise fluidity. The giant organism elongated its body perfectly so it could fly through a narrow section of pylon wires. It reminded Nicholls of a monstrous snake that he had conjured up in his imagination as a small child and had given him countless nightmares. How fitting he thought.

He bent down on the banks of the lake and untied the grocery bag. The snake was reluctant to leave the relative safety of the bag, so Nicholls had to tug it gently to get it to emerge. "Come on you stupid bugger," he said impatiently.

The snake slowly slithered out and seemed to give Nicholl a perfunctory nod. For a moment they stared at each other and Nicholls almost felt a connection, before the snake disappeared into a plump tussock of moss. He stood up slowly and checked his watch. Perfect timing. With a bit of luck, he would be able to stop off and get a coffee before getting to work.

He was about to turn when all of a sudden, he felt a strong force clamp down around his neck and pin his arms to the side. The force of the blow was crushing, and Nicholls was unable to breathe. In blind panic he thrashed his body from side to side and jerked his head back to try and butt the attacker, but it was no use. The attacker was too powerful and negated Nicholls' counter-attack with ease. Nicholls felt his energy ebbing away with each movement as the smothering grip around him tightened like a python constricting a deer. His attacker forced a knee into his back and Nicholls felt his legs buckle. He fell to his knees and tried to take a gasp of air. As he did so, an acrid smelling handkerchief was thrust over his face, burning his nostrils and bringing tears to his eyes. He tried to swing his arms backward, but they were enveloped by his attacker. It was no use. He couldn't believe that this was the way he was going to die.

Holly Maxwell flicked the buttons on the television remote control impatiently. Breakfast programmes were a load of drivel. She hadn't slept much and needed a tonic to quieten her irascible mind. She knew she was suffering from withdrawal symptoms, but that had been expected. Her drug taking had all been part of the plan, a necessary evil to obtain the information she needed. She had put on a convincing show and pretended to take more than she actually did, but there was no hiding it all. Not if she wanted to gain their trust. Now that was all over, she could focus on regaining her strength. She hadn't expected the toll of substance abuse to be so powerful, but she had the resolve and force of mind to overcome these demons. She knew that an even more dangerous task was looming over the horizon. She had to focus on that at the moment. There were people looking for her and if she was found, that could jeopardise the whole enterprise.

The problem was that she had been staring at the drab, boring walls in the flat for the last week with only her own company to amuse herself. She felt suffocated. It was not in her nature to be so withdrawn and her nervous system craved the excitement and stimulation that only human interaction could bring. She tried to force down a few mouthfuls of cereal, but it was so tasteless and bland that she pushed it aside. Her appetite had still not returned and that grinded at her. The prospect of another day on her own was nauseating. What would it hurt to go for a walk by the river? She had an overcoat and a hat that would swallow her slight frame. There was no way anyone would recognise her. She would only be gone thirty minutes, forty-five at the most. Screw it. She had already made up her mind. If she didn't get some fresh air soon, she was going to go crazy.

She dressed quickly. Her pyjamas were drenched in sweat, and she probably smelt awful but that didn't matter. She wouldn't be gone long. She hurriedly exited the room, careful to lock the door and skipped down the steps into the courtyard below. It was still early but the street was slowly waking up. Mechanised shutters were grudgingly being raised in shop entrances to reveal tired looking employees bracing themselves for an arduous day of work. A council litter picker was busy hoovering up debris and human flotsam on the other side of the street. He nodded to Holly as she closed the door, and she flung her head downwards so he didn't see her face.

It felt good to be outside again. The early morning sun mixed with the brisk spring air filled her pores and awakened her senses. She took a deep breath and exhaled slowly, trying to expel the demons that were constantly whispering in her ear. It was a short walk to the river front. There was nobody there. She sat on a bench, alone with her thoughts watching the turbid water drift by. She felt revulsed by what she had done, but ultimately it had been a means to an end. It had been her choice to try and entrap Baldock. No-one else had forced her to do it. The thought of Baldock's sweaty, repulsive face forcing himself upon her had scarred her for life. The vile thoughts could never be totally banished from the dark recesses of her mind, but it had been worth it. Baldock had sporadically surrendered vital pieces of information that she had used to piece together the fragments of her past life and fuel her desire for revenge. It was all coming into place piece by piece. They would all suffer. She just had to be patient that was all.

Jimmy Nicholls slowly came to his senses. At first his vision was consumed by a patchwork of bright colours, and he had to shield his eyes from the glare, but within a few minutes it had returned to normal. His head was pounding, and he had a sharp piercing pain in his lower back but he was definitely still alive. He suddenly remembered that his attacker may still be around, and he frantically scanned his surroundings, but there was no one there. He was all alone.

He stood up slowly trying to gauge his surroundings. He was in a dense thicket of brambles, surrounded by overgrown foliage. There were rows of trees all around him, their bark peppered in a vibrant green moss. A squirrel sensed his presence and darted up a tree right in front of him. He scanned quickly for a trail but there was nothing obvious. He was in a secluded part of the wood that was for certain. It must have taken a huge effort to move him here he thought, and then he remembered the brutal murder of Baldock and his associates. At that moment he couldn't explain why, but he just knew that his attacker had been the same person who had killed these men. The killer had dispatched the men single-handedly. Surely an individual capable of that power could carry a grown man into a wood, with relative ease? He felt a chill tingle his spine at his close brush with death. The burning question though was why had he been left alive and where the hell was he?

He stood on his tip toes to see if he could spot a path and a way out of the brambled prison. A tree branch scraped the side of his face. He pushed it aside, ignoring the thorns that pricked his arm and placed a hand on a leaning tree to support his weight. He could see an opening. He was just about to force his way through when his phone sounded. It made him jump. "For fuck's sake. What is it now?" he said angrily to himself. He glanced at his watch. It was only seven-twenty. If he could figure out where he was, he would probably still just about make to the office before anyone else. He most certainly didn't have time for a phone call now. No caller Id registered on his phone as he pressed the button to accept the call. "Yes," he answered casually, ignoring the fact he was somewhere in a wood, hemmed in on all sides by brambles and with no real idea of how to get out.

There was a long pause. Nicholls could sense someone breathing on the other end of the line. "Detective Inspector Jimmy Nicholls" said a man's voice in a broad Scottish accent. The tone of the voice made it quite clear it was a statement and not a question.

"Yes it is," confirmed Nicholls. "Can I ask who is calling please?"

The caller ignored the question. "I have been waiting a long time to talk with you Jimmy." There was a bubbling excitement in the caller's voice that suggested he was struggling to control his emotions.

Nicholls felt his heart stop beating. This was the man who had abducted him just a few minutes ago. Of that he was certain. "Who the fuck are you?" he said trying desperately not to sound as terrified as he was feeling.

"I'm afraid introductions must wait until a bit later Jimmy. There is something rather pressing that requires our attention first. Don't worry, I have been looking forward to meeting you for a very long time but we must be patient until the time is right." The voice suddenly became more assured and assertive.

Nicholls couldn't believe what he was hearing. He had been abducted, drugged and abandoned in an isolated part of the forest. He needed answers now. "You need to tell me who the fuck you are first. Why have you dragged me here?"

"There's something you need to see, Jimmy. After that we can talk. I am sure you will see my point of view."

"Did you kill Baldock?" Nicholls bleated impatiently.

There was another pause. The caller starting laughing callously. "Well of course, I did, you fucking idiot," he said jovially as if they were sharing a joke over a pint of beer. "When you find out who he was and what he had done, you will be angry that I beat you to it."

"I know what kind of man he was. He was human scum. A lowlife drug dealer who preyed on the weak." He paused. "But that doesn't give you the right to kill him or his gang. Christ. The two boys you killed were barely out of their teens."

"Now you listen to me Detective Inspector Nicholls." There was a sudden surge of anger in his tone. "They all had to die. Do you hear me? They chose to be there that night. No-one forced them to chase me."

Nicholls ignored him. "You know we've got two teams of detectives searching for you right now. You might as well give up now."

The caller laughed again. "Jimmy, we will meet up soon and if you don't like what I've got to say then I promise I will hand myself in and you can do what the fuck you want with me."

Nicholls hesitated, unsure if he was being mocked or not. He decided not to humour him. "How the hell did you know I was coming here? Have you been following me?"

The caller sighed like a teacher trying to appease a petulant student. "Jimmy, we don't have much time if you want to get to work without any questions being asked." Nicholls froze in his steps. How did he know that? "I promise I am being genuine about giving myself up. You just need to do something for me first."

Nicholls decided it was in his best interests to play along. "Go on then. What have I got to lose?" he said, his voice dripping with sarcasm.

"Look directly in front of you. About twenty feet away there is a small grove of birch trees. They are quite conspicuous with their silverly bark."

Nicholls did as he said and instantly saw what he meant. "I think I can see what you mean. One of them has a crooked branch, yes? Almost at a right angle."

The caller didn't acknowledge the question. "Walk over to them now."

The rational part of Nicholls's brain quickly made some computations. If the killer had wanted him dead, then he would already have done that. Curiosity took over. He might as well discover what this psycho wants. He slowly walked over to the trees. The area was overgrown with unruly ferns that grew to his hip height, but that was much preferable to the brambles that had raked his skin. He pushed them aside easily and drew closer to the silver birches. By the first tree there was a patch of disturbed soil. It looked like it had been dug up by animals. He saw there was a ragged plastic sheet crumpled in the mud. He instinctively pulled it aside and gasped. Staring back at him was a discoloured human skull that was half buried in the soil. Nicholls has seen enough murder victims to know that they had probably died from the blunt trauma that had perforated the back the cranium. This was another victim. The spine was partially visible in the mud and Nicholls traced the outline as far as he could see. The rest of the skeleton was still enveloped in the mud. He estimated roughly that this person would have been around five foot tall and by the state of the decomposition, they had been here a while. Virtually all the soft tissue of the body had disintegrated, leaving just disarticulated bones. These are the remains of a very old skeleton thought Nicholls. Perhaps it had been buried here decades.

"Have you found the body?" The voice sounded oddly melancholy.

"Yes, I have," replied Nicholls. "Another of your victims?"

"Not mine, Jimmy. I am not that old."

"Then why did you want me to see it?"

"I needed for you to see it, Jimmy. When you find out who it is, you will share my desire for vengeance and then we can work together." The caller placed strong emphasis on the word "then."

Nicholls grew impatient. "Well, why don't you tell me who it is and save us a whole load of trouble."

"I'm not sure you would believe me Jimmy. And even if you did, I doubt you would be ready for it."

"Try me," chirped Nicholls.

The caller ignored him. "Now is the time for you to listen to me Detective Inspector," he said gravely. "In fifteen minutes, I am going to ring the police as a concerned member of the public and claim my dog has found the grave. At this point you need to be in your car and on your way to the station. There can be no connection with you and this grave. Is that clear."

"If you're asking me to ignore a crime—"

The caller interrupted Nicholls abruptly. "You need to trust me, Jimmy. I am only asking for a few days and then I will lay my soul bare. If you are found here then it will ruin everything and believe me when I say this, your life will be in grave danger."

"Let's just say I do what you tell me. Give me a reason why I should turn a blind eye to this?"

"You need to trust me, Jimmy. If I wanted you dead then you would be dead already. As soon as this call ends you need to go. If you head in a north-easterly direction from the grave site, you will come to the western edge of the lake in about four minutes. I am sure you can find your way to your car from there."

Nicholls clenched his teeth together in exasperation. He didn't know what to do. If he didn't report this crime and people found out he had been here, then the consequences were dire. However morbid curiosity was compelling him to listen to the caller. As a police officer he often relied on his gut instinct when investigating cases and he had an overwhelming visceral feeling in the pit of his stomach that this was a dangerous case and he needed to be out of the spotlight.

"I will do as you say for now. What the fuck happens next?"

"Look in your top jacket pocket," came the immediate reply.

Nicholls fumbled in his pocket and felt a plastic bag. There was something pulpy and soft inside. He pulled it out and gasped. Inside the police style evidence bag were two human ears, complete with diamond rings. Nicholls instantly knew who they belonged to. The flesh around the lobes had turned a mottled brown and the skin had wrinkled like a pair of overripe prunes. "I'm guessing these are Baldock's?"

"Spot on, Jimmy," said the caller sardonically. "There is your proof that I killed Baldock. Now do as I say, and I promise you the truth in just a few days."

Nicholls fought the urge to throw the evidence away and tucked the bag back inside his pocket. He sighed. "I am putting a lot of faith in you. I am not sure why. Who the fuck are you?" He couldn't resist a final question.

"I am your guardian angel Jimmy, that's all you need to know for now."

For the first time since the phone call, Nicholls felt the chill blow of the wind. He slowly put his phone back in his pocket. Had he made a deal with devil? He may be able to convince Flack that he was working to try and secure a conviction if this thing blew back in his face, but he couldn't count on it. He made a decision to confide in Page. At least Page could vouch for him if it went wrong, and he trusted his friendship and advice.

Nicholls must have switched into autopilot because the next thing he knew he was back by the lake where he had released the grass snake. There were a few people milling around, so he instinctively zipped up his jacked and ducked his head as he made his way to the car. From there, it was just a short drive to the police station. When he pulled on to the station road, he was totally unprepared for the utter commotion that confronted him when he got there. The main street was gridlocked with parked cars and slow moving traffic. Bodies disgorged themselves hurriedly from their vehicles. It looked like there were a few news crews there as well, as huddles of workers were straining to carry bulky filming equipment over the road.

"What the fuck is going on?" said Nicholls softly to himself. He parked up and saw a couple of detectives from the Homicide unit in conversation by the gate. "Hey, what's going on?" he called out.

One of the detectives spotted him. "A police officer was shot dead yesterday in a drugs raid," he shouted to Nicholls. "Flack's doing a press conference."

It was not unusual for Flack to do a press conference at Redmead police station, rather than Scotland Yard. The building had a spacious conference room and Flack lived close by. Police officers who worked there were often used to the media showing up for such events, although this time, the atmosphere seemed much more tense than usual.

It was always upsetting when a policeman was killed in the line of duty. The entire force would often grieve and pull together in a show of solidarity. Nicholls said a silent prayer for the policeman even though he didn't know the man. In such situations he felt an enormous wave of sympathy for the bereaved and their family. Usually, police officers who were slain had a partner and a number of dependent children. The sadness they felt must be almost unbearable. He often wondered how Jenny would cope if he died. Would she be devastated? He was sure she would grieve for him but for how long before she moved on? The thought of losing her made him sad and he felt renewed affection for his girlfriend. He still did have very strong feelings for her. Perhaps they could forge a stronger relationship together if they were both prepared to compromise. At the moment their ships were sailing in different directions and if someone didn't act, the bond they once shared would dwindle away to nothingness.

The police station was a hive of activity as Nicholl entered. People of all ranks and departments milled around busily going about their jobs with a steely intensity that was palpable in the air. Nicholls felt suffocated by the pressure that seemed to be building up on him at the moment. He couldn't think straight. He had a case to investigate and a team to lead, even though the murderer had found him first. How was he going to play this? His team were experienced officers. They would smell a rat if he tried to stall them. He was relieved to see Page's greying hair bobbing up and down busily in the corridor.

"Hey Jimmy," he called out seeing his boss. He scampered over to Nicholls and this exertion caused him to start perspiring almost immediately. "The old man is speaking to the media. It's going live in ten minutes," he said with a quick glance at his watch.

"Yeah, I just heard," said Nicholls.

"The team will want to hear him first before we meet. That OK sir?"

"Sure, Kev that's fine. You alright to start it all off today? I've got a migraine brewing here. I've been up all night."

"Yeah, no problem, Sir. You look pretty pale as it happens. I hope Jenny wasn't responsible for your lack of sleep?" Page winked mischievously.

Nicholls smiled wearily and ushed him down the corridor. Both men then made their way to the conference room, narrowly dodging a plethora of onrushing people in the process. The room had already filled up and there was a row of journalists and news reporters jostling for the best positions. The Met Commissioner Daniel Flack was sitting placidly in the centre of a room, his arms resting on a long table covered in a plain white tablecloth. There were two microphones by his elbows and a large blue poster with the insignia of the Metropolitan Police emblazoned in bold white colours behind him. At the edge of the front row, a TV news camera was poised to start filming.

Flack raised his arm and the room immediately fell quiet. His usual affable face had become as stern and implacable as granite. He glanced down at a pre-prepared speech and clenched his jaw.

"It brings me great sadness to inform you that yesterday afternoon, police officer Jack Marsden was killed during an operation to apprehend a criminal gang intent on smuggling drugs into the country." Flack spoke slowly and assuredly and there was a flurry of flashes as journalists took the opportunity to take photos of the Commissioner. Flack paused as a photo of Marsden was projected on to the screen behind him. "Jack was a young man with enormous potential. It had been a dream of his to become a firearms officer in the Met from a young age and it was only last year that he achieved this goal. Jack had boundless energy and a strong sense of decency. He was a kind young man who always wanted to do the right thing and help people when they needed assistance. To lose his life at such a young age is absolutely devastating and our hearts go out to his family at this sad time.

"The goal of yesterday's operation was to take down a dangerous criminal gang and in that respect the operation was successful. Our drug enforcement teams had recently obtained intelligence that a massive shipment of heroin and cocaine was coming into Tilbury docks. Through a mixture of careful planning and excellent police work we were able to infiltrate this gang and catch the criminals as they were unloading the drugs. Despite repeated warnings from our officers to drop their weapons, the criminal gang decided to open fire. It was during this initial exchange of gun fire that officer Marsden was shot in the neck and killed. He was pronounced dead on the scene. His bravery was not in vain. It resulted in the capture of drugs with a street value estimated to be over four hundred million pounds."

Flack looked up and wiped his eye with a handkerchief. A vein in his forehead pulsed. He looked overcome with emotion. "It is drugs like these that are fuelling the crime wave that is unfurling on our shores," he said angrily. "It is drugs like these that are causing young people to kill each other every single day." He paused to let his words sink home. "It is drugs like these that are causing addiction and pain for families up and down the country."

Nicholls ears perked up with acute interest. He had never seen Flack speak so emotionally before. "Our police officers are bravely putting their lives on the line day in and day out in this fight, but we need more support." He thrust his hands forward to emphasise his point. "For years I have sat and watched helplessly as my funding gets slashed and I have fewer officers to help fight crime. We need more resources, and we need more bodies to fight this crime wave. I urge the government to give us the funds to win this war before it is too late."

People looked at each other in surprise. No-one had expected such a candid speech from the Commissioner. It was not his style to be political. There were a few isolated ripples of applause, but people seemed reluctant to commit to anything further. Nicholls imagined the news headlines that evening. Flack's remarks would be dynamite. The Commissioner of the Metropolitan police had publicly criticised the labour government and suggested they were at least partly to blame for the increase in crime of recent years.

Flack still sat impassively in his chair. A reporter raised their hand and Flack nodded his head encouraging the question. "Commissioner Flack, how grave a threat is the drug problem in the capital at the moment and can you handle it?"

"It's something we should be really worried about, Steve. Drugs are flooding the city and are directly and indirectly responsible for a significant amount of the crime we have to deal with. It is a lucrative business I'm afraid and gangs are fighting each other for domination. I have an outstanding force at my disposal, but we need more support if we are to prevail in this war."

Another reporter raised their hand. "Would you support the zero tolerance approach advocated by the Tories?"

Flack raised his hands defensively. "I am certainly not here to talk about politics after one of my brave officers has been killed. However, we do need to get to grips with the situation. We need to take control of our streets again and that does mean being more visible and using tactics like stop and search more effectively. Criminals need to learn that crime doesn't pay."

The same reporter looked quizzically at his notes. "Just one more question, Commissioner. Two years ago, you announced that all armed officers were required to wear head mounted cameras to "provide greater transparency and accountability to the public." What happened to the footage yesterday?"

Flack sighed like an exasperated teacher would at a misbehaving child. "If you had done your research properly then you would have noticed that camera malfunction is a regular occurrence on operations. The technology that we can afford is in my opinion not fit for purpose. I have raised this issue with the Home Secretary. Yesterday afternoon the cameras stopped filming due to a central malfunction and the unit still bravely decided to go ahead with the operation. You'll have to forgive my ignorance when trying to explain such technological matters. If you want, I can get you a meeting with the head of IT? As, most of you are aware, technology is not my forte." There were a few ripples of laughter. "Now, I would all like to thank you for your time this morning. I am sure you will welcome the news that we intend to recognise Jack's Marsden's sacrifice with a memorial. We will liaise with his family and communicate their wishes as soon as we know how they would Jack to be remembered. That is all." Flack stood up and walked away, without bothering to look back at the frenzy he had instigated with his incendiary remarks.

There was a lot of commotion in the conference room after Flack had left. It was highly unusual for the Met Commissioner to talk so frankly about political matters and people were clearly polarised by his comments.

Page looked at Nicholls and raised his eyebrows. "Well sir, I think the shit is about to hit the fan. It might be a good idea to get our heads down and keep a low profile for a while."

Jason Kilbride parked his silver Mercedes carelessly on the side of the road by a huge terraced house. Carlisle Crescent was one of the finest and most sought after residential districts in London. It was typical for house prices here to exceed twenty million pounds. A row of sycamore trees stood imperiously on both sides of the street guarding an assortment of beautiful Edwardian terraced homes that gleamed magnificently in white brick. Each house was surrounded by a gate that contained a beautifully manicured green hedge. This is where I need to end up, said Kilbride to himself enviously.

He had been asked to meet the Tory leader Darren Healey at his home in Carlisle Crescent that morning. Healey was the son of a billionaire industrialist. He had graduated at Oxford before surprising everyone by enlisting in the army. Although this career choice had been a bit of a surprise, Healey had shown real aptitude in the armed forces, and he had risen quickly through the ranks. He had reached the rank of Major before he finally decided to succumb to the repeated requests to join the family business. As the new company chief executive, Healey was able to demonstrate that he was also a shrewd and able businessman and he helped steer his father's company into a very domineering position financially. With the plaudits from his business and military career still ringing loudly in his ears, he had decided to turn to politics in his early forties. He was known for having moderate views and some of his opponents called him a left wing sympathiser. However, Healey was a stubborn, dogmatic man and wouldn't change his principles for anyone. One Healey had made his mind up about something, it was very difficult to convince him to change it. Kilbride was puzzled why the grizzled old man had wanted him to meet him at his family home.

He walked up to Healey's towering four storey mansion. It was an impressive building that had been modernised in the Edwardian Baroque style, a hundred years ago. He pressed a buzzer at the gate house and a voice sounded immediately.

"Good morning, Mr Kilbride. I'll just buzz you through" said a polite voice. Kilbride recognised it immediately as the housekeeper, Mrs Kite. The lock clicked off its latch and Kilbride pushed open the gate and walked up the cobbled pathway to the main entrance. Mrs Kite was there to welcome him. Despite being in her fifties, she had an insatiable energy and a buoyant demeanour. "Mr Healey is expecting you Mr Kilbride. If you'd like to make your way to the reception room he will come and meet you there."

Kilbride nodded politely and followed her through the door. The interior of the house was simply awe inspiring. The entrance hall was furnished with patterned marble paraquet flooring that gleamed as Kilbride stepped across. The walls were painted a pristine dove-grey with bespoke timber mouldings, that sheltered a beautiful mirror that stretched across the far wall. Kilbride was shown to the main reception room and Mrs Kite gestured for him to sit. The reception room was flooded with a stream of natural light courtesy of huge floor to ceiling windows that provided access to the landscaped garden and terrace. Hanging from the ceiling was a bronzed pendant, and carved into the main wall was a polished stone fireplace. There were four dark leather sofas in the centre of the room. Kilbride took a seat in the largest of them and once he had eased himself into a comfortable position, he crossed his legs.

"Would you like a beverage, Mr Kilbride?" said Mrs Kite excitedly. "We have some pain au chocolate too if you are hungry?"

"I'd love an Americano if that's not too much trouble."

"Of course." Mrs Kite left Kilbride alone and returned a few minutes later with his drink.

Kilbride sipped his drink. It was scolding hot. Just the way he liked it. Healey was one of the few leading members of the Conservative Party that he actually had a grudging admiration for. Kilbride thought Healey's political views were a little too progressive at times, but he was blessed with charisma and presence. When Healey spoke, he engaged people, even if they did not believe in his rhetoric. His voice was rich and seemingly had the power to captivate everyone in the room. He had only been conservative leader for the last three years, but his leadership had staunchly galvanised the party and led to the party's popularity increasing markedly in that time.

"Jason, how are you?" His voice dark like chocolate made Kilbride turn unexpectedly as Healey emerged from a hidden doorway by the fireplace. "No don't get up. Let me come to you." Healey shuffled slowly and sat on the sofa adjacent to him. Now they were close, Kilbride was astonished by how gaunt his face looked. His auburn hair was uncharacteristically ruffled, and his skin looked wrinkled and leathery. He was wearing a corduroy jack with leather elbow patches and shabby jeans. It was a world away from the sharply dressed energetic man that led party meetings. "It is good to see you, Jason. Thank you for coming to see me."

"Not at all, Darren" answered Kilbride respectfully. "Are you OK?"

Healey looked at him for a few moments as if he was appraising him. "No Jason, I'm afraid I'm not," he said belatedly. "I've been feeling jaded and lethargic for the last few weeks, but I put it down to the stress of the campaign trail. I can no longer say that I am a spring chicken anymore, hey?" He looked at

Kilbride mischievously and winked. "Unfortunately, I had tests done last week by my physician, and I have been diagnosed with stage two bowel cancer."

"Oh my God" said Kilbride feigning concern. "What does this mean?"

"It means there's still a good chance I can beat it," he said defiantly. "The cancer hasn't spread to any of my other organs. I will need surgery of course, but the doctors are confident they can stop it."

"That's reassuring Darren."

"I have to be prepared for the fact that this process is going to take a lot out of me Jason. I am not sure how my body will react to my current work schedule." Kilbride nodded sympathetically. Healey stiffened. "The public don't need to know of course, just yet. We are doing well in the polls at the moment, and I'd hate to jeopardise anything so close to the election."

"I understand Darren. Is there anything I can do to help you?"

"Not at the moment, Jason. I appreciate your concern though." He patted Kilbride's leg. "I think you are doing a great job, at the moment. The public like you. You speak well and your campaign work has been exemplary. You have all the hallmarks of being a superb home Secretary."

"Thank you, Darren. That means a lot coming from you."

Healey nodded impatiently as if he was in a rush. "But, I also have a responsibility to protect the party. I have to prepare for the possibility that my health will fail so it is vital that there is someone in place to succeed me. It would be a disaster if there is a power struggle when we are so close to achieving our goals." Kilbride felt his heart skip a beat. Did he want him to replace him? Kilbride felt an intense stare boring into his soul. It was as if Healey had invited him here to make a judgement on him as the potential leader of the conservative party.

Healey seemed to have read his mind. "I know you are an ambitious man Jason and I think that can be an admirable quality if it drives you to succeed. But are you a potential leader of the conservatives and possibly a future prime minister? I must confess I do have my reservations. You have a lot of supporters Jason, I will give you that. I don't know quite how you have done it because some people find you arrogant and abrasive. I have also heard some disturbing details about your private life. Perhaps I am being unfair, but I have to be sure about you, if you are to lead my party." He prodded his chest powerfully with his index finger to emphasise the point that he believed that only he had the right to name a successor.

"I need someone to be able to step into my shoes if I can't lead the party. And that person must have the capacity to be magnanimous. They must be able to keep the party aligned and united. That is why labour won the last election and we lost. There were too many cliques and factions in the Tories that couldn't rise above their petty squabbles. If I am to support you as my deputy I need to believe that you have the necessary leadership qualities, that you will be someone who will always put the party first. That means there will be times when you must be able to compromise, even if that goes against your natural beliefs." He laughed ironically. "I appreciate that this might not be the news you were expecting when I invited you round here."

Jason felt the adrenaline surge in his blood stream again. "I would not let you down Darren. I can promise you that."

"Jason before I make any decisions, I wanted to speak to you man to man." His face became deathly serious. "I truly think you have done some fantastic work on the campaign trail and your action plan is excellent. I agree wholeheartedly that we need to get grips with crime in this country. Labour have been too soft, and they have let things get out of hand." Healey took a deep breath as if he was exhaling out some of his deepest worries.

"I am a bit concerned though Jason that you will go too far if you are left unchecked, and that worries me greatly." Kilbride tried to speak but Healey shut him down abruptly with a wave of his hand. "No Jason," he said sternly. "Please let me finish." He paused and stared out into the garden as if his brain was searching for the right words to use.

"Criminality in this country at the moment is like a disease that is contaminating people and rotting away their sense of morality. Criminals have been getting away with their crimes for far too long and they are infecting others with their sickness. We need to restore law and order as one of our main campaign promises and rightly so. And that does mean we must give the police more powers, we must give the courts the power to impose tougher sentences and we do need to build more prisons." He raised his eyebrow ominously at Kilbride as if trying to send him a hidden message.

"But Jason and this is a big but; these measures should only be a temporary measure. Our long term goal must be to take the Criminal Justice System out of the Victorian ages and usher in a new era that focuses on rehabilitation and reform of society. We must look at making our society fairer and more inclusive. If we do that, then crime will take care of itself."

He held out his hand and tapped his fingers one by one. "We must tackle poverty in deprived areas and provide more opportunities for people in these areas to find work. We must improve the education system so every child, regardless of their post code has the same opportunities to succeed and forge a career based on their individual abilities. We must tackle family breakdown in any way we can to stop children from broken families being sucked into a gang culture to gain that sense of belonging. I believe that if we continue to utilise draconian methods of criminal justice for longer than is necessary, then we will create division and resentment. And if that happens then we have failed in our duty to serve the people.

"Christ you only have to look at the American Criminal Justice System to see where we will end up if we are not careful. They just lock people up and throw away the key. Over two million Americans are incarcerated in their prisons. That makes up about twenty percent of the world's prison population. Can you bloody believe it? And they don't do anything to help them rehabilitate while they're in there. That's why they just keep re-offending when they're released. I think the re-offending rates are nearly seventy percent or something silly like that. How on earth can that be acceptable in a civilised society?"

He threw his hands in to the air in a gesture of exasperation and then his eyes narrowed as he stared back at Kilbride. "If I am to choose you as deputy leader of the conservative party, then I must have faith that you will uphold these values. I could not support someone who would choose to protect their own pockets over the country. And, if the worst happens and my health fails me, I need someone to lead the party. My support would be all it takes to make that happen. Could that person be you?"

Kilbride stiffened and looked Cullen in the eye. "We are of one mind Douglas. I can hand on heart say confidently that I agree with everything that you have just said"

Nicholls slumped in his chair. It would be another late day. He had been expecting his attacker to make contact sooner rather than later, but it had been nearly two days now. He had been in a state of constant readiness and expectation that his phone would ring, and he would have to make excuses and a hasty exit. He knew he had seemed distracted and that his instructions to his fellow detectives had been clumsy and vague. He checked his phone for the thousandth time that day. What was he doing? Surely, he had to let Bircham know what had happened to him yesterday morning? Or had it already gone too far? He crumpled some papers on his desk to unleash some tension and hurled them at the door. He was playing a dangerous game and he knew it.

Unbelievably, there had been two bodies discovered at the grave site. The second skeleton had been buried slightly deeper. They were both now undergoing a thorough forensic examination with Schofield. Nicholls had heard that much from the electrified conversations that had been pulsating around the police station. The killer had certainly kept up that end of the bargain and contacted the police with the body's whereabouts almost immediately after their conversation. The talk at the station was that the body was really old. Who could it have been and what were the implications of the death? There were many unsolved murders that were still technically live but had lain dormant for years and even decades as leads and enquiries had all disintegrated. Frenzied speculation about the identity of the victim had dominated much of the talk around the canteen tables and offices all day. Forensics would surely put them out of their misery before too long.

He opened up the Baldock file and stared at the pretty face of Holly Maxwell. There was something about her face that was oddly familiar. It irked him that he couldn't come up with a reason for the feeling. He shook his head. It was probably nothing. Anyway, they hadn't had any luck whatsoever in trying to locate her. The flat she shared with Baldock was empty and two officers had been sat in a parked car watching it all day, to no avail. She had either got wind that there was heat on her or she was already dead. Nicholls guessed the latter.

He picked up his phone again and debated calling Jenny. His thumb hovered briefly over the dial, but he checked and popped it back in his pocket. He heard a knock on the door and Page's head poke round.

"How you doing, sir?" he said jovially.

"I'm OK thanks Kev," remarked Nicholls instinctively.

Page came into the office and closed the door. "Well, who do you think we must have pissed off to get this number sir? This case is rotten to the core. We've got nothing, no forensics, no witnesses and no motives whatsoever. What do we do next, Jimmy?" His voice was almost pleading.

"Kevin, sit down," said Nicholls seriously. He had decided to unburden himself and confide in someone he could trust. He took a deep breath. "What if I were to tell you that the killer knocked me out yesterday morning and then rang me up so he could talk me through how he killed Baldock and the others."

Page stifled a grin. "I'd say that pretty much sums up our luck at the moment.

I'd also say, what the hell are you playing at letting someone knock you out? Have you looked in the mirror lately? You're a bit of a hulking great lump, sir? Perhaps you need to get yourself down the gym."

"I think he drugged a handkerchief, Kev. Then, he dragged me to the murder site at St John's forest. He said that it was significant for me."

"That's lucky then. At least we can add another victim to the list. So, we're dealing with a serial killer then?" said Page playfully.

"I don't think these ones were his. He wanted me to see them first. When the body has been identified, I guess he'll get in contact again."

"Perhaps you'd better start going out with a personal attack alarm, sir, in case he tries to attack you again? I think my missus has got a spare one if you're interested? Are you sure he didn't interfere with you while you were out for the count?" said Page sarcastically.

Nicholls started laughing. He couldn't help it. The situation was ludicrous. "Kev, I'm being deadly serious."

"So am I sir. We need to get on top of this case before Bircham starts breathing down our necks."

Nicholls was just about to respond when Detective Superintendent Daniel Bircham's bulky frame silhouetted against the glass window. He came straight in without bothering to knock. His face was sallow and pallid. "Good afternoon gentlemen." His voice was coarse and croaky like he had been chain smoking cigarettes all day. "Kevin, I could do with speaking with Jimmy alone if that's ok?"

Page got up to leave but Nicholls placed a hand on his shoulder to check him. "Sir, if it's all ok with you I'd like Kev to hear this as well. I am sure he will at some point anyway." Nicholls had a horrible feeling that he couldn't quite explain. It was as if he knew what Bircham was about to say.

Bircham coughed and looked awkward. "That's your decision Jimmy. I think it would be best if you were sitting down though."

Nicholls nodded and sat back down in his chair. His muscles instinctively tensed, and he tried to anchor his weight centrally in the chair to help brace himself for the impact of Bircham's words. "One of the bodies in St John's forest has been identified," he said solemnly. "Forensics were able to use dental records to trace the victim. I'm really sorry Jimmy, but it's your mother."

The news rocked Nicholls like an earthquake. He was hit with a wave of dizziness and nausea that washed over him. He had somehow expected the news, but he couldn't explain why. Bircham was saying something, but there was too much blood pumping through his head to make any sense of the words or what they meant. He felt intensely fragile, as if his entire soul had left his body, leaving only an empty shell that could be blown away by a sudden gust of wind.

Nicholls closed his eyes and tried to breathe slowly. He imagined he was drowning for a few seconds and the vision terrified him. It was a crushing sensation as the pressure of the current consumed him and despite thrashing his arms and legs, he felt himself sinking deeper in the waters below. A strong hand suddenly squeezed his shoulders, and he felt the waters rescind and in an instant he was back to reality.

"I'm really sorry sir," said Page. "I don't have any words for how you must be feeling but if there's anything that I can do, please ask me."

Nicholls nodded gratefully. He didn't try and speak in case his language failed him.

"You need to go home Jimmy. I understand this must be a terrible shock for you," said Bircham. "You need to take as much time off as you need."

"Thank you, sir. I do need to collate the evidence for the Baldock murder but after that I will go home. Don't worry though, I don't intend to have any time off. I think being at work will help take my mind off everything."

Bircham was not known for his compassion as a superior officer. He grunted something incomprehensible that sounded vaguely supportive, and then left the office.

For a long time, Page and Nicholls sat silently in the room trying to process the information. After what seemed like an eternity Page stood up and patted Nicholls' shoulder awkwardly. As the older man he felt he needed to show some support, but was conscious that Nicholls was his superior officer. "Well sir, I guess you weren't shitting me earlier about the Baldock killer."

Nicholls didn't go home straight away. His mind was still ticking like a bomb and at least in the office, he had an outlet to vent his energy by pouring it into the Baldock case. Page didn't want to leave him on his own, and Nicholls almost had to frog march him out the door.

He felt numb, like he had almost let his mother down in some way. Of course, he couldn't remember her. He had not even been two years old when she had gone missing, or so he had been told. His father had been an alcoholic who was incapable of looking after himself, let alone a child so Nicholls had been taken into care and adopted. His childhood had been a happy one, punctuated only by occasional fleeting thoughts about his birth parents and who they were. His adopted family had loved him like he was their own son and given him all the affection and support to make a success of himself.

As he grew as a child, he had been curious about his birth parents and his adopted family had always been candid about the limited information they knew. His mother had gone missing when he was a baby, and they didn't know what had happened to her or where she had gone. Nicholls had always assumed she had abandoned him, so he had built an inner wall of hostility in his mind towards her. Nicholls had also learned through his adopted parents that his father had died of cirrhosis of the liver when he was eight years old and again, he stubbornly refused to feel any compassion towards him. In his head they had both failed in their sacred duty as parents so were unworthy of any of his affection. He had a new family that loved him. He did not need his birth parents and had banished all thoughts of them to the darkest recesses of his mind.

Now he knew the truth, he felt pangs of guilt overwhelm him. His mother had not abandoned him. She had been murdered. Perhaps his father knew something about it or perhaps the grief had destroyed him, and he had turned to drink for comfort. Well anyway, he would surely never know now unless Baldock's killer contacted him. That was now his only connection to the past and he was desperate to know more.

Chapter 4
The Devil and His Disciples

Patrick McGovern looked out of his car window and drunkenly leered at the young prostitutes who were soliciting themselves on the street corner. They were all part of his network of sex workers. He had a lucrative trade deal with the Russian mob who trafficked girls from all over eastern Europe to work in the brothels that he ran from dens in south London. Most of the girls were routinely injected with drugs so they would become addicts. They were more compliable that way and would literally do anything for their next fix. The best-looking girls were shipped off into safe houses throughout the city where they worked to satisfy the sexual needs of his most important clients. Each house was run by one of his "matrons" who ruled the establishment with a rod of iron. These girls were never physically assaulted as that would be bad for business. No-one wanted to fuck a prostitute with a swollen lip and black eyes, but the matrons had learned how to use psychological pressure to make them comply. Most of the girls had families back home and routinely sent money back to them. A well-directed threat to harm a younger sibling or an elderly father usually had the desired effect and resulted in the prostitute doing exactly what was asked of her. There had only been one case where one of the prostitutes had repeatedly refused to have sex with several elderly politicians, and in that instance the severed fingers of her fourteen-year-old brother had eventually done the trick.

Patrick McGovern had made his bones as a young hoodlum, peddling narcotics and acting as a murder for hire entrepreneur for London's criminal bosses. His notorious brutality and savage nature had allowed him to climb the echelons of the capital's underworld at lightning speed. At twenty-five, he had been promoted to underboss of a large organised crime syndicate in east London. He had spent a few years coordinating the cell's criminal activities which included drug and firearm trafficking, prostitution, and armed robbery. At the age of twenty-eight he had organised a brutal coup-d'état of the crime family's hierarchy and replaced them with his most brutal and loyal henchmen. The boss of the family had been gunned down while he ate dinner peaceably with his family in a London restaurant. The wife and two daughters had all been killed in the hit. It didn't bother McGovern in the slightest. It was just collateral damage.

McGovern's rise to power had been total. By the age of fifty-five his empire dominated most of London and southwest England and his criminal network spanned continents. As well as his human trafficking contacts in Eastern Europe, he had a lucrative contract with the Ndrangheta, an Italian mafia franchise to ship drugs into Britain, a firearms deal with Albanian gangsters and with the vast profits from these illegal enterprises, he used Russian criminals to launder dirty money through the city of London's financial institutions. Despite all of this, his lust for power and wealth remained insatiable. He was a vengeful man who thrived on violence, and he ruthlessly exterminated any opponents who dared to cross his path.

Tonight, he was making a rare visit to his den in south London to inspect his newest shipment of women from Russia. The immigrants had all been charged an extortionate amount of money to come to Britain and would be tied to McGovern for the rest of their lives. Many of the women had come from Thailand and Vietnam. The older ones would be worked to the point of exhaustion in a network of nail bars and fast food salons across London, while the younger more attractive ones would be forced into his brothels to ply their trade. McGovern had a voracious sexual appetite and took great pleasure in "breaking in" some of the new girls first. He had been drinking most of the day and he was anxious to find out was on offer for him tonight.

"Get on move on," he growled impatiently to his driver as they pulled into the industrial estate that masqueraded as a cover for his sex den. He was being driven in a luxury grey Mercedes V-Class MPV which had blacked out windows and bullet proof glass. It was not uncommon for McGovern to pick three or four girls to take home for the evening, so he needed a vehicle with plenty of room.

At the southern edge of the industrial estate was an enormous warehouse that bisected a railway line. At first glance it looked just like a typical building found in any old industrial complex, but the unsightly exterior contained the beating heart of McGovern's prostitution business. It was run by an Albanian gang who were known for their brutality and hovered menacingly around the edge of the building like vultures protecting carrion in the African savannah.

Punters called this den "The Ritz" and anyone who could spare a hundred pounds sterling could access the main entrance and have a drink in the seedy bar that was situated in the first-floor lobby. The bar served a small selection of beers, wines and spirits and punters could sit and ogle the naked ladies who served drinks and gyrated on the central podium. These girls were bona fide lap dancers who offered dances for paying customers in the back rooms, but they were only allowed to look and definitely not to touch. Every so often the Albanians had to deal with punters who got a little too rowdy and grabbed a fistful of flesh. Their preferred method was to smash the offending hand with a hammer. Word soon got about that you didn't fuck around in the Ritz.

For another hundred pounds sterling, the punters could be taken to "Broadway." This allowed titillated customers who had been sexually aroused by the lap dancers access to a secure part of the warehouse with banks of curtained booths. In each booth was a drugged-up sex worker who had been trafficked by the Russians. In here, punters could pay for a thirty-minute slot, and this allowed them to do pretty much what they wanted to with the girls, within reason. The Albanians were still of course a constant, menacing presence but the girls were often so insensible they were almost oblivious to the abuse they received, and seldom cried out.

McGovern used a secret side entrance that was manned by a burly Albanian to enter the den. He rarely ventured into the Ritz. He didn't like being seen and had no time for the vermin that the venue often attracted. He was flanked on each side by two huge bodyguards who followed him like a shadow all day. He entered a large foyer that was lit with two banks of industrial lights that effused enough brightness to illuminate the space. In the centre of the area were half a dozen young women, some conspicuously still in their teens, eating a stodgy meal of bread of cheese. They had only just been herded off a lorry that had been their home for the last thirty-six hours. An Albanian matron was responsible for cleaning them up and giving them a meal. Adjacent to the warehouse, hidden out of sight were a series of grotty trailers that provided the living quarters for the sex workers of Broadway. The young women all looked terrified. That was good thought McGovern. That way they would be much easier to control.

McGovern had to hand it to Agnessa the Albanian matron. She only needed a couple of days to get the girls ready to start as sex workers. She was a formidable woman with a face like a bulldog chewing a wasp. Any girl who didn't do as she was told would suffer her wrath. McGovern chuckled. He had seen girls who had argued with Agnessa being beaten within an inch or two of their life. Within a week it was very rare to see even a spark of defiance in the women as they were conditioned to accept their new miserable existence. They soon found out that the streets of London were not paved with gold, and the Eldorado they had dreamed of, was in fact a living nightmare. McGovern did not have any sympathy whatsoever to their plight. They were his commodities, and he would use them as he pleased. They would work for him as sex slaves and when they were too old for this, there would still be lots of nails for them to polish.

He was a big man with a menacing presence. As he stepped closer to the tables where the women were silently eating their food, he felt their fear and he fed on it voraciously, like a shark. It made him feel powerful to intimidate other human beings. A young girl from Vietnam cowered as McGovern crouched over the table and helped himself to a slice of cheese. She recoiled as his face came into the light. It was a weathered face that had so many dents from a life of crime that it resembled an old cast iron stove. She looked into his eyes and felt fear. There was no compassion or empathy in those eyes. They were dangerous eyes and everyone round the table could sense it. They were like the eyes of a wild beast.

McGovern chewed the wad of cheese briefly and then swallowed greedily. He was just about to light a cigar when he saw her. She was sitting on the far side of the table trying to avoid his attention. She had short, cropped brown hair with waif like features and an innocent beauty. Her skin was honeyed, and her hazel brown eyes reminded him of polished amber. She was a real looker. He felt instinctively aroused at the sight of her and wanted her for himself. She was wearing a baggy grey tracksuit, but McGovern could see she had a voluptuous figure as the fabric clung to her pert breasts as if they were magnetic.

McGovern stood up to his full height. He was wearing an Armani suit and a black woollen trench coat. His hair had been shaved by a razor and the light glinted off his bald head to reflect a huge, puckered scar that jagged across his temple. That had been the result of a bar brawl when he was still a teenager. The perpetrator had smashed a glass over McGovern's head, and he been almost blinded by the blood that gushed over his face. If the attacker hadn't hesitated, then perhaps his story would have ended there, but he did, and McGovern had unleashed a flurry of punches that knocked him to the ground. Once on the floor, McGovern had stamped on his head until he had stopped moving. He never found out if the man had ever regained consciousness.

McGovern stepped backwards and signalled Agnessa, who obediently came over to him like a dog to her master. He pointed over at the girl. "What's her story?" he said nonchalantly.

"Romanian, I think," said Agnessa uncertainly. "Early twenties. The driver said she was picked up near Bucharest. She said her father used to beat her and had arranged for her to marry someone she didn't want to. She ran away from home and used everything she owned to pay for the trip." Agnessa smiled wickedly. "Of course, she had to pay some on credit too, so she will be in debt to us until that is paid off."

"She won't be working here that is for certain," said McGovern emphatically. "Bring her to me."

Agnessa nodded and beckoned the girl with a curt command and a jabbing motion of the index finger. The girl saw her and dropped her head submissively. She meekly shuffled over until she stood about a metre away from the towering frame of McGovern and the strapping Albanian.

"What is your name?" asked McGovern. Most Europeans had a good grasp of English, so he spoke clearly and slowly. If the girl didn't understand, Agnessa was more than capable of translating. She spoke a number of languages fluently, although her Romanian was far from perfect.

"My name is Elena," replied the young girl in broken English. She did not take her eyes off the floor as she spoke.

"Look at me girl" said McGovern imperiously.

Elena clenched her jaw and forced her head up until she met the gaze of McGovern. He was a monstrously big man, and she was only just above five foot so she had to arch her neck to accomplish this. McGovern stepped towards her, and Elena flinched. He pressed an enormous finger into the groove of her chin and pushed her head up even higher so he could get a better look. Her skin was immaculately flawless, like velvet. She looked nervous although there was a spark of fire in her doe like brown eyes. That was good he thought. He liked that.

"Elena get your things together. You are coming with me. You are not staying here."

Elena looked at McGovern and nodded complicitly. His lips curved into a menacing grin, and he enveloped her with a huge arm and brought her tight to his chest.

Jimmy Nicholls pulled out a glass decanter from under a cabinet in the hallway. It was full of brandy from the last Christmas. He rarely drank at home, but he needed something to take the edge off the pulsating thoughts that were swirling around in his head. He filled a glass and drained it quickly. The amber liquid burned his throat and he hesitated briefly before pouring another one. He moved warily into the living room carrying the decanter, unsure of whether he could keep his emotions in check. There was an avalanche of grief welling up in his mind and it wouldn't take much for it all to implode.

He sat in an armchair in the pitch black for a long while as he contemplated the devastating news he had just received. At some point the light switched on and the door opened. His girlfriend Jenny entered the room. She was wearing a pink nightie, which left little to the imagination.

"Jimmy, there you are my darling. I thought I heard you come in, but you never came upstairs." Her voice was warm and soothing.

"I needed to sit by myself for a while Jenny," he said sadly.

"That's fine babe." She stepped over to the armchair and started to stroke his hair. "My dad rang me earlier and told me what had happened. I just don't know what to say Jimmy. I'm so very sorry."

It was at this point that the avalanche fissured, and all his emotions erupted at once. He burst into tears and buried his head in Jenny's bosom. He shook violently as the grief cascaded throughout his entire body. It took a few minutes before he could wrestle back control and stop himself sobbing. He looked up at Jenny. She was beautiful. He had forgotten how much he loved her.

Her face also seemed lined with a grief that mirrored his own, but she radiated an innocent beauty. All the arguments of recent weeks and months were dispelled as he gazed into her blue eyes. They were a gateway into her soul, and they shimmered with passion. All of a sudden, she had returned to the young, fragile girl she had been when they first met; a vulnerable woman who was unsure about herself and needed reassurance. He took a moment to take a mental picture of her heart shaped face in his mind, her perfect eyebrows, her petit nose and plump scarlet lips. She had loosened her hair and long golden-brown tresses fell in a wave over her shoulder and across her generous breasts. She was gorgeous and he felt deeply aroused by her.

Without thinking he wrapped his hand around her head and pulled her face towards his, until their lips met. There was a spark of chemistry as the tentative connection became something powerful and the embrace became deeper and more passionate. Jenny groaned as Nicholls kissed her neck and then pulled the nightie over her head. Her breasts were beautiful and achingly swollen as he cupped them with both hands and kissed her pert nipples. Her skin was honeyed and smooth as he traced his hands over her hips and then down her inner thigh until he felt her warmth below. Her body seemed to shudder with ecstasy as he probed further with his fingers. He could barely contain himself and the electrifying feeling that stimulated his entire body had made him as hard as granite. He lowered Jenny slowly on to the carpet and took off the rest of his clothes. As Jenny arched her back in anticipation, he placed one hand under her ribs and eased himself into her. Jenny gave a short squeal but then groaned as he pinned her to the ground. For a brief moment, Nicholls felt almost paralysed as the intense exaltation crippled his senses, but then he began to rock slowly in perfect synchrony with her body. As the pleasure intensified, his thrusts became faster and more vigorous. He couldn't stop himself now even if the earth subsided. Jenny's groans became screams of ecstasy until he was almost breathless with exertion, but he kept going. And then all of a sudden, the pressure reached a volcanic crescendo in his groin, and he climaxed. Nicholls felt a wave of euphoria rush over him and then there was a brief moment of blissful serenity as their sweaty bodies relaxed and detached.

Nicholls stroked Jenny's hair. He felt guilty for not being there for her during the last turbulent months of their relationship. "I'm sorry darling," he said softly.

"Don't worry about that now Jimmy," she replied tenderly. "Come up to bed. You need to rest. I can't imagine what you must be feeling at the moment." She picked up her nightie and took his hand. They were both naked and paused briefly to hold each other affectionately before going up the stairs in the bedroom. They lay together entwined in each other's arms for what seemed like an eternity before Nicholls initiated another round of love making.

Jenny fell asleep soon after, but Nicholls knew that his mind was too out of control for rest tonight. He went downstairs and finished another glass of brandy. He had better be careful. He was beginning to feel very inebriated. If he had many more, he would struggle to be coherent at work tomorrow. Bircham had said he could have as much time off as he wanted, but the thought of being home alone with his thoughts, was a terrifying prospect. He would much rather be at work where there was more productive outlet for his energies.

He looked at his watch. It had just gone past ten. The effects of the brandy were starting to make him feel drowsy. That was good. A drunken sleep was preferable to no sleep at all. He felt his body relaxing when all of a sudden, he was jolted upright with a start. His phone was ringing.

He looked at the screen which displayed the withheld number sign. He accepted the call hurriedly. "Nicholls here. I'm guessing this is the mystery murderer?" he said drunkenly.

"Very funny, Jimmy," came the familiar Scottish voice. "Are you alone?"

Nicholls looked round instinctively as if he expected Jenny to be lying next to him. "I'm alone. I'm hoping you're finally going to tell me what happened to my mother."

The voice sounded sympathetic. "I'm sorry you had to find out that way Jimmy, I really am, but it was the only way I could get your attention."

"Well, let's just say you have got my attention."

"I can tell you everything you want to hear Jimmy, but I need to show you something first."

Nicholls grimaced. He was growing impatient at all these games. "Look you sick fuck," he shouted down the phone. "I kept my promise. I did everything you asked of me. Now I want you tell me right now, what happened to my mum. Who killed her?" Nicholls flinched. He had made more noise than he wanted to and was worried that he might have woken Jenny. That would at the very least provoke an awkward conversation he didn't want to get into at the moment.

"Listen Jimmy, I am on your side. We both want justice for your mother. I can explain everything right now if you want, but you need to meet me somewhere."

Nicholls chuckled. He was more drunk that he thought. What did it matter now? With his luck he would be pulled over for drink driving. "I'm game, Detective Taggart," he said mockingly. "Where am I heading? Do you fancy meeting up for a beer or are you more of a coffee person?"

There was a pause. "Do you know the Capital industrial estate?"

"Yeah, I do," sighed Nicholls. It was a few miles from his home.

"If you drive through the north entrance, by the cinema, there is a café about two hundred yards from the junction on the right. There is a small car park outside. Pull up in there and flash your lights three times. I will meet you there in twenty minutes."

Nicholls needed answers. He was restless and impatient at the best of times and his mind was already a vortex of bubbling theories about what had happened. There was a moment where he briefly contemplated ignoring the call and going to bed with Jenny, but he knew there was no way he could rest with the possibility that he could finally gain some closure. Every sinew in his being drove him out of the house and before he knew it, he had started the engine in his car.

A nagging voice in the back of his head told him to ring Page, but he quickly dispelled it, and within minutes, he was careering drunkenly through the deserted streets in his silver BMW. The knowledge that he might found out about what had happened to his mother had galvanised his focus. He had a fleeting thought about Jenny and what would happen to her if he died, but he didn't feel in any real danger. If this madman had wanted him dead, then he would have had plenty of opportunities to do that already. It was a liberating feeling.

It did not take him long to reach Capital industrial estate. As he expected, it was deserted. There were a few random cars parked in the adjacent cinema, but asides from that it was eerily still and quiet. He found the café easily enough and pulled into a space opposite the front door. He looked out the window, but there was nothing and no-one visible. He flashed his lights impatiently.

All of a sudden, a light switched on in the café and illuminated the courtyard. "What the fuck is this?" exclaimed Nicholls to himself. He stepped cautiously out the car and as he did so, the café door swung open.

A hooded figure stood silhouetted against the door frame. He clapped his hands mockingly. "Well Jesus Fucking Christ Jimmy, I didn't think you would get here at all the state you were in when I rang."

Nicholls strained to see who was speaking to him. Whoever it was, he was wearing a fibre glass resin ice hockey mask to conceal his identity. More games he thought. The desire to seek the truth overrode his natural instinct for self-preservation and he slammed the car door aggressively and gestured angrily to the man. "What the fuck do you want from me?" he growled. "Perhaps I should arrest you right now."

The masked man put his hands up sardonically. "Hey Jimmy, that attitude isn't really necessary. I just want to talk with you."

Nicholls swung his arm contemptuously. He could feel a headache coming on. He was tired and irritable. "Fuck you."

The masked man dipped his arm into a baggy pocket and slowly withdrew a gun. The silver barrel glistened in the moonlight. He saw the look of surprise on Nicholls' face. "Come in Jimmy, I insist. I'll make you something to eat if you want. Don't make me have to use this." He wagged the gun at Nicholls and gestured from him to enter the café.

Nicholls stepped through the door obediently. The masked man moved behind the counter and pointed to a table for him to sit at. It was one of those old-fashioned cafes with simple wooden tables and cheap seats. There was an array of condiments sitting compliantly in a neat box in the centre of the table.

The masked man stood over a grill with a metal spatula and a sizzling frying pan. "How do you like your bacon, Jimmy?" Nicholls couldn't believe what he was witnessing. It was almost farcical. If he hadn't been dealing with the grief of his mother's murder, he might have laughed.

"Nice and crispy please," replied Nicholls sarcastically.

The masked man turned diligently and placed a couple of rashers of bacon in the frying pan. The bacon started sizzling immediately and a mouth-watering aroma soon filled the room. Nicholls felt his stomach rumble. He had barely eaten all day. "Do you fancy a coffee, Jimmy? It might help you sober up."

"Just a splash of milk and a couple of sugars please if you're making one." His voice was dripping with condescension.

The masked man ignored the sarcasm. "No problem Jimmy. It will be just a minute."

Nicholls switched off and his mind instinctively started to drift. He thought about what Jenny would say if she woke up and he wasn't there. He couldn't think of a plausible explanation as to where he had gone in the middle of the night.

The masked man dexterously buttered a slice of bread and scooped out the bacon. He folded the slice over with one hand and poured the contents of a steaming kettle into a large cup next to the plate. He added a couple of sugars and stirred the mug vigorously, before placing the food and the drink on the counter. "Come and get it Jimmy," he said with the nonchalance of a bored cook.

Nicholls didn't need a second invitation. He raced to the counter like an orphan in the Oliver Twist story and hurriedly started to devour the bacon butty before he had even made it back to the table. It tasted good. The grease of the bacon had been soaked up by the bread. Just the way he liked it. Within minutes he had consumed it all. He reclined in his chair and took a mouthful of coffee.

"Did that hit the spot, Jimmy?" Nicholls didn't answer so the masked man stepped past the counter and heaved himself up so he could sit down. He fiddled with his mask and for a split second, Nicholls thought that he was taking it off, so he sat up eagerly in anticipation.

To his disappointment, the mask remained in place. "I am truly sorry that you had to find out about your mother the way you did, Jimmy." The man seemed to speak with genuine sadness, that surprised Nicholls. "But with your help we can avenge her murder. The people that killed her at still at large and still committing evil sins every day. It is finally time to do something about it. If me and you work together, we can bring them all to justice."

Nicholls shook his head. He was tired of going round in circles all the time. "Look," he said impatiently. "At the moment you are holding all the cards. If you want me to help you then you had better start being honest with me. What is your connection to my mother and why do you know so much about her?"

There was a long pause. The masked man had bowed his head for what seemed like an eternity. He loosened a tie at the base of his neck, placed his other hand on the front of the mask to prevent it from slipping off. "I know so much about you Jimmy," he said with his head still bowed, "because I am you."

The last section of the sentence was spoken so softly that for a second Nicholls thought he had misheard. He was about to ask the masked man to repeat himself when the mask dropped to the floor and his face was finally revealed to the light.

Nicholls gasped in shock and horror because it was like looking into a mirror. It was his own face that was staring back at him.

Time seemed to stand still. No-one spoke. Nicholls felt the blood pounding in his head again. He tried to stand but the strength had left his body. It was like he was drunk. What the fuck was going on? Was someone playing a joke on him? The face in front of him remained impassive. It was his face with the striking nose and chiselled jaw line. The raven black hair was longer, more unruly, and the cheeks were more gaunt, but it was still his face. Nicholls closed his eyes and kept them shut. When he opened them, he was expecting the face to have gone, but to his abject horror it was still there. On closer inspection there was a few subtle differences. The eyes of the man in front of him were slate grey, whilst his were brown. The face also had an ugly scar running adjacent to his nose like a riverbank. It was as if he was trapped in a nightmare that didn't seem to make any sense.

Nicholls opened his mouth to speak but no words came out. He thought about the incident in the woods again and seriously debated whether he was actually already dead. Was the man in front of him a demon who had come to torment him for his sins? He stood up slowly. Nicholls could see he was a big man, powerfully built.

"I am your brother Jimmy," he said assertively. The words didn't seem to register in Nicholls's befuddled mind and time seemed to jump forward. The next thing Nicholls was aware of, was that they were both sitting on the same table staring at each other. The gun that had been pointed at him just a few moments ago, was lying next to him, within easy reach. Nicholls amazingly had no urge to try and snatch the weapon.

"My name is Kane," he said softly. "That is your name too, Jimmy. My first name is John."

That at least made sense. Jimmy Nicholls had been the name given to him by his foster parents. "What happened to you?" he said.

Kane sighed. "When our mother died, we were both taken into foster care. Our father was too grief-stricken to cope. He turned to alcohol and in the end, it slowly killed him." He shook his head. "They tried to keep us together, but it just wasn't possible. Apparently, there wasn't a family in the entire country that wanted to adopt a pair of twins," he said angrily. "You were adopted by a local family, and I was taken to Scotland. Hence the difference between our accents," he joked.

"How did I never know about this?" asked Nicholls.

"My story is not a happy one, Jimmy. You were adopted by a loving family. Perhaps they did not want you to find out about me in case it was too painful? I can't speculate about their intentions. My adopted father on the other hand was a brutal man. He abused me in ways that I can still barely even fathom. He turned me into the monster that you see before you today. Yes, in the end I had my revenge, but the damage was already done." Kane's words were laced with raw emotion. For a second, he seemed intensely vulnerable, but then he shook his head and the steely expression returned to his face. "There is plenty of time to talk about my childhood Jimmy, but now is not the time."

"Who killed my mother?" Nicholls blurted. He had almost said "our" rather than "my" but the word just didn't feel right at the moment.

The slate grey eyes stared back at him. They looked like they had seen an ocean of grief in their time. "She was murdered by Patrick McGovern," Kane said solemnly.

Nicholls felt a surge of rage. He had spoken to enough liars in his time to know when someone was being truthful and there was no deceit in Kane's words. He was being genuine with him. He was sure of that. Whether or not it was actually true, was another thing. Kane certainly believed it was and that would have to suffice for the moment. "Why?" Nicholls had wanted to compose a more articulate question, but he was still struggling for the right words.

"Because she was brave," came the reply. Nicholls could detect the pride in his words. "Are you ready for this?" There was a steel to his voice that could carve up the air around them. Nicholls nodded his head.

"Many years ago, Patrick McGovern used to run a brothel not far from this industrial estate. He paid off the police, so he didn't have anyone interfering with the business. He was just the same as he is now, a brutal evil man with an unquenchable thirst for power. One night a prominent businessman's son used one of the prostitutes in the brothel. From what I've heard, she laughed at his prick. Apparently, it was the size of an acorn," he rolled his eyes and smirked. "Now this pathetic excuse for a human being thought it was justified to smack the prostitute around for her remarks." Kane spoke with real contempt and malice in his voice.

"The poor girl was beaten that badly she died from her injuries. McGovern was furious. He came down to the brothel straight away and threatened to smash the boy's head in with a claw hammer. As you can imagine the businessman's son shit himself. He called his father, and they made a deal. Apparently, it cost him over a million pounds for his son's life. Not a good deal if you ask me." Kane said, shrugging his shoulders.

"Of course, the police were in on the crime too," he said angrily. "They had to be. They covered it up for a big sweaty chunk of cash. It was as if her life wasn't worth anything." He turned and looked deep into Nicholls' eyes. "Now our mother was the prostitute's friend. She was a working girl too." He raised an eyebrow at Nicholls. "She was heartbroken when she found out. She wanted justice but she knew what could happen to her and her young family if she said anything. In the end, her conscience got the better of her and she went to the police. The unfortunate thing is that the policeman she dealt with was in the back pocket of McGovern. Instead of helping her, he drove her back to the gangster."

Kane started to well up. There were real tears in his eyes. "McGovern didn't threaten her to keep silent or beat her up. The bastard put a bullet in the back of her head. Then he and the policeman drove her to the grave site you found the other day. It took me a long while to track it down." He wiped away the silvery line of tears that had started to trickle down his cheek.

Nicholls felt numb. It was as if someone had reached into his chest cavity and torn his heart out. "How did you find out where her body was?" His voice was cracking with emotion.

"I found out from Baldock," he said grimly. "Baldock was McGovern's half-brother."

"What the fuck?" spluttered Nicholls. "How does no-one know about this?" he said incredulously.

"McGovern has a lot of connections Jimmy. He was ashamed of his brother. He didn't want him degrading the family name. However, when he was a young man, McGovern and him were close. McGovern wanted Baldock to help run the criminal business. That was why Baldock helped bury our mother. Of course, he was very young back then, but he was still a formidable man. He was a tough guy. They used him primarily to collect debts and from what I've heard, he was pretty good at it. McGovern thought the two of them would rule London together side by side but then Baldock got into drugs. They rotted his brain. He was no use to McGovern after that. A wise man would've killed Baldock. He was a liability. He knew too much about McGovern and how to bring him down."

Kane helped himself to a half-eaten bacon sandwich and chewed fastidiously. "I cut out that information from him bit by bit," he said beaming with satisfaction. "He was still alive though when I inserted the grass snake. The look in his eyes when that slippery bastard slid into his rectum was pure gold. Of course, I had to do a bit of improvisation to make it wide enough first." Kane's eyes twinkled and he started to laugh heartily.

"I needed to speak to you privately, Jimmy and get you to St Johns, so you could find the graves. Somehow, I knew you would take the snake there. I can't explain why. It is in our DNA, a twin thing!" He pointed at his head and crossed his eyes as if he was a madman.

"Now the problem is that our vengeance is a complicated affair." His face became deathly serious again. "The arrangement between McGovern, the policeman and the businessman's son grew like a cancer. If you catch cancer early enough, then often you can beat it, but if you let it grow, then you're fucked. That's what's happened here. The cancer has grown out of control and now these criminals are too dangerous and powerful."

Kane stood up and looked wistfully at the ceiling, as if he could visualise a scene from the future. "It has happened before you know. Two thousand years ago you had Crassus, Caesar and Pompey who ruled the Roman Empire together. Crassus had the money, Caesar was the politician and Pompey was the general. Together they were touchable, but in the end, greed got the better of them and they all fell. That is what we will do to these bastards. We will take them apart piece by piece until there is nothing left." He made his right hand into a fist and smashed it into the palm of his left.

"Who the fuck are we talking about Kane?" said Nicholls. It was the first time he had used his brother's name and it felt unnatural.

"The businessman's son is now the shadow home secretary, Jason Kilbride." He paused. "And the policeman is now the Commander of the Met and your father-in-law, Daniel Flack."

Nicholls was momentarily speechless. It was absurd. The thought that Jenny's father, Daniel Flack was the mastermind of a criminal empire seemed ludicrous. He felt an anger flash through him, and a fierce protective instinct kicked in.

"You're lying, you son of a bitch," he screeched.

Kane remained calm. "Flack is the brains behind their relationship. McGovern can be too hot tempered and rash at times. He needs Flack to keep him under control." He looked accusingly at Nicholls. "How the fuck do you think McGovern has evaded justice for so long? He has a guardian angel watching over him, that's how. Flack takes down McGovern's rivals and keeps him out of jail. He also uses a team of corrupt cops to transport his drugs and illegal firearms around the country. Pretty simple really. Flack takes a massive chunk from the profits of the pie of course and shares it round to the other bent coppers that work for him."

"Are you saying that the entire Met is rotten?" asked Nicholls naively.

Kane looked at Nicholls as if he was stupid. "Come on Detective Inspector. You can't be fucking serious, can you? How the hell do you think Flack does it? He needs a loyal team of acolytes beneath him, planting evidence, botching investigations and bumping off rival gangsters. Remember the Russian gangster who was gunned down recently?" Nicholls nodded his head. "That was Flack's work."

"But the clever part of their business is prostitution you know? McGovern runs a multinational sex trafficking operation. All the prostitutes in the city work for him willingly or not. If you want a cheap hooker to suck you off, then you go to the Ritz." Every policeman worth their salt had heard of it. The name was notorious throughout the city.

"If you've got a bit of money, then you can afford an upmarket girl. They'll only fuck you if you've got five grand burning a hole in your pocket. McGovern

76

uses them on men of power. He'll send over one of his best girls to give them the night of their life. The stupid fuckers never know that they've been filmed. Then, when McGovern or Flack want something, they'll send the stupid dupe a copy of the tape. Christ, he's got politicians, businessman and sports stars all under his thumb. McGovern and Flack are like puppet masters. They pull all the strings in the city. Flack keeps a low profile, but he is the real ring leader. He uses McGovern as a front for everything.

"And Kilbride is their little puppy. They've got evidence on him when he killed the prostitute. He will snap to attention when his masters bark, of that there is no question. And if the Conservatives win the next general election, that will mean Kilbride will be the Home Secretary and the three of them will be fucking untouchable. Who knows, he could even be the next prime minister with McGovern and Flack calling the shots." He threw his arms wildly in the air to emphasise his point.

"How do you know all this?" said Nicholls hurriedly trying to process all the information he had just been told.

"We've been sitting and watching for a long while, Jimmy. We need to know everything before we make our move."

"What do you mean by 'We'?" said Nicholls quickly.

Kane fumbled in his jacket pocket and fished out an old photograph. He passed it to Nicholls. It was a picture of a smiling woman with two boys perched at her shoulders and an older girl sat in the middle. He looked at it studiously trying to ingrain every detail to memory. The woman had long auburn hair and her pretty face was covered in freckles. She looked really happy. The two boys had short black hair and impudent smiles with matching dimples. They were clearly twins. The older girl wasn't smiling but her hazel brown eyes twinkled. Nicholls recognised the eyes immediately although it took him a while to fix a name. It was Baldock's ex-girlfriend, Holly Maxwell.

Kane walked behind Nicholls so he could see the photograph. "I don't know why I ended up with this. Or why my adopted parents let me keep it for that matter." Nicholls looked up at him. "That's the only photo of the four of us. I don't know where dad was for this picture. I like to think it was him that took it, although I can't be sure."

Nicholls gripped the photo tightly, half expecting that Kane was going to snatch it away from him. "I know this girl," he said eagerly. "It's Holly Maxwell. The police are looking for her at the moment."

"Her name is Holly Kane, Jimmy. She's your sister."

Another thunderbolt. This one though, didn't feel quite as severe as the last one, although the earth still moved. "She was Baldock's girlfriend. What the fuck is going on?" His voice had trailed away so it was barely more than a whisper by the time he had finished the sentence.

Kane laughed and there was something patronising and callous about it. "I told you we needed information Jimmy. Your sister thought she could get it from Baldock if she posed as his girlfriend. And to be fair to her she did. That vile pig couldn't help himself. He liked to bully women and show off in front of them. Holly found out from him where our mother was buried. He said he would bury her as well if she didn't please him."

Nicholls stood up and held his hand out like a traffic warden stopping cars. "Hold on a minute. Are you telling me you left our sister with that animal? How could you even contemplate such a thing?"

Kane's gaze hardened. "It was Holly's idea, Jimmy," he said angrily. "I would never have forced her to do it. She suggested it. It was the best way to get the information we needed." He gestured for Nicholls to sit down, and he looked his brother squarely in the eye. "Holly has suffered a lot, Jimmy. When I found her, she was a lost soul. I helped her to heal and to come to terms with everything that has happened. She has a burning desire for vengeance just like me and is prepared to do whatever is necessary."

"Where is she now?" quipped Nicholls hurriedly.

"She is working as a prostitute for McGovern," he said as calmly as if they were discussing the weather. "The last I heard from her, McGovern has moved her into her own house and apparently he likes to visit a lot."

Nicholls felt a sudden surge of rage explode in his head. He picked up the cheap porcelain cup and hurled it over Kane's head, where it smashed into pieces on the adjacent wall. "Are you fucking mad?" he screeched. "What do you think you're playing at? McGovern's a monster. Have you any idea what he will do to her?"

"Relax Jimmy. She has it under control. She is desperate to meet you by the way. We have both been watching you for a very long time."

"You're fucking mad," shrieked Nicholls. "I don't want any part of whatever crazy scheme you are planning."

"We just want justice for our family," screamed Kane. He had started to get angry and spittle bubbled at his mouth. "We didn't have a sheltered upbringing with a family that loved us. We were plunged into a hell that there was no escape from."

He lifted his hoodie and shirt beneath to reveal a grotesque lattice of spidery scars that clung to his torso like a web. Nicholls felt a shiver descend his spine as he contemplated how the wounds had been inflicted. He had seen some horrible domestic abuse cases in his time, but this was something else. It was as if the person responsible had inflicted the wounds out of some sadistic desire to see Kane suffer.

"I have earned the right to my vengeance, Jimmy," he growled. "I want them all to suffer as I have. Every time my adopted father came into my room at night, I endured all the pain and the abuse because I knew there would be a time when I was not weak, a time when I was strong and I could pay everyone back for what they have done. I have waited a long time for my revenge. I have been patient and learned what I could about my enemies. Now is the time to strike."

Nicholls took a deep breath. Kane was psychotic. Of that there was no doubt. He had seen from his line of work how childhood abuse could create monsters. Some of the most depraved individuals he had investigated had suffered horrific abuse when they were children. It moulded them into killers. But he was also his brother. Of that there was no doubt as well. He shared the same genes. How could they be so different? Would he have turned into a monster if their roles had been reversed? A million questions and thoughts flashed through his mind. He suddenly felt an overwhelming desire to protect his siblings.

"John," he said softly. It was the first time he had spoken his brother's name. "I am a policeman. If you have any evidence about their crimes, then you can give it to me, and I will see them face justice."

Kane scoffed. "You are a fool, Jimmy. That is not how this world works. If you try and arrest Flack or McGovern, you'll end up with a bullet in your head. They are too strong to take them down like that." He turned away and looked at a wooden swinging door at the back of the room. "Besides I'd like you to meet someone first." He smiled at Nicholls and shouted at the door. "Marie you can come and see him now."

With near perfect timing, Nicholls turned back, and the wooden doors were flung open. In walked a middle-aged woman dressed all in black. As she drew nearer, Nicholls could see that she had a strong, attractive face that was caked in garish make up, to hide the rigours of a tough life. Her hair was dark brown and flecked with grey. She looked both tough and fragile at the same time.

"This is Marie," said Kane. "She was our mother's friend. It took a long while to find her, but I am sure you will want to hear what she has to say."

Marie stopped at the table where the two brothers were sitting and hovered at the corner as if she was unsure what to do next. Kane pulled a chair out next to him and Marie sat down awkwardly, without taking her eyes off Nicholls. From across the table, Nicholls saw that she had bad skin and that her face was lined with wrinkles. Her eyes were spattered with heavy black eye liner that had already smudged and her lips were covered in a granular pink lipstick. It was as if the cosmetics she used held her face together, so she could never risk taking them off.

"I knew your mother, James," she said at last. Her voice rasped as if she had gravel in her mouth.

Nicholls said nothing and waited for her to continue. "She was my friend. We were both close. I used to look after you, John and Holly when she was working."

Nicholls felt a lump in his throat and his eyes started to fill with tears. "You were always so mischievous James. We couldn't turn our back on you for a second. You wanted to explore everything and by God, you were fearless. I remember one time I went into the kitchen, and you were on top of the TV. Lord knows how you got on there, but you were just about to dive off and break your neck. I only just got there in time and when I held you in my arms, you giggled at me like it was just a game."

She smiled and wagged a finger at him playfully. "And you were a little devil when we wanted you to go to sleep. You used to scream blue murder when we put you down in the cot. You wanted to be held all the time. I used to have to wait hours in the rocking chair before you were fast asleep. If you got too upset, I used to have to rub your belly button to calm you down. I always remember you had a birthmark there like a peach. Do you still have it?"

Nicholls nodded stoically. There was no way this woman was lying. It would have been impossible to have had that knowledge without knowing him personally. It made him terribly sad because it meant everything Kane had said, could be true.

She fished out a handkerchief from her top pocket and dabbed her eyes carefully so as not to damage the gritty make up. Tears were not her friend Nicholls thought. "We were both working girls," she said defiantly. "It was the only way we could support our families, so there was nothing wrong in it. Your father was a bit of a liability then, of course. He drifted in and out of work and spent what money he did have on booze. Yes, me and Julia were close."

Marie placed her hand on Kane's hand, which alarmed Nicholls. These two people were obviously close and shared a connection with his mother that he may never experience. He felt jealous of their bond.

"I always remember the day our lives changed forever," she said sadly. "It was nearly Christmas and there had been lots of snow. Your mother was working a night shift with some Romanian girls. They hadn't been in England long and could barely speak any English. Julia was a kindly soul. She took them under her wing and tried her best to look after them. Then one night she came back from work in floods of tears. One of the Romanian girls had been murdered. She told me it was Kilbride who had done it. He was with some of his posh friends I think; spoilt to the core the lot of them they were. Kilbride was often there. He was an obnoxious weasel, always throwing his father's money around like he was someone. He couldn't have been more than a teenager then, but all the girls hated him. I was fortunate that I never had to service him. He made my skin crawl."

Her voice had started to break up and she sounded like a chain smoker with emphysema. "He beat up one of the girls because she laughed at his prick. She died of her injuries there and then. Her name was Justina, I think. She couldn't have been more than eighteen. I always remember her face. She was a pretty girl with petit features and like all the Romanians, she was stick thin. She thought that England was going to give her a better life. Poor girl never knew what was coming did she?"

"Do you remember anything else about her?" said Nicholls. "What was her surname?"

"James, she was here illegally," said Marie reproachfully. "I'm not even sure Justina was her real name. Your mother Julia was working nearby. She heard the commotion and rushed over but it was all too late by then. Your mother had a fiery temper and by all accounts she kicked off and almost killed Kilbride. She had to be held off him while he cowered in the corner, and even then, she was still trying to kick and scratch him. She said Flack was there as well. We all knew he was a bent copper. He was like an ice man she said. While everyone else was raging he collected evidence and took photos of Kilbride by Justina to incriminate him. They then blackmailed Kilbride's dad, while the poor girl was lying there naked. What kind of cold-blooded arsehole could do such a thing?

"Your mother came home that evening and she told me everything. I told her to keep quiet. Can you believe that? I will have to carry that sin to judgement day. She was a brave lady. I knew she was going to ignore me by the look in her eyes. A couple of days later a policeman came round and she told them everything. I heard it all. We lived in a cheap flat back then and the walls were paper thin. They took her away and that was the last I heard from her."

Marie burst into tears and Kane put his arm around her shoulder. "I only heard what had actually happened years later when John found me," she sobbed loudly.

"And that was the end of our family," said Kane emphatically. "We were all split up. You had the golden ticket and me and Holly got the short straw." There was tangible resentment in his voice.

Nicholls turned back to Marie who was by now a blubbering mess. "Did you see the policeman who took our mother away?"

Marie looked up and dried her eyes. "We knew the policeman very well. We thought he was a good man. His name was Bircham. Daniel Bircham I think."

Chapter 5
Artic Winds

Nicholls vaguely remembered saying goodbye to Marie and being ushered out the door by Kane, but then his mind went blank. The next thing he was aware of was sitting in the passenger side of his BMW with his brother. They were parked up and seemed to be in a rundown industrial estate in another part of the city. He had absolutely no idea where he was and what had happened in between leaving the café and getting to this point. The night sky was still inky black, so it couldn't have been too long. He glanced at his watch. It was a couple of minutes to midnight. Kane was sitting guardedly in the driver's seat, staring intently towards a garage about thirty metres in front of them. The shutters were all down, but Nicholls could see a faint glow of light emanating from a grubby window and he could hear the soft murmur of voices from within the building.

Kane smiled grimly. "It shouldn't be too much longer, Jimmy," he said quietly. "These guys are pretty professional, and their operation runs like clockwork."

"Who are we waiting for John?" Nicholls couldn't disguise the anxiety and agitation in his voice.

"This is the midnight run, Jimmy boy. They have two other collections points every week in other garages in the city, but this is easily the most straightforward and hassle free to monitor."

"Who are you talking about?"

Kane continued to stare at the garage like a predator that was transfixed on its prey and reluctant to let it out of their sight, even for a moment, in case it escaped. "As far as I can work out there are two teams of police officers that traffic drugs for McGovern. One of them is a firearms unit and the other is a drugs one." He nudged his brother playfully in the shoulder. "Kind of ironic don't you think?"

"They pick up the drugs at designated collection points and then distribute them to McGovern's associates at various points around the city. You have to admire the simplicity of it all to be honest. Who would ever think of stopping a marked police vehicle? It's the perfect disguise that ensures McGovern's suppliers get the drugs quickly and risk free."

Nicholls slumped back in his seat. This couldn't be true. All his life he had revered the police's sacred duty to uphold the law and fight against crime. If Kane was correct, then not only were several units in the Met corrupt, but they were worse than most of the criminals that he had sworn to bring to justice.

"Bircham is the architect of it all," Kane continued. "It's rare to see him in person on these operations, but he coordinates everything and sends out all the messages. He's a busy boy that bastard. That's why he gets away with murder as chief of homicide, if you can forgive the pun."

Nicholls had to admit that it did make sense. Bircham was slippery and elusive at the best of times. You could never get hold of him and he always seemed to evade phone calls when you needed him. It was a running joke that he must have possessed compromising photos of senior police chiefs that meant they couldn't afford to sack him; such was his ineptitude as a detective superintendent.

They heard the distant rumble of the engine a long time before the vehicle actually came into view. Kane sat upright in his seat, and he instinctively clenched his jaw as his muscles tensed in anticipation. "Here they come," he said excitedly.

Kane pointed towards the top of the street and right on cue, a large black minibus came into view. At first glance it appeared to be unmarked, but as it came down the road, Nicholls could see a small police sticker just above the wheel arch.

"Inconspicuous, but still unquestionably a police vehicle," hissed Kane. "No-one is ever going to question what a police vehicle is doing. They can do whatever they want with complete freedom."

The minibus drove slowly down the street and at the last minute, turned sharply towards the garage shutters which had already begun to open. Nicholls saw a forest of legs and a whirl of movement from inside the garage before the minibus was through the entrance and the shutters unfolded.

Kane looked at his watch. "In ten minutes that minibus is going to be crammed to the rafters with class A drugs and by tomorrow you and me will be able to buy these drugs on the street. As I said, the operation is a smooth as a baby's bum." Kane raised an eyebrow towards Nicholls as he spoke, expecting him to be surprised at this information but Nicholls stared nondescriptly at the garage as if he was trying to see inside.

"Bircham is Flack's lapdog," continued Kane. "He does all of his dirty work. That way Flack can't be implicated in any of this."

As he was speaking, a small door in the garage opened and a tall man stepped out of the shadows. He was wearing a black overcoat, but Nicholls recognised him immediately. He was an officer in one the Met's firearm units. His name was Clifford. Paul Clifford. Clifford took out a cigarette and lit it up. For a minute he seemed to stare directly into the BMW, causing Nicholls to freeze in horror, but then he turned and paced away in the other direction as a small plume of smoke started to rise slowly above him.

"Relax, Jimmy," snapped Kane. "This is your car and you've got blacked out windows. He can't see a thing."

Nicholls shook his head. He couldn't believe what he was witnessing. It was the ultimate betrayal of everything the police stood for. He felt sick to the pit of his stomach. "They've got to be stopped, John. We can't let them get away with it."

"We will, brother. Don't you worry about that. They will all get their just deserts, but now is not the time. I just wanted to show you the scale of the evil we are up against."

Nicholls looked at his brother pleadingly. "I have a friend in anti-corruption command, John. Tomorrow, I will arrange to meet up with him secretly. I will tell him all about what's been going on and they can bring them down. We don't have to do this on our own anymore."

Kane sighed in exasperation. "You just don't get it do you?" he said angrily. "We can't trust anyone who wears a badge. They will kill you just like that if they think you know anything about this."

"Listen to me," said Nicholls through gritted teeth. It went against his core values to break the law in any way. If people started taking the law into their own hands, then society would disintegrate. "I'm the police officer, not you. From now on, we're going to do things my way."

Kane suddenly grabbed Nicholls' arms and held them still. Nicholls couldn't believe how powerful his brother was. Kane looked at him, his grey eyes flickering with menace, like embers of burning coal. "No, you are going to listen to me brother," he said defiantly. "I have everything under control and I'm not going to have my plans put in jeopardy because of you." His grip on Nicholls intensified until all of a sudden, he exhaled deeply and released his brother as his rage evaporated as quickly as it had appeared.

"You just have to trust me Jimmy," he said quietly.

"And what if I don't want to go ahead with what you've got planned?"

Kane sighed and slumped back in his seat. "I was hoping it wouldn't come to this." A look of regret appeared on his implacable face. "After I had killed Baldock and his men, I scraped their fingernails on my arm until it opened up my skin." He paused to slide down his shirt to reveal some faint scratches on his forearm. "Your forensic team know what they're doing. They will already have identified my DNA from the dried blood and fragments of skin under the fingernails and will be looking for a match."

"I don't understand," said Nicholls.

"The problem for you, Jimmy is that we are identical twins, and we share the same DNA. There is no record that I even exist. I took care to destroy the adoption records some time ago. Now, what do you think would happen if someone made an anonymous phone call to the police, pointing the finger of blame for Baldock at you? How are you going to explain why your DNA and footprints were found at the scene? Are you really going to blame your identical twin brother who technically doesn't exist? I'm no police officer, but I guess it will also look pretty damning when the police find some of Baldock's body parts hidden in your house."

Nicholls felt a cold shiver trickle down his spine. "Why you son of a bitch." He fought back the urge to strike his brother. He felt completely powerless. Kane seemed to have planned everything.

"You just need to trust me, Jimmy," said Kane almost apologetically. "I have this under control. I just needed some insurance to get you to understand who holds the cards. I will make the evidence disappear when the time is right." As he spoke the shutters opened again and the police minibus emerged. It slowly trundled down the road until it had disappeared around the corner.

"Now, we could go and follow these bastards around the city dropping off their drugs until it gets light, or I have a better idea about we can do."

Nicholls looked at his brother. "What's that?"

"I can drop you off home and you can get some sleep. Tonight, has been eventful enough."

Nicholls woke up on the sofa to a text message from the Met Commissioner Daniel Flack. It read: **We need to meet up. A car will pick you up at 7:30.**

He looked at his watch. It was a few minutes after seven. He heard some movement in the kitchen. Jenny was evidently already up. He wondered if she had noticed that he had driven off last night or did she think he had fallen asleep downstairs? He moved sheepishly into the kitchen. Jenny was looking out of the window as the kettle boiled.

"I'm sorry that I didn't come up, honey," he said tiredly. "I guess I must have fallen asleep on the sofa."

Jenny turned towards him. She smiled and nodded understandably. "That's fine. You have a lot on your plate at the moment. I don't think alcohol is going to be much help though," she said reproachfully, staring pointedly at the half empty decanter of brandy in the living room. "Why don't you take the day off with me? No-one would expect you to go into work today."

Nicholls shook his head. "Your father has just messaged me. He wants to meet up this morning. I'm getting picked up in twenty minutes."

"Jimmy, you've just found out that your mum has been murdered. There's no way you should be in a stressful work environment at the moment. You need time to come to terms with what's happened."

"Let me meet up with your father and see what he says. I'll give you a ring when I've spoken to him."

Jenny sighed and tucked her golden-brown hair behind her ears. "That's fine. I'll speak to you later then."

Nicholls walked over to her and embraced her softly on the cheek. He didn't say anything else. By the time he'd changed and brushed his teeth, Flack's car was parked outside.

It was a short drive to Flack's favourite Italian restaurant. The owner and Flack were friends so it wouldn't be open to anyone else until later. As Nicholls walked through the door, he saw the Met Commissioner on the far side of the room. He was sat crossed legged on a leather couch in conversation with the balding, Italian owner and was smoking a cigarette. When he saw Nicholls, he stood up swiftly and gestured for him to come over. Flack face looked pained and full of sorrow.

"Jimmy, my boy," he said sadly. "I am so sorry for your loss. You must be devastated." His voice was rich, like expensive dark chocolate.

Flack brushed the restaurant owner aside, who obediently left the two men together, and enveloped Nicholls in a comforting hug. Nicholls looked down at the diminutive figure. It didn't seem possible that Flack was a criminal mastermind. If what Kane told him were true, then Flack was indeed the devil incarnate and the architect of his family's misery. Perhaps his brother and Maria had got it wrong. Nicholls' mind desperately tried to conjure up an explanation that would exonerate Flack but nothing plausible would materialise. As a police officer, Nicholls didn't believe in coincidences and there were simply too many for this to be a mistake. But why had Flack taken him in and treated him like a son? He had even set him up with his daughter. None of it made any sense at all.

Flack ushered Nicholls on to the leather sofa and pointed towards the restaurant owner. "Enrico here will make anything you want. I recommend the poached eggs. The sauce is irresistible."

"Could I just have a strong coffee, please Daniel," said Nicholls politely. He always referred to the commissioner by his first name when they were off duty.

Flack nodded compliantly and stroked his white beard as the restaurant owner disappeared into the kitchen. Nicholls met Flack's gaze as he sat down. Outwardly the commissioner seemed relaxed and calm, but his blue eyes betrayed an apprehension that Nicholls had never seen before.

"How are you son?" said Flack.

"To be honest, I can't quite believe what has happened," said Nicholls truthfully. "I guess I'm in a state of shock at the moment. I just want to know what happened to her."

Flack nodded sympathetically. "That is quite understandable my boy. I have no words to assuage your grief or that would do justice to how you must be feeling at the moment. What I can promise you is that we will find the truth. I have put one of our best murder teams on your mother's investigation and I am sure they will uncover what has happened to her. We will do everything to bring her killer to justice. Of that you can be assured."

Nicholls hesitated. He didn't know how to respond. If he said the wrong thing, would Flack be able to tell? Luckily the restaurant owner, miraculously appeared with his coffee, giving Nicholls time to contemplate his answer. "Thank you, Daniel. I am grateful for everything you have done for me. You have been like family and always treated me like a son. Hopefully one day I will be able to repay you fully for all your kindness."

Flack paused to light up another cigarette. "Think nothing of it my boy. I saw your potential when I met you at school all those years ago and every day you make me proud of the person you have become." He patted Nicholls on the knee affectionately. "Now, tell me how this damned Baldock case is going?"

"It's not going well to be honest. We have no leads and very little in the way of forensic evidence."

Flack ignored the answer. "Do you think you are still up to leading the investigation? By your own admittance, you are in a state of shock at the moment. My advice would be to take some time off and come to terms with your grief. There is no expectation for you to come into work at the moment. I have detective superintendent Bircham poised and ready to take over the case."

Nicholls shook his head defiantly. "I think work would be good for me at the moment. It will help me take my mind off things. I don't want to sit at home and let the pain take hold."

Flack nodded his head in agreement. "As you wish, my boy. But if it gets too much for you, then you only have to say the word and we will support you any way we can."

"Thank you, Daniel. It is very much appreciated," said Nicholls calmly.

Nicholls drank his coffee quickly, before making his excuses and leaving the restaurant.

Flack grinned and hungrily ate the rest of his breakfast. He had been nervous about meeting up with Nicholls beforehand, but the young man was still clearly oblivious. The discovery of his mother's body had been unfortunate and badly timed but perhaps it presented Flack with another opportunity. He would think about how he could work it to his advantage at a later date. There was something far more important and pressing to deal with later on that day.

The eagle's nest penthouse suite consumed the entire seventh floor of the Highbury hotel. As well as having two master bedrooms, the suite also provided access to a beautifully furnished dining room, a large bar, a solarium and a modern gym with sauna. Huge wall to ceiling windows allowed light to flood into the lounge area. This was where Flack had arranged to meet McGovern and Kilbride. When he got there, he found the two men sitting around a white marble dining table on luxury reclining Italian sofas. McGovern was drinking a whisky and water even though it was only mid-morning while Kilbride was nursing a frothy cappuccino.

The three men were here to see the Russian oligarch Sergei Ivankov who was in London for business. Ivankov had been described in the United States as the "boss of bosses of the Russian mafia." He had first come to prominence after the

Soviet Union began to crumble in the late eighties and he had coordinated a lucrative black-market economy. As his power grew, he branched out into drugs, prostitution and gun running. He was notorious throughout Eastern Europe and had developed a reputation for a brutality that was unparalleled even in the Russian mafia. He famously used ex-Afghanistan war veterans as enforcers. These men had been forged in a brutal and savage war and they crushed any opposition to Ivankov with merciless violence. In recent years, Ivankov had tried to rehabilitate his reputation and had poured his money into legitimate enterprises. He had managed to build bridges in the Kremlin and forge a strong relationship with the Russian president. This had been confirmed last year when Ivankov's pipe company had won a contract to transfer oil all over Russia.

Flack had never met Ivankov before in person, but the Russian was a close business partner of McGovern. As Commander of the Met, he was taking a huge risk in meeting two notorious gangsters in a south London hotel. Even with his nimble brain it would be very difficult to explain away their encounter if there were any uncompromising pictures taken of the four of them together. He closed his eyes and imagined the headlines in the morning papers. McGovern had arranged the security and they had all entered through a secret side entrance of the hotel. There shouldn't be any problems, but you just never knew. The prize at stake was definitely worth the risk.

It would be down to McGovern to make the introductions. He and Ivankov had worked together for years, coordinating the human trafficking operation across Europe. Flack hoped that they were both still on good terms. If this meeting went well, then everyone in the room was going to be set for the rest of their lives.

He had arranged for Ivankov to join them a little later that morning. He had important business to discuss with McGovern and Kilbride first.

"I'm sorry to hear about your brother Patrick," said Flack sincerely. McGovern flashed an angry glance at him as if he had hit a raw nerve.

"I'm not sorry that he is dead Danny boy, so neither should you be," said McGovern defiantly. "He was a drug addict and an oxygen thief. I offered him the world, yet he chose to squander all of that getting high every day. The man was a loser pure and simple, and I am glad that my family is finally shot of him."

"He was still your brother Patrick."

"Half-brother," interrupted McGovern. "Have you boys found out who did it yet? Probably some drug addict that he ripped off. I've got my people on the case as well and I'll wager a pretty penny that they find them quicker than your boys in blue. Either way, you hand them over to me if you get them first, and I'll tear them apart bit by bit. They will be praying for death by the end. You don't fuck with my family and get away with it."

Flack ignored McGovern's request and changed the subject abruptly. "Have you both heard about Julia Kane?"

Kilbride shifted uneasily in his seat, while McGovern's face was resolute. "We both saw the headlines on the news," he said taking a big gulp of whisky.

"Is there anything we need to worry about?" said Kilbride nervously to Flack.

McGovern grunted impatiently. "Relax Jason. There is nothing that can be found to link the two bodies to any of us. That was another of my brother's fuck ups. I told him to burn them and then there would have been no way of identifying the bodies. He couldn't even do that properly."

McGovern looked accusingly at Flack. "I would be more concerned that the Commissioner here has taken such an interest in her son. I just don't get why you would do that, Danny? By all accounts it was you that fast tracked him up the ranks. You even set him up with your daughter. It doesn't make any sense, that's all"

Flack smiled which only seemed to antagonise McGovern further, and he scowled like a petulant child. "Patrick, I've looked after you all these years and when have I ever let you down? You just need to trust me, that's all. The boy will be our insurance policy, if things go sour. I know what I'm doing."

McGovern shrugged his shoulders. "That's your business, Daniel. I can't say I understand your thinking though."

"You don't need to Patrick. Thinking things through rationally has never been your strong point." He swung his hand abruptly like an executioner's axe to indicate that the topic was finished. "Now gentleman, are you happy with our proposal for Ivankov? This is big. If we make this deal, then it can make us richer and more powerful than our wildest dreams?"

Both men nodded. That was the easy part, thought Flack.

Sergei Ivankov was a huge, corpulent man with heavy cheeks like two slabs of mahogany wood. He had a swollen, bulbous nose and a red face that were both aggravated by his penchant for vodka. His face was rugged, and his thick auburn hair was wild and unruly like a Siberian Forest.

Although his facial features were unremarkable, his clothing exuded an alpha male quality. He wore an immaculate slate grey Brioni suit that glimmered when it caught the light, and he was adorned from head to toe in expensive jewellery, with a diamond encrusted Rolex watch around his wrist. He was flanked by two huge bodyguards who looked like they could grind metal into dust with their teeth alone. Walking behind him was a small, wiry middle-aged man with brown leathery skin.

Ivankov smiled menacingly when he entered the room. There was something dangerous about the man that commanded everyone's attention. He was a predator, of that there was no doubt. Kilbride shifted nervously in his seat as if the presence of Ivankov had triggered a prehistoric survival instinct. The wiry, tanned man scuttled over to the bar and clumsily scrambled on to a bar stool that was too high for him. Ivankov moved slowly over to the sofas where Flack, McGovern and Kilbride were sitting. His face was grim and expressionless. When he saw McGovern stand to greet him, his lips curled into a cavernous smile to reveal blood red gums and a gold tooth that glinted in the light.

"Patrick, it is good to see you my friend," he said in a heavily accented voice that reverberated around the room. He wrapped two huge arms around McGovern and pulled him into an embrace. McGovern was a big man, but Ivankov seemed to tower over him.

"It has been too long, Sergei," croaked McGovern who had been smothered in the Russian's vice like grip. "Come and have some whisky with me."

Ivankov glanced reprovingly at the half empty bottle of whisky on the table. "I will respectfully wait until after our business has concluded, Patrick. After that I will gladly have some vodka with you." He looked at Flack and Kilbride and smiled. "You can take the boy out of Russia they say but you can't take Russia out of the boy." He spread his arms mockingly and started to laugh heartily.

His eyes moved over to Flack. "And you must be the chief of Police that I have heard so much about," he said warmly. Flack stood up and offered his hand which Ivankov gratefully enveloped and shook vigorously.

"It is good to finally meet you Sergei," said Flack. "I think we can do great things together." He motioned over to Kilbride. "I'd like you to meet Jason Kilbride. He will be the next Home Secretary after the General election. He will be a good friend of ours."

Kilbride stood up nervously and shook Ivankov's hand. He knew that Ivankov was a cold-blooded killer. Ivankov did not say anything but stared coldly into Kilbride's eyes as if he was weighing him up.

"I must offer my thanks for your help in dealing with Pavel Kornilov,

Sergei," said McGovern pouring himself another whisky.

Ivankov took his eyes off Kilbride and sighed. "A regrettable business I'm afraid. He used to be like a son to me, but alas he got greedy. I should have dealt with him in Russia, but I turned a blind eye and let him slip away. Perhaps I am getting too sentimental in my old age. If we had let him loose in London, then he would've been a threat to my friend Patrick. The man was a snake. I know, I taught him everything he knew." Ivankov smiled but it quickly transformed into a grimace, disguised with fake melancholy. "I had to help you Patrick, even though his death pained me greatly."

Ivankov turned and sat on the last sofa. "But life must go on I suppose and that is why I am here today." He turned towards the huge bodyguard on his right. "Yuri, get me a coffee please." The bodyguard nodded his head and obediently disappeared behind the bar.

"As you all know, myself and Patrick have been business partners for many years. It has been a profitable arrangement for both of us." He looked at McGovern and smiled. "We have also become good friends in that time, and I value his friendship greatly. We talk often as friends do and I have shared with him some of my troubles. He mentioned that the Chief of Police had a proposition that I might be interested in, and he vouched for you Mr Flack. That is good enough for me to come and meet you and hear what you have to say."

Flack smiled. He looked at McGovern who encouraged him to speak for them all with a flick of his hand. "Firstly, I would like to thank you for taking the time to meet with us today, Sergei. You honour us greatly," said Flack respectfully. "You are a businessman, and I will do you the honour of being frank with you. We have had you in mind for a long time as a potential investor in our project. I will not lie to you, myself and Patrick have been planning this for years."

The fact that Flack did not mention Kilbride was not lost on Ivankov. It was plainly obvious that Kilbride was the subordinate person in their arrangement. "We feel that very shortly we will be in a position to make our move, and that is why we needed to speak with you Sergei, as your help will allow us to finish the puzzle. We have positioned our pieces on the chessboard and now we are ready to go in for the kill."

"I am always open to any business opportunities that will increase my holdings," replied Ivankov candidly. "Please enlighten me as to what you are proposing? You certainly have my attention."

"We want you to help us build a prison system," said Flack so quietly that the wiry accountant, Sykes almost fell from his stool as he strained to hear.

Ivankov laughed. "I know a lot about prisons Mr Flack. In Russia we have proper prisons, not like the holiday camps you run over here. But I fail to see how this is a good business opportunity for me."

Flack's face acquired a steely resolve. "Sergei, I know from Patrick how you follow international politics religiously, so I do not need to elaborate about the dire state of affairs that Britain finds itself in at the moment. We are in the midst of a recession; unemployment is not far off record levels and the country is being ravaged by a rampant crime wave." He paused. "A crime wave I might add, that Patrick and myself have helped to cultivate and encourage."

"I know this. I watch the news. The lack of order I see is decidedly anti-British. I do not understand why you are encouraging this lawlessness. Surely it is bad for business?"

"We have our eyes set on the general election Sergei," said Flack with a rueful smile. "We want to ensure that the Labour government are castigated for this mess, so the Conservatives win the election. When that happens, we will use Mr Kilbride here to help us complete our vision."

Ivankov grinned. "At last, it begins to make sense. I saw your interview on the news recently Mr Flack where you were critical of the government and the funding your force was being given. I thought at the time that it was highly unusual for a policeman to speak out against the establishment, but I would never have guessed that this is what you had in mind. It made Labour slip further down the polls if I am not mistaken." He wagged his finger at Flack and smiled. "This is quite brilliant gentleman. Very Machiavellian. My Italian friends would be most impressed."

"And when the Conservatives come to power, we stamp out the crime wave, just like that. Patrick here will pull the strings to accomplish this, but the plaudits will of course go to the new Home secretary here and the reforms he helped introduce." Flack motioned towards Kilbride. "The country will be galvanised, and we use this momentum to make our move."

"I am intrigued," said Ivankov. "Please continue."

"The new government will be given a mandate to clean up the country and sort crime out for good. Jason, as Home Secretary will spearhead this drive. We build prisons up and down the country using your money Sergei and we create new laws to fill these prisons up with criminals. The prisoners will make us our fortune."

Ivankov grinned excitedly on the sofa. "As I am sure you are aware Mr Flack, I bring a lot of money to these shores every year. Like all Russians I have to answer to the tax man and every year he tries to take a bigger bite from my arse. I have friends who trust me to invest their money wisely when they need it cleaned and that is why I use Mr Sykes here."

He pointed to the wiry man sitting upright on a stool by the bar. Sykes' body seemed taut with the tensile strength of a cobra that was poised to strike. He looked tough and uncompromising. "Mr Sykes is my accountant, gentleman. I don't invite him to these meetings for his company as he bores me to tears," he said laughing. Flack and McGovern looked surprised. Sykes had a cruel and callous demeanour that suggested he was one of Ivankov's main enforcers, rather than a money man.

"He is my financial wizard gentlemen, an American unfortunately, but we can't hold that against him if he does a good job, can we now? I don't know what he does with my money, but it goes from Russia to the Bahamas, Gibraltar even, and then he invests it in London and around the world. I own real estate, restaurants, flats and even fucking sports teams all over London. You name a street around here and I'll bet you I own something on it. I have more English politicians, businessmen and lawyers and bankers on my payroll than I have employees in the whole of Russia!"

He took a sip of coffee and inhaled a deep breath. "But Mr Sykes tells me this arrangement is getting precarious. There is too much money apparently to clean. Can you believe that! What a problem to have, I suppose you might say. The Americans have started to stick their nose into business that doesn't concern them. They claim that our legitimate business ventures are funding organised crime in their country. They whinge like women to the Kremlin and I end up getting it in the neck. Last year they froze the assets on a Russian bank and stopped us doing business. The Americans are like a spoiled child when they do not get their way. They go home with the ball and stop everyone else playing.

"And then there are people who are skimming from our accounts like common thieves! Can you believe that? People fucking stealing from me! Do you know what I do to people who do that in Russia? Mr Sykes says this is negligible and we have to accept some losses, but it is the principle of the thing. Perhaps I am too proud. But then I have people to answer to in the Kremlin. They ask me Sergei, where is our money and I show them the accounts, but they question every transaction like they are paupers on the street watching every ruble, as if their lives depended on it. It is all very tiresome Mr Flack. I am getting old, and I don't need the hassle anymore."

Flack reached under the table and pulled out a leather file. "With respect Sergei, this could be the only investment you need to make in the future." He tossed the file over to the other side of the table where Ivankov was sitting.

Ivankov scooped it up greedily and pulled out a pair of diamond studded Cartier glasses from his top pocket, that he skilfully flipped over his nose with one hand. He opened the file and scanned the documents intensely. After a few minutes, he looked Flack in the eye. "What is Secur8 Mr Flack and why should I be interested in this company?"

"Secure8 is a fledging security company that is currently owned by myself and Patrick. The headquarters are only a stone's throw away from where we are sitting now. With your help Sergei we will turn Secure8 into the world's leading security company. When the Conservatives win the next election, we will build a ring of prisons around the country and Secure8 will get the contract to run them all."

Ivankov looked unfazed. "What are the costs Mr Flack?"

"For ten prisons initially we're looking at somewhere in the region of six hundred to seven hundred million pounds. You have to remember that Secure8 will own the prisons outright so they will not be leased by the government. It is an investment for the future Sergei. And don't forget they will also provide an easy way to clean your money, and I can assure you that you won't have any prying government eyes into your affairs."

Ivankov looked impressed. "You have obviously done your homework Mr Flack. But please tell me how owning these prisons will make me and my partners money?"

"First of all, you receive a generous stipend from the government for each prisoner," said Flack. "But the real coup de grace are the reforms we will make through parliament. We intend to revolutionise the prison system under Kilbride. Our prisons are too soft. Prisoners can watch television, play computer games, go to the gym. Hell, they can play ping pong all day if they want to. From now on we are going to put them to work and make them sweat, and that Mr Ivankov is how we are going to make our money."

Flack pointed at the leather file that Ivankov was now clutching close to his chest. "If you look through the file you can see all the ways we can exploit prison labour for profit. We get prisoners to make clothes, office furniture, staff call centres, put them to work in the fields like good old fashioned chain gangs. We've even got a potential contract in the pipeline to get them to make missile parts and put them together! How ironic! Prisoners assembling weapons that could bring about the world's destruction! And the beauty of this all Sergei is that we can pay them pittance. They are our slaves to do with as we please. Forget third world sweat shops. This will be more lucrative than even those, and you won't get the human rights brigade involved because we're dealing with criminals. These are people who have committed crimes and need to make amends to society."

Flack rocked back in the sofa and smiled cruelly. "And it doesn't even end there. Read on," he said excitedly. "We can then outsource a list of services to private companies that we control; telecommunication companies for example. Prisoners will still want to make phone calls. We just hike up the price if they want to speak to loved ones." Flack spread his left hand and tapped each finger methodically. "Health care, food, clothing, building contractors, cleaning services; to name but a few. So, every prisoner is a potential cash cow for us. You look at the American system; they call it mass incarceration. They've got over two million prisoners in jails over there. Can you believe that? That's nearly twenty-five percent of the entire world prison population. It's a billion-dollar industry and no one gives a fuck because they're just prisoners.

"Of course, we are playing catch up, but the current climate gives our justice system the perfect excuse to lock criminals in jail and throw away the key. We are just cleaning up society and protecting the public. Who can argue with that?" Flack looked over at Kilbride. "Jason here will put together a new sentencing law, an indeterminate sentence he will call it."

Ivankov held up his hand. "What is an indeterminate sentence, Mr Flack?" he said slowly, mouthing the unfamiliar word.

"An indeterminate sentence is a sentence that allows judges to lock criminals up indefinitely. We say it's for public protection. Any criminal who is deemed a danger to society gets an indeterminate sentence. They are locked up until they can prove to a parole board that they are no longer a danger to society. We move the goal posts to make this process as difficult as possible to achieve and encourage judges to hand out these sentences like sweets in a candy shop. Before long the prison population gets bigger, and society gets safer. We will have to get this law passed by parliament, but we control enough politicians to get through a vote.

"We have around ninety-thousand prisoners in our jails at the moment. In ten years, that figure could be over half a million. We will make more money in a year than we have in a lifetime. And of course, as soon as someone is jailed, they get disenfranchised by society. They lose their ability to vote for ever and the Conservatives stay in power for the foreseeable future. That will again have to be ticked off by parliament, but that is not a problem if we control it."

Ivankov nodded his head and his body rocked as if Flack's ideas had energised his spirit. He was clearly very excited by the proposal, but he had not achieved all he had in life by showing his hand too early. "We have a saying in Russia, Mr Flack. If you're scared of wolves, don't go into the woods. It means nothing ventured, nothing gained. It is a code I have lived with all my life, and it has served me well. But as I get older, I get more pragmatic and I see obstacles whereas when I was younger, it was only opportunities. I am a rich man. Life has been good to me, so why should I risk it all on this new adventure?"

He sat silently for a few moments and pondered everything he had heard. After what seemed like an eternity, he looked at the three men. They were hanging off his decision now and he fed voraciously on that anxiety. He knew they needed him and his money or these ideas would never come to fruition. Like an experienced gameshow host trying to draw out the tension for as long as possible, he made his face impassive. Then his lips began to curl into an almighty smile, and he started to chuckle. The tension in the room dissipated.

"I love your ideas gentleman," he boomed enthusiastically. "They are inspired!" He addressed them all, but his wolf eyes narrowed in on Flack. "You are a puppet master of truly diabolical genius Mr Flack," he said with genuine admiration.

Flack nodded his head respectfully. "Patrick, fuck the vodka," laughed Ivankov. "Pour me a whisky. I am that impressed with your ideas, I will have what you are drinking."

McGovern stepped forward and slapped Ivankov on the shoulders playfully. He pulled out a glass tumbler from under the table and poured out a generous measure of the amber liquid and handed it to Ivankov. Ivankov took a tentative sip, and he pursed his lips in disdain as it flowed down his gullet.

"Give me vodka any day, Patrick," he chuckled. "Your whisky is not for me." He put the drink down and looked again at Kilbride. "I know you well, Patrick. You are my friend and I trust you with my life. He speaks highly of you

Mr Flack and having met you today, I can see why. I am good at judging people. It is one of my strengths. I know if I can trust someone and whether they have balls of steel when I meet them, from the look in their eyes. You have titanium balls Mr Flack. I can see that now. You will see this through, of that I have no doubt. In the communist era, you would most definitely have been shot as a capitalist pig! But Mr Kilbride here is a bit of an unknown quantity to me." He looked down at the tumbler and traced a huge finger around the tip of the glass, so it began to hum.

"So much of this plan rests on his shoulders. If he fucks up, then what then? I have to know what his balls are made of."

Kilbride reclined in the chair and crossed his legs. He interlocked his fingers and looked Ivankov in the eye. "You can trust me, Mr Ivankov. I will do whatever is necessary to help us achieve our goals. The public love me. You only have to type my name into google to see that. I have clawed and scrambled all my life to get into this position and I do not intend to stop now. With the support of everyone in this room, I will continue to rise, and I know how to look after my friends. The Spanish call it 'cojones' and you can be assured that I have plenty of it. You do not have to worry about me."

Ivankov nodded. "If Patrick and Mr Flack vouch for you, then that is enough for me at the moment." He took another sip of whisky and smiled. "That time it was not so bad! Perhaps this whisky is an acquired taste that I can get used to?

"Before we celebrate too early, there is still much still to discuss gentlemen." He looked again at Flack. "This plan depends on the Conservatives winning the next general election. If they lose, then we are all screwed."

Flack nodded his head. "I have seen the polls. Labour are being pummelled like a weak boxer at the moment. It looks like the fight is nearly over and they are waiting for their trainer to throw in the white towel. But politics is like boxing. It is corrupt and fickle. You don't need me to tell you that. A boxer can be dead on their feet, but one lucky punch in the final round and they can still be victorious.

"We cannot take any chances with the result of the general election. Luckily, I have contacts within the Kremlin who are experts at manipulating the results of elections around the world. We can use fake social media accounts to undermine the Labour campaign and sew conspiracy theories about the government. This is something we have become very adept at. Disinformation is a very profitable business in Russia. And why not? We want to ensure we work with governments that will cooperate fully with Russian interests." He took a big sip of whisky. "In the past we have even hacked into American voting machines to record votes. If voters have weak encryption and bad passwords, then they only have themselves to blame," he chuckled. "Of course, that is a risky game. I will have to defer to my contacts in the Kremlin for their tactics. They are the experts after all."

"That would be most appreciated," said Kilbride hurriedly, trying to show that he did have some say in the meeting.

Ivankov smiled. "But I do have another concern gentlemen that I would like to address. Darren Healey is the leader of the Tories. He is known for his more moderate views, shall we say. You would not expect him to support such a draconian prison system." He shuffled in his seat, trying to search for the right words to use. "Will he be a problem to our plans?"

Kilbride looked quickly at Flack, who gestured for him to speak. "Hats off to you Sergei. You clearly are very well informed about British politics. Darren Healey would not be supportive of our plans. Of that you are correct." Ivankov's face dropped as if he had uncovered a major flaw in their plans that could jeopardise everything.

"But what no-one knows is that he is gravely ill," said Kilbride enthusiastically. "He has cancer and is not responding particularly well to treatment. He has already taken a back seat on the campaign front. He doesn't want to make it public just yet, in case it jeopardises the election, but it is looking very likely that he will have to step down, if he becomes prime minister."

"And who would take over from him?" said Ivankov astutely.

Kilbride smiled at him. Ivankov sighed with palpable relief. "So, there is a silver lining on the horizon after all then? You are confident of this?"

"Absolutely," quipped Kilbride. "I met with him last week and he confirmed that I would be deputy party leader. Besides I have enough supporters I could count on if there were any issues to this."

Ivankov raised his glass to Kilbride. "My congratulations to you, Mr Vice-President! You clearly have this well in hand. But again, we must be vigilant. Healey is a strong man. If he recovers fully then this will throw another spanner in the works."

"What do you have in mind, Sergei?" asked McGovern.

"We have to monitor this situation very closely. You are right. If Healey steps down now, it could be dangerous for the general election. We need to drag him over the line if needs be, but he is a danger to our plans. I will need to speak to my contacts in the Kremlin. If he refuses to die, then we may have to encourage him to do so. Our agents are experts at creating a 'natural death'. We have nerve agents and toxins that can induce death, yet give the impression the deceased has died naturally. That is of course a last resort and a decision that will not be taken lightly."

Kilbride flinched at the unpalatable subject. No-one noticed but Ivankov, who sipped quietly on his whisky. "It has been a pleasure to meet with you today gentleman and I must confess that you have taken me by surprise with this beautiful idea. I will read your proposal in detail later and I will convey it to my friends in Moscow. Let us have a drink to cement our friendship."

McGovern poured Flack and Kilbride a drink and refilled his and Ivankov's glass. The men all stood up. "Nasdrovia my friends," boomed Ivankov, draining his drink in one go. "May this be the start of a beautiful relationship."

Chapter 6
Reconciliation

Jimmy Nicholls had a pounding headache which had gotten worse steadily throughout the day as he considered how his life had been turned upside down in just a matter of days. He was sitting in his office at the station, nursing a cup of tepid water that was fizzing away with two dissolving paracetamol tablets. He had somehow managed to stumble through the day, since his meeting with Flack, but he felt sick to the pit of his stomach. His whole life had been ripped apart to the point at which, it was hard to discern what was true anymore.

His mother had not run away. She had been murdered. He had a twin brother and an older sister. The architect of this destruction was his boss and father to his girlfriend, Jenny. It was quite simply the stuff of nightmares, yet even some of his dreams seemed more plausible than his reality at the moment.

He heard a tap on the window of his office and he looked up to see the bloated face of Detective Superintendent Daniel Bircham pressed up against the glass. Nicholls felt a wave of revulsion at the man, and he clenched his teeth in anger. He had always considered Bircham as an inconsequential nobody, who had stumbled his way into a position of power by forces outside of his control. But if Kane and Marie were right, he had been Flack's willing lapdog and had driven his own mother to her death. Nicholls felt sick to the pit of his stomach, but he forced himself to smile feebly at his senior colleague.

"May I sit down Jimmy?" asked Bircham awkwardly. When Nicholls nodded, Bircham pulled out a chair and sat opposite him.

Bircham's face was pale, and his eyes were bloodshot. He looked pathetic. There were times in the past when Nicholls had felt sorry for him. Now the only feeling he had for the man, was a burning hatred that boiled and bubbled inside his guts. He wanted to scream at him, to pummel his face into a bloody mess with the force of his fists, but at the last minute he heard Kane's words resounding around his head. "Don't do anything yet Jimmy. We move our pieces into position first." Nicholls stifled his anger and curled his hands into a fist under the table.

"Look, Jimmy," said Bircham fidgeting uncomfortably in his seat. "You've had a tough few days."

That was an understatement thought Nicholls.

"Your head is clearly all over the place at the moment," he continued. "I think it's for the best if you have some time off to sort yourself out. I spoke to Flack earlier on. I told him that you weren't in the right frame of mind to do your job properly and he agreed. I know you spoke to him earlier on today and he said you could carry on, but he's changed his mind. He wants you to take some time off. That's an order by the way, so don't think of arguing."

Arguing was the last thing on Nicholls's mind. "Fine," he said meekly.

Bircham had clearly braced himself for some resistance to the order and he was visibly surprised by Nicholls's response. "I'm glad that you're seeing sense, son," he said. "You need to get to grips with your loss. Why don't you take Jenny away for a few days and try to recharge your batteries? How does that sound?"

Nicholls pondered the information he had just heard. He didn't feel any natural hostility towards the suggestion. In fact, he could use the time to speak to Kane and try and dissuade him from the suicidal course he was surely planning.

"I think you're right sir," he said quietly after a lengthy silence. "My head is all over the place at the moment. I know it's affecting my work and that's not fair on the team."

Bircham looked visibly relieved and relaxed in the chair. "That's good Jimmy. Take my advice and leave everything behind. Turn your phone off and try to refocus on what's important. You don't need any distractions at the moment." He stood up hurriedly and tucked in the end of his shirt which had come loose. "Give me a ring when you're ready to come back, but I won't answer if it's less than two weeks from today." He smiled and patted Nicholls on the shoulder. "Look after yourself son, and I'll see you soon."

Nicholls quickly gathered up a few personal belongings before making his way through the door. Conveniently, there was a fire escape adjacent to his office and a set of stairs to the ground floor that were seldom used. It meant he could exit the building quickly and avoid any awkward conversations with colleagues. He briefly considered ringing Page to let him know what had transpired but thought better of it. Page was perhaps the only person he could trust in the whole force.

He had just pulled out on to the main road when his phone rang. It was a no number, so he instinctively knew who was calling him. He pressed the hands-free button on the steering wheel and braced himself for the next bombshell.

"Jimmy, are you alright to talk?" said Kane.

"Yes, go ahead John," sighed Nicholls. "The force has put me on leave so I will have quite a bit of free time for the foreseeable future. Apparently, it was Flack's idea."

"Good," replied Kane bluntly, patently ignoring his last remark. "Can you remember how to get to the café on the Capital estate?"

"Yes, I do. Why?"

"Meet me there as soon as you can." Kane hung up the phone before Nicholls had time to answer.

Nicholls shook his head. He wanted to ignore him and go home but the nagging voice in the back of his head was never going to let that happen. He indicated right and performed a sharp U-turn in a narrow junction to change direction and before long he was parked outside the peculiar café again. The industrial estate looked deserted. There was something eerily strange about the dilapidated concrete buildings. When Nicholls had last been here it was late at night, but this time it was still only mid-afternoon. Most industrial estates in London radiated a voracious energy as employees worked around the clock in an endless cycle of assembly and shipping. But this place was soulless. It was as if the life blood had been sucked out by a supernatural being. Nicholls shuddered.

He parked up quickly. There were a handful of cars dotted around and a few lights flickering in warehouse buildings, but no-one seemed to notice his arrival. He walked briskly up to the café and the door swung open to greet him. It was uncanny how Kane seemed to anticipate everything.

"Get in quickly," he said impatiently, holding the door open for Nicholls.

Nicholls brushed past him. "Got any bacon on the go? I'm starving."

"You can help yourself to some food in a bit," said Kane impatiently. "There's something I wanted to show you. Then you and me need to talk."

Nicholls funnelled his arms into a point. "Lead the way John," he said sarcastically.

Kane placed his hand on Nicholls' shoulder and led him through the wooden doors at the back of the room, from which Marie had emerged. It was a dimly lit storeroom with pallets and boxes piled messily in the corners.

Nicholls' attention was drawn instinctively to a compact shape in the centre of the room that was covered by a grubby blue sheet. Kane gestured for Nicholls to take a seat in a plastic backed chair by the entrance. He walked over to the blue sheet.

"What's this all about John?" asked Nicholls.

Kane held his hand out to silence him. He took a hold of the blue sheet and whipped it off to reveal a clump of sweaty, matted brown hair. At first, he thought it was a hairdresser's wig, but to his horror he quickly realised that it was a man's head. He felt a chill tingle down his spine. His first instinct was that this was another of Kane's victims but then he saw the man's head bobbing gently to the rhythmic movements of the chest, as he breathed in and out.

"Jesus fucking Christ," he exclaimed. "Who's that?" He leaned over to get a better look at the figure, whose head was slumped over to the side. He looked vaguely familiar although Nicholls couldn't place his name. He was quite short and powerfully built with a flattened nose and a puckered scar down one side of his face. As Nicholls drew closer, he could see that his brown hair was peppered with grey, and his stubble was as white as hoarfrost.

"His name is Gary Darnell," said Kane calmly. "He's a commander in one of the Met's armed units. A real nasty piece of work if ever there was one. He's Flack's lapdog and as bent as they come."

"You've abducted a police officer," shrieked Nicholls. "Are you fucking mad? The whole force will be searching for him."

"Relax, Jimmy. He's on leave too. Nobody will be looking for him."

"What have you done to him, John? Does he need a doctor?"

Kane moved swiftly over to a table on the far side of the room and picked up a small box. He opened it up and withdrew a syringe. He checked the syringe worked and plunged it into a medicinal bottle that was lying nearby. "I used the opioid etorphine to knock him out a few hours ago," said Kane methodically. "He should be coming round anytime now but this antidote will bring him up to speed pretty quickly if I can inject it straight into his carotid artery. The problem is that I don't have ultrasound to guide me, so it's a bit of a gamble."

Kane traced his fingers over Darnell's neck until he was satisfied that he had found the right spot. He pressed the syringe into the skin and injected the antidote.

"What now?" said Nicholls anxiously.

"We wait, Jimmy." Kane walked back to the table and removed a remote control from one of the drawers. He pointed it up at the ceiling and a projector whirled into life. He pressed another button and an electrical whiteboard unfurled along the far wall. It made Nicholls jump. He had not noticed it before. The technology was totally incongruous with the old-fashioned demeanour of the café. Kane opened the drawers of the table to reveal a modern looking computer. He pulled out a data stick from his pocket and placed it delicately in the flash drive.

Darnell suddenly started to splutter, and his head jerked up. He spat a mouthful of phlegm onto the floor and coughed violently. Kane moved over menacingly into his eye line.

"Who the fuck are you?" growled Darnell. "What have you done to me?" His face was still partially immobilised by the effects of the drugs and his eyes were drooping, but he was fighting hard to regain control of his body. The veins that ran along his forehead were pulsating in rage. He tried desperately to step out of the chair, but his legs and arms had been securely fastened to the back seat.

"It doesn't matter who I am," said Kane icily. "You need to listen very carefully to what I've got to say if you want to make it out of here alive." Nicholls shuddered.

"Do you know who the fuck I am? You're a fucking dead man when I get out of here." He noticed Nicholls out of the corner of his eye. "You're both fucking dead. Do you hear me you bastards?"

Kane smiled wryly and then very slowly and very deliberately, he walked over to Darnell and stooped so he could look him squarely in the eyes. Darnell tried to head butt him, but he was still too dazed by the agent to get any power, so his thrust was disjointed and pathetic. Kane easily stepped back to avoid the butt, and then in a fluent motion he slapped him hard across the face. Nicholls felt the force of the blow where he was sitting.

"Now you listen to me, you cunt you," hissed Kane. "If I wanted you dead then you would be dead already. I want you to watch the screen and then after that we will talk."

Darnell's jaw tensed as he accepted the futility of his situation. Like it or not, he was at the mercy of his captors. Kane walked over to the computer and opened up a video clip that appeared on the projector screen. The picture quality wasn't perfect, but Nicholls could make out a fuzzy lorry that was surrounded by a dozen or so armed men.

"What's this?" growled Darnell.

"My apologies, Gary," said Kane mockingly. "I should have explained. It's not the best quality as you can see but it's a video of your last operation to bring down a Russian drug dealer. I think it paints a pretty damning picture to be honest."

Darnell shifted uncomfortably in his seat. "Where did you get this?" he stammered nervously.

"That doesn't matter now, Gary," said Kane dismissively. "Let's just watch it and see what happens next." Kane excitedly pressed the remote and the video whirled into life. The footage was grainy and the sound was partially distorted but Nicolls could see quite clearly that the armed men were police officers courtesy of the distinctive police issue body armour and black helmets. The police officers were shouting aggressively at a small group of men who hovered around a section of wooden pallets. The footage suddenly zoomed in on a central figure who was barking orders at the others. He was a squat man with a strong jaw line and a flattened nose.

Kane paused the video. "Now, I know that the picture isn't perfect Gary, but I think you'd be hard pressed to convince a court that isn't you. What do you think Detective Inspector?"

Kane deliberately stressed the "Detective Inspector" part of the sentence. Darnell's gaze fixed on Nicholls. He was clearly surprised that Nicholls was also a police officer and didn't understand what the implications were for him. Nicholls could clearly see the doubt and anxiety that was etched on his face.

"A very strong likeness if you ask me," responded Nicholls staring ponderously at the screen.

"You will be very interested to see what happens next, Detective Inspector?" Kane started the video playing again. The shouting was beginning to get quite intense, and you could feel the tension permeating the room as the police officers levelled their weapons at the criminals.

Nicholls looked on in fascination. Where had Kane obtained this video from? He remembered that a police officer had died during the operation, and he wondered whether they would be able to see that on the video.

Darnell barked an order at the men. It sounded like an ultimatum. There was a brief stand-off before the criminals nervously dropped their weapons and placed their hands on their heads. Darnell ordered them to kneel. That command was perfectly audible.

The police officers edged closer to the criminals with guns primed, like sharks circling their prey. The criminals had all given up and seemed resigned to their fate. Darnell moved on his own towards one of the men who was furthest forward. He seemed to bend down to speak with him. He then turned towards his unit, shouted something inaudible and all of a sudden, the police officers opened fire. The sound of gunfire was deafening and even though it was a recording, Nicholls jolted upright in his seat. The criminals dropped to the floor one by one like dominoes. Nicholls couldn't believe what he was seeing. This was cold-blooded murder.

"I don't fucking believe it," exclaimed Nicholls in shock. "What is going on here?" He shook his head in incredulity.

"Now that evidence is pretty damning isn't it, Gary?" said Kane. "That looks like you've just ordered the murder of a group of men who had given themselves up. I don't know how you would convince anyone who sees that video that you were acting in self-defence."

Darnell's face recoiled in disgust. "Alright you bastard. You've got me. Turn it off now."

"Now why would I do that Gary when the best is still to come" said Kane coldly.

Nicholls's gaze was transfixed on the screen. He couldn't take his eyes off it. Darnell had now moved over towards the lead figure, who was twitching spasmodically on the floor. He watched as Darnell picked up a gun. Even on the video the black cannister shimmered in the light. Another figure came into view. He was shouting and remonstrating with Darnell. A police officer who wasn't part of the plan thought Nicholls. And then amazingly Darnell slowly pointed the gun at the police officer and fired. The man staggered back a few steps and clutched his neck. Nicholls could see blood spilling through his hand and dripping on the floor. He waved his other hand tentatively at Darnell in disbelief before collapsing on the floor.

Nicholls stared at Darnell. The police offer couldn't meet his glare and looked down at the floor. To shoot another police officer so coldly and callously was the work of an inhuman monster. Nicholls pictured the headlines the next day and the total furore his death had caused. What was his name again? It took him a second before he remembered. It was Jack Marsden. He had died during the operation; shot and killed by the criminals. That was what had been claimed by the Met. But that was rubbish. He had been killed by his own men, possibly for disagreeing with the brutal execution of the prisoners.

Nicholls visualised the press conference the following day, when Flack had launched into an unexpected and vehement assault on the government. He had criticised the funding the Met had received in recent years and pointed the finger of blame squarely at the government for not giving the police the necessary resources to fight the drug fuelled crime wave. It was all a lie, but why on earth would someone do that? And then just like that the answer hit him with the force of a steam train.

There had been times during Nicholls's career as a police officer when his brain was so befuddled with theories that it had created a fog in his mind, and he was completely unable to think straight. When he was in this state of blindness, he would often miss crucial details, that were right in front of his face. Nicholls had been operating in this mindset for the last week. He had been trapped in a prison of his own imagination and dark thoughts that was impossible to escape. Now, seeing that video, it was as if someone had turned a light on his head which had cleared the room in an instant. He finally understood what was going on. The drug lord was a criminal rival to McGovern, so he had conspired with Flack to take him out. Poor Jack Marsden had been killed to fuel more opposition to an under-fire government and potentially damage their credibility to the point at which it was irreparable. And what would happen next? The conservatives would win the general election, Kilbride would become the next prime minister and McGovern and Flack would be untouchable. Nicholls knew then that he had to stop it, even if that meant working with his brother to do so.

"What do you think, Detective Inspector?" asked Kane.

Nicholls felt a vehement hatred for Darnell surge through his veins. He was a physical embodiment of the evil, corrupt system that had ensnared the city of London. That same system had killed his mother because she wanted to speak out against it. He wanted to smash him into oblivion and when his face was a bloody mess of broken tissue, drag him to jail and throw away the key.

He stared at Darnell with a look of utter contempt on his face. "I think we need to take this video to anti-corruption. This piece of shit can rot in jail for the rest of his life"

Darnell shifted uncomfortably in his seat. He prided himself on being a tough man, but the thought of a life sentence in jail was terrifying.

"If we do that Detective Inspector, the real villains will get away with their crimes. Darnell here isn't stupid. He knows full well what will happen to his family if he testifies against McGovern and Flack." He stared venomously at Darnell whose eyes betrayed his fear. "I bet you couldn't give two hoots about your estranged wife, Sarah, but I would imagine your daughters are a different story. What were their names again?" Kane scratched his head and pretended to think for a second. "Poppy and Abby, if I remember correctly. Isn't that right, Gary?"

"If you hurt my kids, I swear to god I'll kill you," hissed Darnell.

"I'm not in the business of hurting innocent people," hissed Kane. "I don't punish children for the sins of their parents. I'm just reminding you what's at stake here. The people you work for wouldn't have any qualms about killing children though and I think you know that." He stood up and moved away from Darnell as if he was disgusted by his very presence.

"Listen you piece of shit. I don't care about what happens to you. You sold your soul to the devil and now you have nothing left to sell. I have taken over the debt, and I am offering you a way out which is something you definitely don't deserve." Kane paused to take a deep breath.

"It is McGovern and Flack that I want, not you. It is not quite time to take them down yet, but it will be soon. They never need to know about our arrangement, so your daughters will be safe. You are free to go back to your sinful life, but I will come back for you, and you will do exactly as I say when that time comes. And just remember that I own you Gary." He pointed towards the screen which had been paused to display Marsden's death, to emphasise his point. "If the authorities get even a whiff of this video, then it will be prison for you for the rest of your life. Do you know what happens to corrupt police officers there, Gary?

"And if you even think of betraying me to McGovern and Flack you son of a bitch, then I swear that I will come and snatch your life as you walk down the street."

Darnell didn't answer. His powerful jaw muscles were strained as he clenched his teeth in impotent frustration. Kane moved over to the table and fiddled with a bottle. He took something out of his pocket but his back blocked Nicholls's view so he couldn't see what he was doing.

Kane took Darnell's silence as confirmation he was on board. "Good decision, Gary. You will not regret it." He patted his back mockingly. "Now if I'm honest I've had quite enough of your vile presence. It's time for you to go back to sleep."

Darnell instinctively knew what was coming and thrashed his head away from Kane, but he was too strong. He wrapped a huge arm around his neck and forced his head upwards. With his spare hand he pulled out a handkerchief from his pocket and plunged it over Darnell's mouth.

Within seconds, Darnell's arms stopped flapping and his whole body sagged as he succumbed to the chemicals.

Nicholls stood up. "Where did you get that video John? It's dynamite. If the public see that, there will be anarchy in the streets."

"I had a tip off the operation was about to go down," said Kane casually. "I used a drone to film it all. Turns out I got more than I expected." Kane pulled out a Stanley knife from his pocket and cut the binds that had secured Darnell to the back of the chair. "Now, listen Jimmy. I need to get this piece of shit out of here, but I won't be too long. There are some beers in the fridge in the kitchen. Why don't you make a start on them and I'll join you in a bit?"

Nicholls nodded somewhat reluctantly. He would definitely get it in the neck from Jenny if he did not get home soon. "Don't be too long," he said.

Kane grinned mischievously and winked at Nicholls. He took hold of the frame of the chair and tipped it backwards, before dragging Darnell towards a door on the far wall. "Leave some for me."

Nicholls grimaced. He could scarcely believe the scale of the nefarious scheme devised by Flack and McGovern. How on earth could Kane fight against these evil men who controlled such vast resources? It was like fighting against the might of the Roman Empire with sling shots and bows and arrows. Kane seemed to have it all in hand and wasn't at all fazed by the enormity of the task that he faced, but surely that had to be a smokescreen. He was just one man; a dangerous, unhinged man that was for sure, but what could one person do against such evil.

Nicholls ambled into the kitchen and opened the large industrial refrigerator. He pulled out the bottom tray to reveal a box of Foster's lager that had already been opened. Without thinking he withdrew an ice-cold can and pulled on the tab. The soothing liquid had a slightly bitter flavour with a sweet after taste that invigorated him. He hadn't realised he was so thirsty. He took another hearty drink and moved back into the dining area. He sat down and removed his phone. Jenny had already rung, and he had two missed calls from her. His finger hovered over the redial button but then he hesitated. What was he going to say to her? A phone call would provoke too many questions that he wouldn't be able to answer.

He sent her a quick text message that he was out for a drink with a friend and then he turned his phone off. The inevitable argument would have to wait until tomorrow.

Nicholls picked up his can. To his surprise it was already empty. He went back to the fridge and pulled out two more. Kane had better get back quickly or he would already be drunk. He opened the second can and before he realised, he had drained that one too. He was beginning to feel slightly inebriated and for the first time in weeks, he started to relax. Not for the first time, Nicholls began to wonder about Kane's life and what had happened to mould him into the person he was today. He felt an overwhelming desire to learn more about his family and emphasise with his brother. The dark thoughts that had been gnawing away at his soul began to gradually subside.

Nicholls looked at his watch. It was nearly seven o'clock. There was no point in going back home now until Jenny was asleep. He would have to call a taxi as well and fetch his car in the morning. More awkward questions that would have to be answered. He resolved to forget about his troubles for the time being and banish them to the dark recesses of his mind where they would lurk, waiting to emerge and terrorise him at another time.

The refrigerator seemed to be drawing him in like a magnet. This time he fancied a change of drink. There were a few unopened bottles of wine in the inner door but that would have to be a last resort, as it made him bloated and gassy. He checked again and saw a bottle of gin that had already been opened. He remembered that he had seen some bottles of tonic water on the kitchen top. They would complement each other perfectly.

"I don't mind if I do," he said excitedly to himself. He raided the cupboards and quickly found some glasses. They looked dusty but he wiped the rim hurriedly with his finger and decided that would be sufficient.

"Pour me one too," said a voice from behind him.

Nicholls almost jumped out of his skin in surprise. He dropped the glass which smashed into fragments on the floor. He turned around and his jaw almost hit the floor. Standing in front of him was a beautiful young woman. She was wearing a slate grey baggy jumper with ripped blue jeans and gleaming white sports trainers. Her face was oval with razor sharp cheek bones and alluring brown eyes that glinted like amber. She ran her hand through her short, cropped brown hair and smiled mischievously at him.

Nicholls was stunned and felt drained of his powers of speech. The silence between them seemed to grow into an awkward crescendo before Nicholls was able to stutter, "hello Holly. How are you?"

His sister looked at him and her amber eyes were suddenly saturated with emotion. "Hello Jimmy," she said softly. "It's so good to see you. I have been waiting for this moment for such a long time."

She stepped towards him and stopped about a metre away. She was small and slender with immaculate olive skin that glinted in the light. When she looked up at him, her voluptuous lips curled into a warm and genuine smile. He opened his arms invitingly and she plunged headfirst into his caress. They held each other without speaking for a few minutes. Holly felt as delicate as a snowflake and Nicholls was wary not to grip her too tight in case she cracked.

"I remember you, Jimmy," she said nuzzling into Nicholls' chest. "I remember you and John. I remember our parents. They are only hazy, fleeting memories but no-one can take them away from me." Nicholls felt unable to speak. He didn't want this moment to ever end.

Holly led him back to the dining area of the café and gently pulled him down into the chair he had been sitting on. "You wait here, and I'll fix us a drink. I don't trust you do it properly after what I've just seen," she said playfully, pointing at the smashed glass on the floor. "I take it you were making a gin and tonic?"

Nicholls nodded. He turned and wiped a tear away from his eye so Holly couldn't see. She returned shortly with two generous glasses of gin and tonic. She sat down on the chair next to Nicholls and gently caressed his knee.

"I've rehearsed what I would say when I first met you a thousand times, but here we are and I'm afraid to say that I'm lost," said Holly a little nervously.

"I only found out I had a twin brother and a sister a few days ago," replied Nicholls. "Needless to say I have found it quite a shock." He wanted to find out everything about her and what her life had been like, but there was one nagging question that he just couldn't ignore. "When did you meet John?" he said, a little too intensely than he had meant to.

Holly pulled back fractionally in her chair, surprised by his directness. "I met John a few years back. I was in a pretty dark place at the time." Her voice started to tremble, as if the question had evoked painful memories.

"I always knew I had a family, but I just didn't know what had happened to it," she said candidly. "One day I had a mum and a dad and two brothers and the next day I woke up in a foster home. No-one told me why or where they had gone. It was as if my memories had all been a dream. I was much too young to question what was going on so I just kind of accepted it."

Nicholls nodded sympathetically. He didn't know what to say. "My adopted parents weren't good to me," Holly continued. "They were very strict, and my dad used to beat me if I disobeyed him. I hated it there. The family had two older sisters who were their natural children. I don't know why they wanted to adopt another child. The sisters were horrible to me. I couldn't wait to get out. I ran away from home when I was sixteen. I spent a few years dossing with friends and then I really got in with a bad crowd." She turned away from Nicholls as if she was really ashamed.

"I took drugs, I stole. I even had to sell my body to get by. I didn't care about anybody or anything. It was then that John found me." She paused to take a long sip from her gin and tonic. "I don't know quite how he tracked me down, but if he hadn't, then I know I wouldn't still be here today. He's damaged goods as well. He's been through some terrible shit, but it's given him a strength that I could barely even fathom. He took care of me, and he helped me get myself clean. He told me what had happened to our family, and he told me about you."

Nicholls irked slightly. How long had they known about him before coming to find him? "I had no idea about any of this, Holly."

She smiled reassuringly. "Of course, you didn't. How could you? Each of us was plucked from our family and given a different upbringing. You had love and look what happened to you." There was a hint of resentment in her tone.

"I am sorry for everything, Holly" he said gently.

She turned and looked at him quizzically. "It is not your fault, Jimmy. Our family has been torn apart by a terrible evil. We must have our revenge for what they have taken from us. John and I have been planning this for a long time. When this is over, there will be time for us to get to know each other properly."

What had they been planning? Nicholls felt bitter that he had been kept out of the loop for so long. He was torn between his desire to reconcile and his enmity from being excluded for so long. He tried to change the subject. "What do you remember about our parents, Holly?"

Holly smiled. "I remember our mother's face and the way she looked when she was happy. She was a beautiful lady, Jimmy. When she smiled, her eyes shone with joy and her laugh was infectious. She used to light up any room when she walked in. Our father was a quiet man with hooded eyebrows and fair hair. He wasn't particularly affectionate, but he always had time to play with us." She stared through Nicholls as if he was transparent, picturing the scene in her memory. "We were loved Jimmy. We had a happy family, and they took it all from us."

Holly buried her head in her hands and sobbed loudly. Nicholls was about to go and comfort her when he heard the door swing open and Kane walked in. He was grinning like a Cheshire cat, as if he didn't have a care in the world. "Ahh good," he said nonchalantly. "You are both here. I hope you saved some beers for me." He must have seen that Holly was upset about something, but he patently ignored it.

He disappeared into the kitchen and emerged with a couple of cans of lager. "Now before we get started, we need to deal with the important stuff first." He slammed both cans aggressively on the table and sat next to Nicholls. "What football team do you support Jimmy?" he said bellowing with laughter.

Nicholls laughed. "I'm a goner, John. Is that okay?"

"I suppose it will have to do. They aren't a big club like the mighty Celtic though!" He opened the can and took a few huge mouthfuls, glancing at the empty cans and half-finished bottle of gin. "It looks like I am playing catch up after all!" He wiped his mouth and sat back in the seat. "Now isn't this something," he said winking at Holly. "The Kanes are finally all reunited together as a family for the first time in forever. It is enough to make you quite emotional."

"I grew up thinking that I didn't have a family" replied Nicholls. "I want nothing more than to get to know you both."

"There will be time for that soon. Who knows, perhaps we can all become close in the future? But at the moment there is a terrible injustice that we need to right first. We cannot look to the future until our vengeance is complete."

"It doesn't sound like much of a democracy at the moment. It's just you two calling the shots and I have to hold on for dear life in case I fall off."

Kane ignored the rebuke. "I apologise for keeping you in the dark, Jimmy. There were things that needed to be put into place first. I won't keep you out of the loop again, I promise."

"And what about Holly?" he said angrily. "If I've got this right, she's hooked up with McGovern masquerading as a Russian prostitute? What kind of fucked up plan is that?"

"Actually, I'm a Romanian prostitute," quipped Holly in an exaggerated East European accent.

Kane laughed hysterically and spat out a mouthful of beer. Nicholls looked at the pair of them and couldn't contain his amusement either. He smiled and had to work hard to suppress his laughter at the ridiculous situation.

"It was all my idea, Jimmy," she responded hurriedly. "And it's worked. McGovern is besotted by me. I've got him wrapped around my little finger at the moment. The poor, innocent immigrant girl routine is working like a charm." She reached into her hooded jumper and pulled out a notepad that she hurled casually onto the table between Nicholls and Kane. "I copied this from his computer yesterday."

Kane raised his eyebrow compelling her to elaborate. "It's his diary entries for the next week or so. It details who he's meeting and where."

Her brazen comments seemed to have a sobering effect on Nicholls. "Holly, please be careful," he said nervously. "McGovern is an evil man. The thought of you with him terrifies me. You don't need to do this."

"You don't need to worry, Jimmy," she snapped unexpectedly, ignoring his concern. "It's a means to an end. McGovern is so complacent the risks are really quite small. He is obsessed by me. I have the keys to a flat in Kensington, but I spend most evenings with him at his home. He thinks I am grateful to him for rescuing me."

She laughed and took a mouthful of her drink. "Can you believe that? The arrogant son of a bitch. He leaves me on my own and I am given free reign round his estate. The bastard thinks he is untouchable. I am going to find out all his dirty secrets and use them to bring him down."

Nicholls looked at Kane for support. "And you are happy with this?"

"Hey, don't look at me Jimmy." He spread his hands mockingly. "Holly won't listen to anyone when her mind is made up."

"Well, I want to hear what your grand plan is then, John. What are we going to do in the meantime while we wait for McGovern to hang himself?"

"You and I are going to send him a message, Jimmy lad," said Kane excitedly. "Have you heard about the Ritz?" Nicholls nodded. Everyone had heard of the Ritz. It was McGovern's lap dancing club. "We're going to take the place down and then carve up his evil empire bit by bit till he's on his knees. How does that sound for a plan?"

"Us three and whose army?" said Nicholls a little more sarcastically than he had meant to.

Kane shrugged nonchalantly. "Why don't I show you, Jimmy? Come with me." Kane stood up clutching his beer can. He gestured for Nicholls to join him and then started to move towards the back room where Darnell had been kept prisoner. Nicholls looked behind him. Holly had stayed put. Whatever it was, she had already seen it.

"The kindest thing that I can say about my childhood was that I survived it, Jimmy," said Kane as the pair of men stepped through the storeroom. Kane opened a wooden door at the base of the room which allowed a stream of light to pour through. Kane stood to the side to let Nicholls go through first. He found himself in a gated compound that was strewn with weeds and strangled by overgrown trees that clung to the metal fence. There were two old rusty cars partially concealed by a grubby brown weather cover that Nicholls noticed first. The cover was too small, and the exposed metal had turned a mottled orange as it rusted.

"The family that adopted me were monsters. They abused me in more ways than I could imagine," said Kane sadly. "But I supposed I should be grateful because in the end, they helped make me strong and ruthless. I left home at the earliest opportunity. I spent about a year on the mean streets of Glasgow before I decided to join the army."

He looked at Nicholls and smiled. "What a pitiful creature I must have been at the start. By that time, I was almost feral. It was a miracle I wasn't kicked out during training. I didn't like taking orders from anyone. I wanted to fight the world. If it wasn't for my sergeant, then I'm sure they would've have done. He was a tough man, but he was fair. He must have seen something in me that no-one else did. Anyway, it was him that helped me deal with my anger and channel it into a strength. It turns out that I was actually quite a good soldier, Jimmy. Can you believe that? My first tour was Iraq. It was a tough place. In my second week there, we were caught up in an ambush and we had to fight our way out. Some of the lads didn't make it but I was guess I was one of the lucky ones. I was never scared of dying like some of the others. I suppose that is quite a useful quality for a soldier, if you can harness it. It helps me to think clearly under pressure. I have made peace with death so there is nothing else that can hurt me. I should have been a philosophy lecturer instead of a soldier, shouldn't I?"

He pointed to a dingy old green caravan that was slumped in the corner of the compound and camouflaged by an overgrown tree. The wooden panels were covered in mildew and the frameless acrylic plastic windows were chipped in several places. The fibreglass frame was pockmarked with dents like the face of an old and broken boxer.

"It's not quite the Savoy but it will do for now," said Kane buoyantly. "As I was saying, being a soldier somehow came easy to me. I had found a profession where I could excel and for the first time in my life I had a purpose, and I was content."

The pair of them had reached the caravan. Kane rubbed his hand fastidiously over a patch of mould on the front as if he could wipe away the fungus with mere elbow grease. "I got promoted quickly and it wasn't long before I became a sergeant. Apparently, I was one of the youngest people ever to achieve the rank," he said proudly. "But that wasn't enough for me. I wanted another challenge and after six tough months in Brecon I passed selection to the SAS."

Nicholls stopped in his tracks, clearly surprised by the revelation. "Hold on! Are you telling me you were in the SAS?"

Kane put his finger to his lips. "I am but please don't tell anyone. It's supposed to be a secret," he said playfully. "I had two tours in Afghanistan, one in Sierra Leone, a hostage rescue in Baghdad and my last mission involved fighting ISIS in Syria."

"Jesus Christ," yelped Nicholls, suitably impressed. "That sounds pretty hardcore. I can't believe it."

"It was dangerous work don't get me wrong," said Kane. "At one point ISIS captured fifty Kurdish soldiers who provided us with support during an operation. We found their severed heads impaled on spikes all the way down the main street of some god forsaken town we were fighting over. They didn't care about dying as long as they could take some of us with them. My best friend in the unit was blown up by a suicide bomber. The only good thing was that he didn't know anything about it. There was scarcely enough left of him to fill a shopping bag at the end."

Nicholls didn't know what to say. No wonder Kane was scarred. "I was a good soldier, Jimmy. I never let anyone down. I could handle the blood, the guts and the gore but there was something missing in my life that I couldn't quite explain. My brain couldn't handle it when I was on leave. Some of the other men were single but they seemed to adapt pretty well to civvy life. I couldn't. I ended up turning to the bottle. It was only after one botched suicide attempt that I decided I had to find out where I came from. I didn't have to do much digging to find out who I was Jimmy and what happened to my family." He finished his first can and hurled it over the compound.

"I couldn't accept it, Jimmy. It made my blood boil to think about it. I tracked down Marie and she told me everything she knew. I couldn't let them get away with it. I just couldn't." Kane's anger all of a sudden became very palpable. He clenched his jaw in fury and kicked a bit of metal flotsam that was peeling off the caravan.

Kane took a deep breath and refocussed. His moods were particularly temperamental thought Nicholls. Anyone could see that he had anger issues, and it was almost a constant battle for him to keep control of the demons within. "I left the army almost straight away," said Kane. "I had saved a bit of money and I used it to buy this café. Who knows, perhaps one day I can make a go of it and have a nice quiet life. Does that ever happen in your experience, Jimmy?"

Nicholls nodded but didn't say anything. His brother was clearly very disturbed. He had already murdered four men, and they were only the ones he knew about. Severe mental illness and an idyllic life were very rarely compatible, but Nicholls didn't see the point in explaining that to his brother. Kane's anger seemed to give him a focus and determination that made him stronger than anyone he had ever met in his life. There were times when he appeared quite calculating and rational but other times it made him capricious and volatile. Kane was clearly a dangerous man. He was a trained killer; of that there was no doubt. You didn't make it into the SAS without having exceptional qualities. Would those qualities be enough to bring down Flack and McGovern? Nicholls highly doubted that. But what choice did he have but to try and support his brother and sister even if it meant travelling down this perilous path that seemed destined to end in their destruction? He wasn't sure if he could talk them out of their quest for vengeance and the more he thought about it, the less he wanted to.

Kane stepped onto a wooden pallet that acted as a temporary doorstep and prised open the door. They were both big men so had to stoop to avoid banging their heads. The air inside was stale and musty and the interior was badly outdated. Garish blue wallpaper dominated the tiny front room. It had already begun to peel in places and there were sporadic outbreaks of mould that clung to the coving and ceiling like jungle foliage. There was a tiny table in the middle of the room that was surrounded by an old brown sofa with protruding springs. Both items of furniture were piled high with a mountain of paperwork that looked ready to topple over at any moment.

Nicholls' attention was drawn to an intricate set of photos and newspaper articles that were mounted on a chipboard frame and dotted along the entire length of the interior wall. Each photo was dated with a description on a postage note underneath that was bisected by a string timeline. Nicholls noticed that the stringline was fastened to the wooden door frame and began in 1993 with a photo of their mother. The postage note had the single word "murdered" scrawled in conspicuous black ink. He felt a lump form in his throat. As he moved along the wall, he saw the storyboard was dominated with photos of McGovern and Flack, charting their rise to power. Most of the photos were of people he could easily identify like Bircham and Baldock but there were a few he had never seen before. Kane had clearly gone to great lengths to compose this storyboard and obtain as much information as possible.

As he moved to the end of the stringline, he noticed that there were four photos grouped together. The date the photos were taken appeared to have only been yesterday, and all the men looked like they were entering the same building. McGovern, Flack and Kilbride were easy to recognise although they all seemed to be attempting to disguise their entry. The fourth person was a large, corpulent man with thick auburn hair. Nicholls had never seen him before. He looked at the postage stamp and saw a name that seemed familiar but one that he couldn't quite place.

"Who is Sergei Ivankov and what he is doing at the Highbury hotel?"

Kane didn't respond immediately. He was in the tiny front room looking for something. He picked up a brown folder. "Ahh, this is it," he said excitedly. He passed it to Nicholls. "Sergei Ivankov is a Russian mafia boss. He's the biggest shark in the sea; a right fucking megalodon. He traffics the girls that McGovern uses in his brothels. I don't know what McGovern and Flack were meeting him about but I'm sure it's going to be bad news. It's real cloak and dagger stuff you know? They all arranged to meet at the Highbury hotel and made great pains to avoid being seen. I don't like the sound of it one bit. Holly is going to do her best to find out as much as she can in the meantime."

Nicholls nodded and opened the folder. It was a dossier containing photos of an industrial estate, including aerials. He wondered how Kane had obtained them. There also seemed to be photos of a lap dancing club which presumably had been taken on a hidden camera.

"It's photos of McGovern's prostitution business and schematics of the complex. You can take it home if you want to look over. I've committed it to memory."

"How do you know all this, John?" asked Nicholls.

Kane smiled and opened a door in the hallway. "Come and let me show you," he said proudly.

The bedroom, if you could call it that, looked like a mobile police surveillance unit. There was no bed, just a large wooden table that was crammed with computers and strange technology that Nicholls had never seen before. On a bedside cabinet was a box containing a dark black shape with four motor driven propellers that reminded Nicholls of gun turrets. As he walked over, he realised it was a drone. The black metal gleamed in the sparce light that came in through a dirty window. This must be what he had used to film Darnell's unit thought Nicholls.

Kane could sense Nicholls' curiosity blossom as he looked in puzzlement at the alien devices. "McGovern uses an encryption service on his phone that he thinks allows him to send secure messages to other criminals. It's a kind of WhatsApp chat that gangsters use to conceal their activities because they think no one is watching. Unfortunately for McGovern, Holly was able to put a cloning device on his phone, so all of his messages pop up on this computer. It's been very handy in learning his plans. We've also got some GPS tracking devices planted in his cars so we can keep track of his movements. Even if McGovern finds them, there's no way he can trace them back to Holly, so relax Jimmy. I don't want you getting upset again."

Kane pointed to a weathered old wardrobe at the back of the room. "Now, this is the real coup de gras. Why don't you open that up and have a look at what's in there?"

Nicholls obediently moved towards the wardrobe, forcing himself to squeeze through the narrow gap between the table and the cabinet. He pulled open the stiff double doors and gasped in surprise. The wardrobe was crammed with an array of deadly weapons and assault rifles that seemed to leap out at him.

Kane smiled. "Don't worry Jimmy. I know how to use them in case you're worried. My favourite is the C8 carbine assault rifle. That's the one closest to you. It's versatile and reliable. We can take it out later and you can shoot it, if you want?"

Nicholls didn't answer. He opened a chest of drawers beneath the main weapons to reveal a stack of handguns. "I've got Glocks, a couple of Brownings and a Sig Sauer. Not to mention all the custom-made fighting knives in the bottom drawer. I bet you can't work out which one carved up Baldock can you?" laughed Kane. "Those fuckers ain't going to know what hit them."

Nicholls felt a wave of nausea hit him as he stared at the deadly weapons. He bundled past Kane and scrambled to the dingy bathroom at the far end of the caravan, where he emptied his guts.

Chapter 7
The Die Is Cast

Kane peered out of the window of his caravan into the main compound. The sky was slate grey and swelled with menacing looking rain clouds. It had been good to spend some time together with his brother and sister and the alcohol had certainly lubricated some of the shackles that had restrained their previous attempts at intimacy.

Nicholls had drunk too much and had ended up spending the night in the caravan on the sofa. His face had been an unhealthy green pallor in the morning that matched the lime-coloured wall tiles in the bathroom. He had been sick at least twice already and was currently making himself some breakfast in the café, although Kane seriously doubted he would be able to keep much of it down for long.

That was good. There was something he had to do, something he didn't want Nicholls knowing about just yet. He moved into the bedroom and closed the door firmly. Instinctively he placed a small table by the door to act as an obstacle if Nicholls tried to enter unexpectedly. He opened the nearest cupboard and removed a leather bag. Inside was a laptop that he placed carefully on the large table in the centre of the room. He turned it on and dialled a number that had been burned into his brain and he could recall from memory.

The computer link was encrypted and provided a secure line that couldn't be traced if the laptop was seized. Kane snatched a bottle of water from the floor and drained it quickly. He kneeled over the computer like a coiled spring.

The dial tone stopped ringing as someone answered. "Can you hear me?" said Kane robustly.

The cursor on the screen flickered temporarily. Kane scratched his neck nervously and rubbed his jawline as he waited. With seconds, text appeared on the screen to answer his question.

I am here John.

"Good," replied Kane. "I sent you an email last night sir containing the names of the corrupt politicians and businessman we have been looking to unmask. Holly obtained them from McGovern's black book, and it looks like he has them all under his thumb. Some of them have clearly been bribed but others may have been blackmailed. McGovern entices them with his prostitutes and when they've indulged in their sexual debauchery, they find out that everything's been filmed. After that, they're puppets dancing to McGovern's tunc. Holly says that McGovern likes to use underage girls in his brothels for the really big fish."

Another pause as the person on the other end of the line typed his response.

I have received the list. Thank you for this. There are some interesting names here. Some of them, I half expected but others have taken me by surprise. We have to be very careful about who we can trust at this point onwards.

"What have you found out about Ivankov, sir?" said Kane, changing the subject.

Very little. Russian money laundering has being going on in London for years. Ivankov is undoubtedly a key figure in this operation, but he seems to have divine protection. His involvement is a concern. Can you find out more?

Kane stood up but kept his hands firmly on the table. "I can try, sir. I will see what Holly can find out, but I don't want to place her in any more danger than is absolutely necessary." Kane rubbed his hands fastidiously. He was ready, but were they?

"Would you like me to move forward with the next stage of the plan, sir?"

There was a longer pause. **Go ahead, John. It is time to kick the hornet's nest and see what stirs.**

It had not been a good morning for Nicholls. Not only had he woken up with a pounding headache, but his insides churned like agitated sea snakes. It had been amazing to meet his sister, but that excitement paled at the realisation of the terrible danger she had placed herself in.

He had turned his phone on in the morning to be bombarded by a stream of messages from his girlfriend. They had started off as relatively civil enquiries, but as he had not replied, they had quickly deteriorated in to raw, vitriolic abuse. When Nicholls had driven home later that morning he was not surprised, and to be honest a little relieved to find that Jenny had packed up her belongings and moved out. There was a hastily scribbled message pinned on the fridge informing him that she had gone to stay with her sister until he "sorted himself out."

Patrick McGovern stretched out his limbs. He felt relaxed and exhilarated, all at the same time. It was a warm, spring day with an invigorating breeze that caressed his body as he lay on the mattress. Elena lay next to him. She was asleep. He traced the outline of her sensuous figure with his hand through the silk bedsheet. He shuddered with ecstasy at the thought of the supple, bronzed body underneath. It would only take a flick of his hand to expose her nakedness, but something checked him from doing so. He wanted to absorb every detail of the way she looked and commit it to memory. She was perfect. Her brown hair shimmered in the afternoon light like a polished mahogany cabinet. When he had first met her a few months ago, her hair was short, but it had grown quickly and now covered her neck and most of her shoulders. Her face was partially buried in the pillow, but her olive skin and voluptuous lips seemed to illuminate the entire room.

McGovern sighed. He had never felt so happy. He knew that she was not with him for his looks but perhaps she was attracted to the power he wielded over other men. He protected her and made sure she wanted for nothing. Perhaps that could be enough. He had even started to confide in her some of the plans he had made with Flack and Ivankov. Just snippets of information at first, but she always listened attentively, offering sound advice when asked and gradually, little by little, he started to reveal more and more to her. McGovern found the conversations with Elena cathartic. He felt energised by talking to her. No topic was off limits. One day he might be speaking about his childhood and the next day he was asking for advice about how to maximise his money laundering operation. Elena was always calm and composed and seemed to possess a wisdom beyond her years.

McGovern often thought about the future, and he couldn't imagine his life without Elena. He felt slightly abashed that she had captivated him to such a degree, but he couldn't help his feelings. He was a man who could order another person's death without a flicker of remorse, yet at the same time, Elena had reduced him to the same levels as a lovestruck teenager. He had even considered starting a new family with her. He had two adult sons with his first wife, yet they were coarse and did not have the intelligence to take over his criminal empire. He wasn't too old to have more children and Elena was young, beautiful and in the prime of her life. The thought of a new family with Elena rejuvenated him and made him feel young again. The future glimmered with all manner of opportunities. The plans that he had made with Flack and Ivankov were tantalisingly close. He could almost touch them. Darren Healey, the leader of the conservatives was appearing less and less in the media and with the election only a matter of months away, there were rumours that he was gravely ill. Even that would not stop the conservative juggernaut storming to power. He and Flack had seen to that by steadily undermining confidence in the labour government for the last few years, by encouraging the crime wave that had engulfed the nation. All they had to do was wait for Kilbride to take over, become prime minister and then they would be untouchable. Even Al Capone never enjoyed such power, with the supreme leader of the country, under his thumb. They would be the puppet masters who controlled the political apparatus of the entire country, and all they had to do was wait.

He stood up out of bed and rubbed a lattice of angry scars that adorned his ribs. He had been stabbed in an argument during his early twenties and by all accounts he had been lucky to survive. He wore these scars as a badge of honour, a symbol of what he gone through in his rise to power. There was a half empty bottle of champagne on the cabinet next to the bed. He grabbed the bottle and took a greedy slurp without bothering to use the two glasses that were in easy reach of him. Elena was still fast asleep. McGovern had deliberately not made any plans for the day as he wanted to saviour as much of Elena's company as he could. Perhaps he would book a table at the plush Italian restaurant that Ivankov owned in Kensington. He would make sure that they would be the only customers there that evening. Money was no object. He didn't want to share Elena with anyone else. The booking would have to be made as late as possible. There was still the rest of the afternoon to have sex with her and he wanted to ensure that his voracious sexual appetite had been well and truly sated before they sat down for food.

He put on some trousers and a shirt that had been causally discarded on the floor. Elena could sleep whilst he had a bite to eat downstairs. There was bread and cheese in the fridge and a large basket of strawberries. He would have an early dinner and watch the Arsenal versus Tottenham match from last night to kill some time.

McGovern was a complacent man. He did not fear anyone and why should he? This was his city, and he was the undisputed alpha male. Why should the wolf be concerned about any of the other animals that lived in his territory? He did not see the need to be cautious and often he sent his bodyguards home if he knew he would not be going out that day. His luxury apartment in Kensington was secure and had its own private security guards that manned the main foyer downstairs. No-one could gain access if they hadn't made a prior appointment and he couldn't think of anyone who would be foolish enough to disturb him here when he was here with Elena.

He took out his phone from his trouser pocket and scanned it nonchalantly. He had received no calls or messages in the last hour which struck him as slightly unusual. The television was blaring but he couldn't remember switching it on. Elena had led him into the bedroom as soon as he had arrived so it definitely wouldn't have been him. All of a sudden, he started to feel quite nauseous and lightheaded. There was no way he could be drunk. They had barely finished the bottle of champagne before having sex and McGovern prided himself on being a hardened drinker. He moved into the kitchen swiftly and placed both hands on the sink to steady himself. His head was swimming, and his vision was starting to blur. Within seconds, his stomach began to churn and before he knew it, he had vomited into the sink.

McGovern didn't hear the assassin who had been hiding in the kitchen cupboard all morning. As McGovern was spewing his guts up, he silently crept up on him with the stealth of an experienced tiger. With a flash of his hands, he looped the wire garrotte over McGovern's head and pulled tight. The weapon was specially designed with a double loop feature. If the victim pulled at one of the loops, then he would only succeed in tightening the other and subsequently hasten his own demise.

McGovern jerked upright in an instant. The pressure around his throat was excruciating as the deadly wire bit into his neck and choked the air from his lungs. It felt like his head was going to explode. He tried to scream but nothing would come out. He frantically clawed at the wire that clamped down on his throat, but his attempts were futile. McGovern desperately tried to catch his assailant with a flailing arm, but his blows simply brushed off the attacker. He felt the life slipping away from him as he slumped to his knees and felt the attacker's weight directly on top of him. Summoning his last reserves of energy, he thrashed his head back with as much force as possessed. He felt a crunching sensation as the attacker's nose broke, and then all of a sudden, the colossal pressure on top of him dissipated as the assailant was flung backwards by the force of the blow.

McGovern snatched the weapon from around his neck and threw it at his attacker who was lying dazed on the floor a few feet away. He was pervaded with a burning hatred and anger to kill the person in front of him, but he was still weak and disorientated. Strangely he thought about Elena and if he died now, what might happen to her. The threat to her safety galvanised his thoughts. He would not be rash and throw away his life. McGovern stumbled to his feet and faced his attacker, who was obviously still feeling the effects of the head butt.

The man looked McGovern squarely in the eye. He looked oddly familiar. He was about the same age as McGovern with greying hair and granite like cheeks. There was a prominent scar that stretched across the side of his face. He looked dogged and determined.

"You'd best hope that I kill you now," growled McGovern insensibly. "If I take you alive, my men will make you suffer like you would never believe."

McGovern half expected the man to run off. He had failed in his first assault and McGovern knew he was formidable fighter even at the worst of times. Instead, to his surprise, the assassin pulled out a hunting knife from his belt that glinted in the afternoon light. McGovern felt a pang of fear creep up his spine. One of them would die today, of that there was no doubt.

The man slowly moved towards McGovern, as if gauging his strengths and weaknesses. He held out the knife as if he was going to plunge it through McGovern's chest, but it was a feint. Instead, he shifted his weight on to his back foot and thrush an uppercut into McGovern's ribs that seemed to drain the air from his entire body. McGovern would have fallen backwards if the kitchen table had not got in the way and supported his weight. He thrust his right hand backwards to steady himself and at the same time managed to catch the assailant's knife arm with his left hand as it veered towards his unprotected throat.

There was a brief respite as both men strained to outpower the other. McGovern clutched at the man's wrist with all his might, but his attacker was strong, and the knife inched slowly towards his face. McGovern thrashed out fiercely with a savage kick and caught the man in the groin. He groaned and wheeled backwards. Sensing a change in momentum, McGovern acted quickly to secure the initiative. He stepped over and pummelled him with an enormous right hook that caught him on the temple. The man's knife flew out of his grip, and he lay motionless on the floor. McGovern assumed that he had knocked him out, such was the force of the blow. He rolled him over to get a better look at his attacker, but it all had clearly been a ruse, for in the same motion, the man spun round and fished out a smaller knife from his pocket that he plunged into McGovern's stomach.

Time seemed to stand still for McGovern. He felt his legs buckle and he sank to his knees. He was stunned, temporarily incapable of understanding what had happened, until he saw the shaft of the blade embedded in his flesh. The man slowly stood up, looking bizarrely expressionless. He wiped away a trickle of blood from his nose and moved over to the larger knife that was lying on the floor, a few feet away.

"Fuck you, you bastard," hissed McGovern defiantly.

The man calmly walked up and behind McGovern. The criminal felt his collar being yanked backwards and the cold, steel blade of the knife pressed firmly against his neck. McGovern tried to shake his head free, but the grip was too tight. He closed his eyes. There was surely nothing that could save him now. Suddenly, a gunshot reverberated throughout the room. McGovern closed his eyes. For a split second he thought was dead. He gingerly opened his eyes to see Elena standing in the door frame, with a gun. She was shaking with the fragility of a leaf in the wind.

McGovern turned his head. His attacker staggered a few steps backward. A crimson lake erupted in his shirt, around a single wound in his chest. He looked at Elena and then back to McGovern with a look of sheer puzzlement in his eyes. He took one more step, before crashing to the floor. McGovern couldn't understand what had happened. He closed his eyes before darkness took him.

Nicholls shifted uncomfortably on the sofa. His stomach churned and he had a sour taste in the back of his throat due to the copious alcohol he had consumed the previous evening. His phone was ringing. He didn't even have to look to know that it was Kane. Kane had told him he would be coming round that evening. Nicholls hadn't said anything to discourage him at the time, but he would demonstrate his displeasure by blatantly refusing to answer the phone to him now. It rang off. Nicholls closed his eyes, but his mind was ticking like a bomb. Being on his own tonight would not be conducive to a restful evening. Perhaps it would be better to spend it with Kane instead.

Within minutes, there was a sharp knock on the door. Nicholls sighed. His brother would clearly not take no for an answer. He stood up gingerly and walked slowly to answer the door. Kane was standing there impatiently with a black baseball hat and a navy-blue overcoat, covering a pair of worn Levi jeans.

"We need to go, Jimmy," he said curtly as if Nicholls was late for an urgent appointment.

"Where are we going, John?" responded Nicholls tiredly. He feigned disinterest but in reality, he was really rather curious.

"We're going for a drink. Have a quick wash and a shave because you look like shit. I'll see you in ten minutes. The car is parked out front." Kane smirked conspicuously and turned away.

Nicholls deliberately took his time. He had a shower and ironed his clothes before meeting Kane in the car. No-one spoke during the brief journey into town. Kane seemed to have an ingrained knowledge of where to go that impressed Nicholls. He had lived here all his life, but he still often got lost and had to rely on his sat nav. They parked up and walked around the corner to a rough looking pub called the Boar's Head. The peeling red paint that licked the doors and the dirty windows suggested the clientele weren't too fussed about appearances. Kane ordered two pints of Guinness and then they both sat at a small table by a dilapidated old pool table. There were three other men sat at the bar, but they barely raised their heads to acknowledge the newcomers.

Kane took a deep sip from his drink leaving a whispery foam residue above his lips. Nicholls had a much smaller sip and then recoiled at the bitter taste that didn't compliment his hangover.

"I'll get you a knife and fork with that if you want?" chuckled Kane. "You're not my brother though if you can't handle a few drinks on a night out!"

Nicholls smiled. Kane had an infectious humour about him. He was almost impossible not to like. "I'm just out of practice, that's all." He took a bigger sip to emphasise his point before putting the glass down firmly. "What is next John? Where the fuck do we go from here?"

Kane grimaced. "After tonight I think, you will start to see things more clearly brother."

Nicholls shook his head angrily. "Why won't you tell me what you're planning, John? You expect me to help you and come at your beck and call, but you give me nothing in return. What kind of a relationship is that?"

Kane smiled wryly which only infuriated his brother further. "Listen, Jimmy.

You just have to trust me. There's a lot of stuff that I can't tell you for your safety. I've got it all planned. You don't need to worry."

"You've turned my life upside down since I met you. One month ago, I thought I was an orphan. Now I've found out I've got a twin brother and an older sister, and my mother was murdered by the father of my girlfriend. It's hard to imagine how things could get anymore fucked up!" Nicholls stared at Kane intensely pleading for an answer, but Kane could barely look him in the eye.

"Now you want to take down a crime syndicate that is run by the Met commissioner, the biggest gangster in the country and a Russian godfather. You're delusional if you think we have a chance in hell of winning?"

"Are you certain about that?" said Kane quietly.

Nicholls absorbed the question briefly before nodding his head firmly. "Yes, I am sure John. This can't end well."

Kane abruptly changed tack. "Jimmy, I know you like your sport. Let's see if you know the answer to this question." He clasped his hands together, so it looked for a second like he was praying. "In athletics, what is the world record for the mile?"

Nicholls thought for a second. "That's easy John. It's around three minutes forty-three. Hicham El Guerrouj, if I'm not mistaken."

"You're certain that's the fastest mile ever run in an athletics event."

"Yes, John, I am. You can't beat me in a sports quiz," he said smugly.

Kane smiled. "What if I told you that the fastest mile ever run was by a man called Craig Wheeler who ran it in three minutes twenty-four in 1993." Nicholls was about to vehemently object until Kane silenced him with a raised palm. "It was a downhill mile you see, Jimmy. Not officially recognised but the fastest mile nonetheless."

Nicholls scoffed. "That's a load of bullshit John."

"Maybe it is Jimmy. But my point is that you shouldn't be certain about something until you know all the facts."

"What are all the facts?" interrupted Nicholls.

"You have to trust me, brother. I can't give you all the facts yet, but I will do when the time is right." Nicholls looked away petulantly, so Kane banged the table, causing him to turn back. "You think that I'm some psychotic war veteran who's out of control and after revenge, right? Well, you might very well be very close to the mark. I do have demons inside of me, but I know how to chain them up. Everything is under control, brother. I have planned for every eventuality and let me assure you, we will bring those bastards down. Every single one of them."

Kane's eyes were full of an intensity that Nicholls had never seen before. He wasn't sure if he imagined it but for a split second, they appeared to fill with blood. Kane left to go to the toilet and by the time he returned, his expression was back to normal.

The next couple of hours seemed to fly by. A few more punters came into the pub, but they sat at the bar and left the two brothers alone. They had a few more drinks but Kane who seemed to dictate the pace, slowed right down and Nicholls did not feel inebriated in the slightest. He even started to feel a lot better within himself. They played a couple of games of pool, but the table had several patches of ripped felt and leaned to the left, so the matches were generally decided by fortune rather than skill.

Before Nicholls knew it, the landlord was ringing the bell for last orders. Kane looked at his watch. "It's time, Jimmy," he said solemnly.

"Time for what John?"

"It's time to show you the evil that we are going to stop." He fastidiously placed the two pool cues back in their racks and guided Nicholls towards the door.

Kane walked through a dingy side street which opened up in front of a kebab house. There were two old Mondeo cars parked in the nearby lay-by. Kane strode confidently to the first one and tapped gently on the driver's window with his knuckles. The driver wound down the window and raised a bushy eyebrow.

Kane stooped so he could look the driver in the eye. "Can you take us to the Ritz?" he said.

The driver barely had enough time to answer before Kane had opened up the passenger side door and pulled Nicholls in. Everyone knew where the Ritz was, and unlicensed taxis were often the only way to get there.

Kane's demeanour had changed as soon as he had left the Boar's head. He had a steely, determined look fixed upon his face. He meant business.

The driver had clearly been to the Ritz before because he didn't need any directions. They drove most of the way in silence. The area around the bar was a decaying urban jungle that had been starved of development and finance for years. Derelict buildings and abandoned businesses punctuated the quiet streets. The driver turned around a corner and Kane shot upright.

"You can drop us off here," he said sternly.

The driver obediently pulled over. Kane gave the man a fifty-pound note which was clearly way too much; a robust message not to tell anyone where he had been that night and who he had dropped off.

Kane jerked his head towards Nicholls, indicating he should follow him. They strode down a dimly lit alleyway. Nicholls felt a few droplets of rain on his face. He looked up. Although it was dark, he could still see some menacingly dark clouds swelling in the sky above them. He pulled up the zip on his jacket and hoped that they would make it to their destination before the heavens opened. Neither man spoke. Again, Nicholls was stunned by Kane's sense of direction. He struggled to keep up with him as he crossed two deserted streets before darting down another side street. His innate guidance system seemed to be flawless.

They came to the end of the alley which was enclosed by old wire mesh fence. Kane stood to the side and pulled the wires apart so Nicholls could squeeze through. As they stepped on to the street, Nicholls could hear the commotion before he saw anything. About two hundred metres away was the Ritz. It was a huge warehouse that backed on to an old railway line and was surrounded by decaying buildings on either side. There was something palpable in the air; a malicious miasma that assaulted the senses. Nicholls could almost taste it. There was an evil presence here, of that there was no doubt.

The road that led to the Ritz was freshly tarmacked and looked oddly out of place amongst the derelict surroundings. Nicholls could see a large, throng of people queuing up, by what he assumed to be the main entrance. That was where he could hear the noise coming from.

Kane put his hand on Nicholls' shoulder and his face acquired a serious look. Nicholls noticed that he clenched his cheeks when he did this.

"We're about to enter the gates of hell, brother," he said quietly and deliberately slowly. "You have to trust me." There was a pleading look in his eyes. Nicholls nodded to acknowledge the gesture. "I promise you that I have all this under control. Whatever I do in there is down to me. I don't need you to help me. In fact, I want you to stay out of the way. There's a lot of stuff that you need to see, Jimmy. It will help you to understand everything." He grabbed Nicholls' arm tightly to emphasise his point. "Promise me brother, you will leave everything to me?"

Nicholls wanted to disagree, and the words started to form in his mouth but then he looked into Kane's eyes and sighed. "Yes, John I promise," conceded Nicholls.

As they got closer to the main entrance, Nicholls could see that the queue comprised of a ragtag selection of different people. Naturally they were all men, but some were young and in groups, and others were middle-aged or even older and conspicuously on their own. The loudest were a group of youngish drunks who had clearly been out in town beforehand, courtesy of their smart, alcohol saturated attire. They were at the front of the queue beneath a set of stone steps that ascended up to the main entrance. Kane and Nicholls quietly walked by them and joined the back of the queue.

At the bottom of the steps were two huge security men. Even from twenty feet away, they looked formidable. They were both powerfully built with taut muscles that bulged out of their black clothes. The nearest one had a flattened spade-like nose and the other one seemed to be missing his ear. They were both looking distastefully at the group of drunk young men in front of them who had started to get a little rowdy. Nicholls couldn't hear the conversation, but something was clearly said and one of the youths foolishly squared up to the bouncer. It looked ridiculous. The youth was a small figure with a slim frame, while both bouncers were colossal behemoths. It was obvious to everyone what would happen next.

The first huge bouncer simply grabbed the youth by the collar of his shirt with an enormous hand and started to raise him off the ground. The youth tried to squirm free, but the bouncer slapped him hard across the face and he instantly stopped twitching. Then, with astonishing power the bouncer hurled him headfirst into the wall of the building. There was a sickening crunch as the youth's head crashed against the brickwork, before he collapsed in a heap on the floor. One of his friends tried to step in front of the bouncer to protest, but he was brushed away dismissively by a decisive swipe of the arm by the other bouncer. The injured youth tried to stand but was clearly dazed and had to contend with a deep gash in his forehead that gushed a torrent of blood. His other friends went over to help him to his feet. They all looked pleadingly at the other men in the queue for some sort of assistance, but no-one would meet their gaze. There was little alternative for the group but to shuffle over to the other side of the road and try and coordinate their journey to hospital.

Kane looked on at the spectacle impassively. He didn't say a word as the queue shuffled forward. It took about another ten minutes before they reached the steps. Kane was in front. The first bouncer growled something incoherently to him and Kane nodded as if he understood the request. After a brief delay they

134

were both allowed to go through. The steps were quite steep, and Nicholls almost felt out of breath as they stepped through the main door and reached a till that was nestled in the corner of the entrance.

It was manned by a petit redhead with voluptuous lips. She smiled seductively at both men. The cost was fifty pounds each to gain entry. Kane reached into his pocket and pulled out a wad of crumpled notes. He threw them playfully on the table and waited. The redhead quickly counted the money and beckoned them to go through the steel double doors behind her.

Nicholls was not surprised to discover that the Ritz was just like all the seedy, grotty lap dancing venues he had been to in the past, albeit on a much larger scale. The doors opened up to a large, rectangular room with a brightly coloured podium at the far end. A scantily clad woman who was caked in too much fake tan, was gyrating on a pole to the obvious pleasure of a few customers at the front. Nicholls quickly scanned the room. It didn't look to be overly busy. There were banks of tables arranged in neat lines parallel to the main podium. Only about half the tables were occupied and dancers bustled busily around these customers trying to entice them for a private show.

At one end of the room was a long bar and on the adjacent side was a DJ, spurting out a stream of Hip Hop tunes. The walls were emblazoned with large mirrors that reflected a stream of lights that flashed above their heads.

Kane motioned for Nicholls to follow him, and they sat at the far side of the main bar. A weathered looking barman with long grey hair came over and Kane ordered a couple of beers.

"Have you ever been here before?" said Kane. Nicholls shook his head. "This is McGovern's business. On the face of it, it looks like any old harmless lap dancing club. Everything is done by the book in this part. You pay to watch the girls but there's no touching." He pointed to a couple of muscular doormen perched by the podium. "They'd have no problem taking you out back and giving you a good hiding if you misbehave here."

He paused to take a drink from his beer. "However, that door over there will take you to the depths of hell, Jimmy. It shows what these bastards are really capable of and why they must be stopped." He pointed to a small, inconspicuous door in the corner of the room that was manned by a wiry looking man with a pitiful moustache.

"What happens through there, John?"

"That's where the sex workers ply their trade, Jimmy. Girls that McGovern has illegally trafficked from all over the world. They're pumped full of drugs all day to keep them compliant and then stuffed into cubicles to be abused by the men who come here first."

As they spoke, a portly middle-aged man wearing a tweed jacket, nervously shuffled up to the door. He gave the wiry man some money, and the door was opened for him to go through.

"Jesus, are you serious John? That's terrible. What are we going to do about it?"

Kane smiled. "I was hoping you'd say that." He took a long, final sip of his beer. "Stick close to me and do exactly what I tell you."

Kane catapulted himself off the stool by the bar and walked purposively towards the DJ booth. The moustached man cast him a wry glance as he strode by. The DJ was staring intently at something on his phone and didn't even acknowledge Kane's presence. Nicholls stood in his brother's shadow, and he could literally feel the raw hatred emanating from him as he stood there.

"Oi," shouted Kane angrily at the DJ. "Can you not see me you, muppet?"

The DJ was a small middle-aged man with dark, receding hair that he had grown long at the back. He was wearing a garish designer jacket and ripped jeans that made him look ridiculous. He looked at Kane with unbridled condescension. "If you speak to me again like that, I'll have you thrown out." He pointed at the two muscular doorman who had sensed the hostility in the air and were watching the scene intently. "Don't you know who runs this place you idiot?" He shook his head with contempt and looked back at his phone.

Kane ignored him. "Can you please play some decent music for a change. I'm fed up with the rubbish you've been playing. Put some Metallica on for Christ's sake."

The DJ looked at Kane with utter incredulity. "This is a strip bar you idiot. If you don't like the music, then fuck off!"

Kane reached up into the booth and picked up a CD. He then hurled it with incredible accuracy at the DJ. The CD hit the DJ squarely on the forehead and the force of the blow propelled him backwards.

The two doormen reacted quickly. They both relished any opportunity to use physical violence to assert their dominance. Within seconds they had reached the DJ booth and were intent on making Kane pay for his impertinence. The first doorman was in his mid-twenties and fuelled by testosterone, he flung himself at Kane with the ferocity of a grizzly bear. Kane neatly sidestepped his lunge and swivelled to take hold of the doorman's arm with one hand and the base of his neck with the other. Kane then used his momentum to slam the doorman's head powerfully into the wooden frame of the booth. It knocked him out cold.

This caused the second doorman to hesitate and check his assault. He stopped a few feet away from Kane to contemplate his next move. Kane mockingly beckoned him on with a flick of his fingers which had the desired effect. Enraged by Kane's arrogance, the doorman rushed at him and swung wildly at his head. Kane dodged each blow with consummate ease. As the doorman tired, Kane ducked under his punch and then with the force of an unleashed coiled spring, he connected with a huge uppercut which dislodged several of the doorman's teeth. He was unconscious before he hit the floor.

Nicholls had been primed to assist his brother, but he had been quite simply hypnotised by the clinical brutality of the display unfolding before his eyes. He looked at the two doormen who were lying comatose on the floor.

"Jesus Christ," he said in amazement. "My brother's Rambo."

For a brief moment, the room was cocooned in silence. The music had stopped. Nicholls quickly glanced round. Everyone was transfixed by Kane. The excessively tanned girl on stage had stopped her dance and was staring open mouthed at the two doormen. The wiry, moustached man who guarded the side door to the brothel was frantically communicating into his headset. The shit is about to hit the fan now thought Nicholls ominously.

Kane then slowly wheeled round so he was in full view of everyone and then he very deliberately and obviously, withdrew a handgun from his pocket. He raised the gun and fired a shot into the ceiling. The sound was deafening. The DJ looked visibly petrified as Kane turned his attention towards him. Nicholls noticed a large wet patch appearing on the crotch of his jeans as he lost control of his bodily functions.

"You should've played Metallica when you had the chance, you muppet," laughed Kane. He pointed the gun menacingly at the DJ, who was cowering where he was stood. "Now get the fuck out of here while you've got the chance," he growled. He then turned to the rest of the room. "Did you not hear me?" he thundered. "Get out of here now."

People didn't need a second invitation. A stream of customers and near naked women scrambled out of the double doors in a frenzied panic. Within seconds, the room was nearly empty. Kane looked at Nicholls and pointed towards the black metal door that opened up to the booth.

"Take cover behind there, Jimmy," warned Kane, instinctively sensing the imminent danger.

Almost on cue, the side door crashed open and two burly figures exploded from the entrance firing wildly at the brothers. One of them dived under the nearest table, while the other used the metal door as a shield. Kane had been expecting this. He upturned a table to use as cover and fired some warning shots at the entrance. One of them hit the moustached man in the thigh as he was scrambling for cover, and he squealed in pain like a stuck pig.

Nicholls watched Kane from his vantage point. He was both terrified and enthralled at the same time. Kane seemed to have everything under control. He watched Kane assess the situation and weigh up his next course of action like a seasoned general. One of the men taking cover behind the table, hadn't realised that his foot was exposed. Kane didn't need a second invitation. He shot three bullets at this target and two of them tore away the flesh of the lower heel. The man screamed and instinctively jumped up, which allowed Kane to finish him off with a well-aimed bullet to the neck.

The man behind the door screamed in anguish at the death of his companion. Perhaps they had been related, thought Nicholls. He leaned over the door to get more leverage, but this opened his torso and Kane's accuracy was deadly. The first shot hit him in the shoulder and launched him into the open. His eyes widened with fear as he realised the danger, he was in. Kane was in no mood for mercy. He calmly aimed his gun and the bullet bludgeoned through his eye and exited through the back of the head. Fragments of brain, flesh and brain were splattered on the door.

Kane whistled loudly. "Come on Jimmy. It's clear now." He pushed over the table, and it crashed to the ground. Nicholls stepped out into the open cautiously, fully aware of the danger they were still in. As they approached the door, there was a trail of blood leading through the entrance and up the corridor. The moustached man was desperately trying to crawl away on his injured leg, but each movement released a torrent of blood from his wound.

It took a couple of steps for Kane to catch up with him. He stooped down and took a grip of his shirt and yanked him roughly to his feet. The moustached man squealed in agony. "Where are the girls you bastard?" hissed Kane.

The moustached man spluttered and tried to jerk free, but Kane was too strong. He pointed tentatively up the corridor. Kane simply dragged him forward as he walked.

The corridor was dimly lit, with an old-fashioned purple carpet that made crunching sounds as they walked. The walls were painted yellow, and they were decorated with random pictures of naked women in artistic poses. It was a long corridor, perhaps sixty feet or so before they reached a wooden door at the end. The moustached man was now almost practically sobbing through a combination of pain and fear. He pleaded desperately for his life, but Kane didn't even acknowledge him as he dragged him along.

As they drew closer to the door, it suddenly flung open and shots fired. Nicholls felt a whirl of air as a bullet passed by his head. Kane used one arm to drag his brother closer to him, but he still kept pressing forward. He crouched behind the moustached man as if he was a human shield and shot back through the entrance.

Two more shots fired. One of them hit the moustached man in the stomach and he shrieked in pain. Still Kane kept hold of him. They were under the doorway now. Nicholls could see a large open space but little else as his vison narrowed and he took shelter behind the door. Kane hurled his human shield through the entrance and joined his brother. "That was close, Jimmy. We were sitting ducks there," he said with a grin on his face.

Kane peered out. The moustached man had been shot again in the head and was by now very much dead. The shooter was on the far side of the room. For some reason it was very bright all of a sudden. Nicholls could see comfortable sofas, tables and a small bar in front of them. It reminded him of a hospital waiting room. Kane looked up. There were banks of plastic lights protruding from the ceiling. He took aim and fired. The bullets disintegrated the cheap, plaster ceiling and one of the large light cases fell to the ground. There was a shout of pain as a maelstrom of debris collapsed on to the shooter. Kane was up quickly and pumped two bullets into the legs of the man as he wrestled with the light case.

As they drew closer, Nicholls saw that it was one of the huge doormen they had seen when they were queuing for entry. Kane kept his gun firmly pointed at the man's head as he walked over. He was dazed and incapacitated but aware enough to hiss some insults at Kane as he came into view. Kane kicked away his gun which had slipped from his grasp as the light landed on his head. There was a moment of silence that seemed to last for an eternity.

All of a sudden, there was a loud, visceral roar and a flash of movement from the small bar next to them. A huge shape exploded into view and darted for Kane.

Nicholls struggled to make sense of what was happening. The large shape barged into Kane and knocked him over. His gun was knocked out of his hands. Nicholls could see a glint of light flashing from a knife in his hand that was poised to slash down on his brother's head. It was the other massive doorman, who had remained hidden throughout the shooting. Kane had somehow caught the doorman's wrist, but he was kneeling on the floor and being overpowered.

Nicholls heard a grunt behind him. The other doorman was scrambling for his gun. He panicked, unsure about what to do. Kane's gun was a couple of feet away from him. He dived to the ground and scooped up the weapon. At the same time, Kane skilfully swivelled on his knees and the doorman overbalanced and toppled over. In the same movement, Kane snatched the knife and plunged it into the unprotected neck of the bouncer.

Nicholls glanced at the other doorman. He had picked up the gun and was scrambling to his knees. Kane had his back to him, so was oblivious to the danger he was now in. There was no time to think. Nicholls aimed and squeezed the trigger repeatedly.

The bullets tore into the doorman's chest and abdomen. His body was hurled backwards, and he died instantly. Nicholls' arm locked stiff at the moment the gun was fired. He was clutching the gun so tightly that the blood drained from his fingers, and they turned white. Kane walked over to him and patted him on the shoulder. He plucked the gun from his hands.

The other doorman was clutching his neck, but blood was erupting over his hands and bubbling out of his mouth. His whole body was shaking.

"Leave the bastard. He's done for," said Kane casually. Nicholls could barely make sense of what had happened. He had never killed anyone before and was struggling to come to terms with his actions. Kane noticed his discomfort. "That was a good shot by the way, Jimmy. You probably saved my life there."

He placed his hand on Nicholls' shoulder. "Do you know what this place is, Jimmy? It's where the perverts can relax before they visit the girls. It's like a private doctor's surgery. They wait here and then they get a call. Simple as that really." He pointed to a set of double doors in the corner. "Now my guess is that's where they head through when they get the call. Shall we go and investigate?"

Nicholls was almost too stunned to speak. The nearest doorman was convulsing noisily on the floor next to them, as he gurgled out his dying breaths. Kane pulled on his brother's arm and led him towards the doors.

Kane kept his gun raised as he pushed on the door. There was no-one in sight. Soft, classical music welcomed them into the room. It was like they had entered the foyer of a budget hotel. In front of them was a desk and a computer and beyond were rows of cubicles arranged on either side of the floor. Nicholls could hear faint moans from within the cubicles that were only partially drowned out by the music.

"Sound-proof panels, look Jimmy," said Kane pointing at the heavily insulated padding that coated the walls. As they approached the first cubicle, they heard a clinking sound. Kane extended his gun arm in the direction of the sound. One of the walls opened up into a narrow annex, which led to a set of descending stairs and a heavily padlocked door. It clearly allowed the brothel to be accessed from outside as well.

The sounds were coming from a powerfully built lady who was frantically trying to unlock the padlock and get out of the building. "Turn around," shouted Kane aggressively.

The woman stopped and slowly turned round. She was a really large, formidable looking lady with muscular shoulders and short brown hair that had been shaved at the sides and the back.

"Don't shoot me please," she pleaded in heavily accentuated English. "I'm just a cleaner here."

Nicholls couldn't explain why but he instinctively knew that she was lying. There was something about her that seemed cold and callous. She had the flattened nose of a boxer and small duplicitous eyes that were encased in a corpulent face.

"We've hit the jackpot here Jimmy," said Kane inexpressively. "This is the devil queen herself. Her name is Agnessa. She is in charge here."

"No, no, no," sobbed the woman. "You've got it wrong. I just clean up here."

Kane's voice became cold and sinister. "No, I'm afraid I have not got it wrong Agnessa. I have been watching you very closely these last few months and I know exactly who you are and what you do."

"Please don't kill me," she said desperately. "I beg of you." She started to climb back up the steps towards them. She held her arms out submissively to show that she wasn't a threat. "They made me do it. I didn't want to, but I had no choice. They said they would kill me if I didn't."

She was now only a couple of feet away. "Tell me Agnessa. How much does it cost to spend some time with the girls in here?"

Agnessa looked deep in thought as she pondered the question. "It's one hundred pounds for one hour."

"So that money allows men to do whatever they want with them, right?" Agnessa didn't answer. "And who drugs the girls?"

Agnessa shook her head. "No, you are wrong sir. We do not drug the girls. Some of them have problems with drugs and we try and wean them off it. It is not good for them if they go, how you say cold turkey? I look after the girls. That is correct but we do not make them work here. They are free to leave at any time."

Kane stepped right into Agnessa's face. She tried to cower away, but he took a firm hold of her arm. "Agnessa, you're a lying bitch." He smashed her in the face with the butt of his gun. She collapsed on the floor in a pitiful heap, caressing a broken nose.

Nicholls tried to object but Kane silenced him with a venomous stare. "Now let's see what the girls say shall we. Don't move a muscle you bitch, or I'll cut out your lying tongue."

Kane beckoned Nicholls to follow him. They walked up to the first cubicle. Kane pressed his hand on the wall and there was a slight wobble. They were cheap, plasterboard walls supported by a timber frame. He reached for the handle and opened the door. The music was much louder inside the cubicles courtesy of the speaker system that was wired through ugly holes that had been hacked in the ceiling. This could be why the occupants in the booth obviously hadn't heard the commotion outside and jumped up in alarm as Kane and Nicholls entered.

"What the hell do you think you're doing?" shouted a half-naked man who leapt off a bed and into the air. Nicholls saw that it was the portly, middle-aged man who they had seen in the strip bar about half an hour ago. He was lathered in sweat and his receding hair was plastered on the side of his head, so it looked like he was wearing a hat. The man was still wearing his shirt, but his pants were off and exposed his tiny manhood, which was only partially aroused. Lying on the bed was a young Asian girl. She had sat upright when the men had entered but her glazed eyes suggested she didn't have much awareness of what was going on. She was naked except for a tiny thong and black leather boots.

The middle-aged man started to look irate until he saw the deadly look that had formed on Kane's face and the gun hanging by his side. He tried to say something but thought better of it and hurriedly tried to pull on his trousers. Kane raised the gun at his head. "Don't even think about getting dressed. Get out of here now or I'll blow your head off." The man dropped his trousers and scurried out of the cubicle, whimpering as he ran.

Nicholls tried to smile at the girl, but she didn't respond. She stared vacantly out the door as if she was completely oblivious to what was going on. She was clearly, heavily sedated with drugs. He picked up a coat which was hanging on a clothes frame by the side of the small room and wrapped it around her shoulders. He noticed that there were numerous punctures wounds and bruises that peppered her arms. From experience, he knew that these track marks were consistent with someone who had been injecting heroin.

Kane motioned for them to go so Nicholls carefully helped her to her feet. As they walked out of the door, the young girl saw Agnessa and recoiled in fear. "Just as I thought," said Kane loudly. He turned to the girl. "Don't worry. That bitch can't hurt you now." Nicholls doubted whether she understood anything he said, but he smiled warmly, and the girl nodded. Kane pulled out a sofa and gestured for her to sit down. "Stay with her, Jimmy. I'll go and see the rest."

Kane found eight girls in total. All of them were heavily drugged and displayed the same track marks on their arms.

"Jimmy, we need some help," said Kane. "You need to take all of these girls outside. If you can, get them to wear something warm. There's plenty of clothes round here. Once you've done that, I need you ring your friend Kevin Page and get him down here."

Nicholls looked surprised at the mention of his partner's names. "How do you know Kevin?"

Kane sighed. "Kevin's a good guy Jimmy. He'll explain everything when he gets here."

"I don't understand what's going on here?" said Nicholls as Kane made to leave. "What are you doing now?"

"I'm going to explore the premises, Jimmy. Don't worry, I'll be out soon."

It took Nicholls about twenty minutes to coax all of the girls out of the building. Some of the more coherent girls were able to assist and support the others. Once they were all out, the girls huddled together on the far pavement. There was no-one else in sight. Nicholls couldn't believe how rapidly the building had disgorged itself of people.

Nicholls did as Kane asked and rang Page. He answered the phone immediately as if he was expecting the call. He said he would be down in around ten minutes.

The night sky was ghostly dark, although the moon glimmered defiantly in the distance casting silvery hues over the street. A few of the girls could speak fragments of broken English, but most didn't understand his attempts at communication at all. He tried to explain that he was a police officer and that they were safe, but he doubted whether the message got through. They generally seemed content to sit in silence watching the night sky, although the presence of Agnessa caused visible distress to more than a few of them. Before he had departed, Kane had tied the Albanian matron roughly to a metal gate with a piece of coarse rope on the other side of the pavement. Still, no-one dared meet her eye.

Kane emerged moments later. He looked grim. Before he had crossed the street, Nicholls saw tentacles of smoke drifting out of the building. They were light and wispy to start but within minutes they became sooty-black billowing plumes that swirled majestically into the sky.

"What have you done, John?" bleated Nicholls anxiously. "There's dead bodies and evidence in there!"

"Relax Jimmy. There's nothing in there that I don't know. Besides we need to send a message and make sure the whole country takes notice."

The acrid stench of the fire had already begun to burn Nicholls' throat and nose. There was a smashing sound as the front windows broke and red and orange flames began to hungrily lick the walls and sweep across the roof.

The two men stared in silence as the building burned. A few of the girls seemed to smile and one of the more coherent ones, even began to clap. It was only a faint ripple at first, but this seemed to ignite the confidence of others, and before long most of them were cheering loudly.

It was against this unusual backdrop that Page arrived in two blacked out people carriers. Nicholls watched in surprise as armed men jumped out of the vehicles wearing blue rain jackets that were emblazoned conspicuously with the lettering "NCA" across the front and back. It took Nicholls an eternity to realise as they drew closer that these were officers of the National Crime Agency.

Page looked totally different to his normal role as a quiet, unassuming detective in the Met police. He strode over with vigour and purpose. His greying, whispery hair was gelled back and glistened in the moonlight, and he was wearing a bullet proof vest over his jacket. He made a beeline for the two brothers and pulled Kane aside, barely acknowledging Nicholls' presence. The other armed men split off into two groups with the first half tending to the women and the other half pacing impotently outside the burning building.

Page and Kane were locked in heated conversation much to Nicholls' consternation. How did they know each other and what was all this about? His mind was ticking like a bomb. Kane looked cool and composed but Page was visibly agitated. It was totally out of character to see Page so strained.

Nicholls felt his anger rising. Why was he always kept out of the loop? He walked over to the pair and looked questionably at Page. Page felt the glare of intense scrutiny upon him and broke off his conversation.

Kane smiled. "Ahh, Jimmy, you know Kevin don't you?" he said sarcastically.

"I thought I did," replied Nicholls bitterly. "Is everyone I know lying to me?"

Page ignored the acidity of the comment. He smiled half-heartedly at Nicholls, but his eyes were stony grey. Nicholls could sense something ruthless about his aura that was completely alien to him. Page was his affable, good-natured partner who could always make him laugh with his acerbic wit. He didn't recognise the man in front of him now.

"I'm sorry that we had to keep you in the dark, Jimmy," said Page. There was a noted emphasis on the "we" part, as if he and Kane had been in collusion for a long time. "It was for your own protection."

"Don't give me that bullshit," interrupted Nicholls angrily. "I've had enough of it from my brother," he hissed. "I just want the truth. I put my life in danger today. I think that I've earned the right for you to level with me."

Kane placed a hand on his shoulder to calm him down. "I promise you I will tell you everything tonight, Jimmy. To be honest, there's not much more to tell. Kev is not a detective in the Met. He is an undercover agent in the National Crime Agency. I met him around three years ago when he was coordinating an operation into organised crime and police corruption in the Met. As you know I have a particular set of skills and family contacts that have proved very helpful during the course of the investigation."

"John wanted to get you in the team earlier on, but we couldn't risk jeopardising the operation," said Page. "We didn't know if you were in league with McGovern or if you had even been brainwashed by Flack. For Christ's sake, you were engaged to his daughter. To put it bluntly, we didn't know where your loyalties were."

"I vouched for you, brother," smiled Kane. "There was no way a brother of mine was dirty."

Nicholls stiffened at Kane's attempt to goad him, but he didn't respond. He paused and thought carefully about what to ask. "How did you two meet?" he asked finally.

"For a long time now the National Crime Agency has been investigating institutional corruption in the Met and links to organised crime," said Page candidly. "Flack has been under suspicion for decades, but he is a slippery fucker, that one. We could never get anything concrete on him. He's got powerful friends that protect him at every corner. Three years ago, a top-secret task force was created to bring him and McGovern down. It's a small team due to the secretive nature of the investigation. That's where I met your brother. We are both part of the same task force, recruited by the same person, who's running the entire operation. If John wants to tell you who that is, then that's fine by me, but that's on his head." Page looked warningly at Kane.

"As you can imagine, some of our tactics haven't been totally legal and I have disagreed vehemently with some of your brother's actions." He kept his gaze fixed on Kane as he spoke. "But your brother has the support of the "boss" and that gives him the freedom to satisfy some of his vengeful impulses." An image of Baldock's blood-soaked corpse, flashed through Nicholls' mind.

"Our investigation is entirely off the record. If we fuck anything up, then it's on our heads, not the government. Plausible deniability they call it. They can deny everything so we can't make any mistakes in any of this." He turned to look at Nicholls. "Now did you see why we kept you in the dark? It is for your own safety.

Our country is riddled with a cancer that has been growing stronger and more powerful every single day. It's our job to cut it all out however we can, even if we have to break the law to do so."

"But if we break the law, how can we punish them?" interrupted Nicholls.

Page flashed Nicholls an angry glance. "You of all people must want your revenge on these bastards," he growled. "This might the only way that you're going to get it. They are too strong and too well insulated to take down legally." He sighed tiredly. "Listen now both of you. We can clean up here although it won't be long before the press gets wind of the fire, so you need to get out of here right away before your faces appear on the news. I'm sure that if you do have any questions, Jimmy then your brother can answer them in his own inimitable way. We've got a busy day tomorrow. There's no going back now." Page took out his phone from his pocket and turned away from the brothers, indicating that the conversation was finished.

Nicholls bristled at the slight from Page. He had dozens more questions that he wanted answering. He was just about to pull Page round and demand answers when Kane took hold of his arm. "Jimmy, we're going to get started on McGovern tomorrow. I'll tell you all about it on the way home." Nicholls swore under his breath, loudly enough for Page to hear but he didn't respond. He was in mid conversation with someone on the phone.

As Kane led Nicholls away, Page paused as if he had remembered something he wanted to say. "Hey Jimmy," he shouted from across the street. Nicholls turned towards him. "You are an excellent police officer by the way. Maybe a little too naïve for my liking, but it was a pleasure to work with you."

Chapter 8
Operation Sea Lion

Patrick McGovern could hear the murmuring sound of voices all around him. He tried to open his eyes, but his vision was haloed by a bright light that forced them shut. Nothing would come into focus except a few fuzzy silhouettes that seemed to be moving slowly from side to side. His head ached and he had a sharp pain emanating from his stomach, that sent a stabbing sensation across his entire body every time he moved. He was groggy and felt as weak as a kitten.

The voices kept getting louder and every now and then, he was able to comprehend a familiar word. Gradually his vison began to come into focus and the grainy shapes in front of him began to take form. He was lying in a bed but that was about all he could say for certain. There were two figures on the periphery of the room, both wearing white coats. They were not paying any attention to him, and McGovern couldn't see what they were up to. Directly in front of him on the far wall was a large mirror that reflected the light, and it was this that had blinded him initially when he had opened his eyes. He tried to sit up, but as he moved, he felt a sharp pain in his arm. McGovern fumbled clumsily at his arm where the pain was, and he felt a thin plastic tube that had been inserted there. He looked up at the mirror and saw how the plastic tube connected to a pump on a metallic stand next to the bed. It took him about a minute to comprehend that he was on an IV drip so that must mean he was in a hospital somewhere.

His next thoughts were of Elena. Her beautiful face appeared in his mind's eye, and he felt a terrible fear that something bad had happened to her. The last thing he could remember was seeing her shaking like a leaf as she clutched a gun that was pointed in his direction. His brain desperately tried to make sense of the jumbled images that were appearing in his mind, like the still frames of an old movie. Had she shot him? Was she responsible for the injuries he had received?

And then there was another whirl of memories of the preceding moments. He had been in a fight for his life with a mystery attacker. He touched his neck and felt the raw burn mark that had been left by the garrot of his attacker. He winced at the pain as his fingers aggravated the torn skin and bruising. That was it. Elena had saved his life by shooting the attacker. He felt a surge of relief flood through his body. He was a tough man, and he would recover from his injuries. All that mattered to him at that moment was that Elena had proved her love for him. They were destined to be together.

"Good afternoon, Patrick," said a quiet voice immediately next to him. McGovern almost jumped out of his skin in alarm. There was a small figure, partially camouflaged by the IV stand, sitting very casually in the armchair next to him. McGovern opened his mouth to respond but his larynx had obviously been crushed when his attacker had tried to strangle him, and the words wouldn't come out.

"Would you like a drink?" said the small man gesturing towards a large jug of water on the table next to him.

McGovern shook his head and grunted. The man in front of him was particularly nondescript and unthreatening. He was small and rotund with grey whispery hair. McGovern estimated he was probably in his early fifties, but he could potentially have aged prematurely, and been a lot younger than that.

The man stood up and brushed down the wrinkles that had creased his suit trousers when sitting down. He reached into his jacket pocket and pulled out an ID badge. "My name is Kevin Page and I'm an officer in the National Crime Agency," he said. "You are very lucky to be alive, Patrick. You were stabbed in the lower abdomen and the injury perforated your lower intestine. Thankfully, the skilful team of surgeons we have here were able to stem the bleeding and repair the damage." Page swung his arms in the direction of the white coated doctors behind him to acknowledge their efforts, but they ignored him and carried on working diligently in the background.

McGovern grimaced. He tried to speak again but the exertion was like chewing razor blades. "Who stabbed me?" he croaked eventually.

Page nodded and pulled out a photograph from his jacket pocket. He held it out to show McGovern who snatched it out of his hand impatiently. He looked at the image of the man on the photograph and recognised him immediately. It was definitely the man who had tried to kill him in his apartment. He was a tough, grizzled looking man with greying hair and a scar that ran down the corner of his face. He had seen him before, but he couldn't remember where it was.

"This is Gary Darnell, Patrick. He's a firearms officer in the Met. You should know him as he's being doing contract killing for you for some years now," said Page sarcastically. "He's one of Flack's lap dogs. Of course, we can't prove that."

The realisation of who he was sent an icy chill down McGovern's spine. That was where he remembered him from. If Darnell had been sent to kill him, there could only have been one person who had given the order. McGovern looked away from Page as he tried to make sense of the situation. It couldn't be true. Why would Flack want him dead? He was his oldest associate. They had risen to power together, their fortunes intertwined.

Page took a seat on the bed and pulled out a recorder from his pocket. "We managed to obtain this intelligence if you don't believe me." He pressed a button, and the device made a scratchy, crackling sound. At first, McGovern could only hear inaudible voices but then there was a pause and he heard someone laughing heartily. He recognised it immediately. It was Ivankov. There was another pause and then Ivankov said, "McGovern's time is up. We have to take him out if this is going to work."

McGovern's heart sank. He couldn't believe it. Ivankov had been his friend too. They had been partners for over thirty years. How could he betray him like this?

Page waited patiently for the realisation to sink in. "We have an informant who has been supplying us with intelligence, so we know you've got something big planned with Ivankov and Flack. Perhaps they no longer needed you anymore and you were surplus to requirements, so to speak? Anyway, I wouldn't want to speculate about that, but it looks like the only way you can have a future is to cooperate with us now. If you go back on the streets, then you're as good as dead. Even you can't compete with a whale like Ivankov. We do have a lifeline though that might work in your favour." Page looked at McGovern and smiled. He reached on to a side table and snatched up a television remote control. He pointed it at a screen above McGovern's head and the screen flickered into life.

It was the news headlines. McGovern watched as a pretty news reporter stood outside the smouldering ruins of his club. The news ticker underneath displayed the revolving text;

London crime boss McGovern feared dead as his club is burned down

in suspected gangland attack.

McGovern went numb. For a second, he couldn't quite believe what he was seeing. He retched but nothing came out. Page pressed the volume controls and the reporter started to speak. "At the moment we are getting very sketchy information about what has actually happened. It would appear that the National Crime Agency have taken jurisdiction of this case and are not, repeat not working with the Metropolitan police. Patrick McGovern the notorious gangster, who it is alleged runs this club has gone missing. We have had unconfirmed reports that this was a gangland attack, and that McGovern has been shot dead last night. We are still waiting for a statement at the moment from the National Crime Agency, so I reiterate that none of this is confirmed at present."

Page turned off the television and smiled sanctimoniously. "You're dead, Patrick. We managed to leak that to the media this morning, which gives us a bit of breathing space. Now I would imagine that your first response when asked to help law enforcement would be to "go fuck ourselves" right?"

Page didn't wait for McGovern to reply. "So, lets save us all a bit of time and pretend that we've already done this part, so we can move on shall we? We only want three things from you, Patrick. Firstly, we want you to tell us everything about your criminal empire and how it works. Secondly, we want to know which cops and politicians are dirty and do your bidding. I'm particularly keen to hear about how the police transport your drugs around the city. Thirdly, we want to know about what you've got planned with Ivankov and Flack. They are who we are after now, and don't forget that they've just tried to kill you. The prize for you, Patrick, is that you get to live and disappear to some tropical beach to live out the rest of your days in anonymity drinking cocktails. You won't need to spend a minute in jail!"

McGovern looked at Page venomously. He wanted to get up and punch this cocky arsehole in the face, but he seriously doubted whether he could even get himself out of bed. How could it have come to this? Could he seriously make a deal with law enforcement to save his own skin?

Page seemed to relish the new-found power he suddenly held over the crime boss. McGovern didn't have any other options. Everyone in the room knew that. "Now, of course the cost of witness protection isn't going to be cheap," said Page gleefully. "The Home Office will have to seize most of your assets over here, unless of course you can prove you acquired them legally? However, I'm sure a sensible gangster like yourself has managed to squirrel away a bit of money in an offshore account somewhere? Perhaps to use for a rainy day?" McGovern ignored Page's sarcastic tones and turned, stony faced away from him.

"Come of Patrick, I'm just toying with you. There's no need to be like that!" laughed Page. "We don't care about any of your offshore accounts, if you cooperate with us. You can literally disappear off the face of the earth. I'm sure you've got enough money to buy yourself some nice property and maybe a nightclub or restaurant or two to keep you busy. You might also want to consider getting some plastic surgery and maybe a hair transplant too! The Russian mob will think you're dead, but it wouldn't hurt to change your appearance. You know what those guys are capable of."

Page leaned over so he was almost whispering in McGovern's ear. "Maybe you've even got a special someone you can take with you to start a new life together?"

A sudden adrenaline rush caused McGovern's heart to skip a beat as he thought about Elena. If she was with him then everything would be alright. They could make it work together. She had proved she loved him when she shot Darnell. McGovern flinched forward and took hold of Page's wrist. He looked pleadingly into his eyes. "Elena?" he croaked. "Where is she?"

"Yes, I did think you had a soft spot for that one, Patrick. She truly is a stunningly beautiful girl," said Page. "She's barely left your side since you were admitted here."

McGovern felt a surge of relief that she was safe and close by. The nervous tension dissipated from his body. He released his grip on Page's arm and sat back on his pillow.

"Would you like a bit of privacy to speak with her, Patrick?" asked Page walking towards the door. McGovern's eyes widened with joy at the thought of seeing her. Page opened the door and there she was, looking as beautiful as the first day he had seen her. There was still that innocent fragility about her. She was biting her lip nervously and her doe like eyes seemed to twinkle in the light. She looked at Page who nodded to her, and she smiled and ran over to McGovern, jumping on the bed to embrace him. The pain was excruciating but he didn't care at all as she nuzzled into his chest.

Page silently smiled and walked over to the far side of the room. He pulled aside a curtain to reveal a hidden door, which he opened as quietly as he could. The door led to a small annex which was dimly lit and crammed full of people who had been watching the interchange between him and McGovern intently. McGovern was completely oblivious to the one-way window and saw only a mirror on his side of the room.

Page nodded to Kane and Nicholls, who were standing in front of the window. "I think we've got the bastard on board," he whispered triumphantly. "It's game on now."

Page worked with McGovern for the rest of the evening. McGovern begrudgingly revealed the inner machinations of his criminal empire, although he steadfastly refused to say anything on tape or give specific names of international crime bosses he dealt with. Instead, Page and a couple of National Crime Agency officers frantically scribbled down the information on pads of paper. He told them about his human trafficking operation with Ivankov and dealings with the Ndrangheta, an Italian mafia franchise to ship drugs into Britain. He told them about how he trafficked illegal firearms into the country with Albanian gangsters and how he used shell companies and front men to reinvest illegal gains in the legitimate economy.

The scale of corruption was staggering. McGovern had simply too many people on his payroll to recount them all by memory so instead, he gave up the location of his safe house in the city. It was an obscure, Georgian terrace in a quiet suburban neighbourhood but the treasure trove it revealed was incredible. On the third floor of the building was a specially constructed panic room which required a key card and code to enter. Inside the room were electronic files and letters that linked hundreds of politicians and prominent figures to McGovern's criminal operations. They found a leather-bound book containing banking transactions in a filing cabinet, which showed that several prominent police officers in the Met received regular lump sums from McGovern every month. It was in this room he also kept the evidence that he used for blackmailing purposes. There were countless video files of people engaging in illicit activities. In one of the first videos Page watched, he saw the industrialist, Doug White being spanked by a woman in full dominatrix gear, before having a dildo inserted up his bottom. It would take a team of analysts, days to trawl through all the information here.

The sun was just breaking when McGovern began to talk about their plans to install Kilbride as the next prime minister. He told them about Secure8 and the plans to launder Russian money through a privatised prison system that would make them all insanely wealthy. Even Page was shocked by the scale of their ambition, but he thought quickly on his feet.

"That's why they want you dead, Patrick," he told the mobster. "If this scheme is going to work then there can't be any ties with organised crime. Imagine the publicity if one of the most notorious gangsters in London becomes a shareholder for a private security company that's running all the prisons in the country. You're a liability to them if they want to go legitimate. There's no place for sentiment in business I'm afraid and you were expendable."

Until that moment, there was still a niggling doubt burrowing away at McGovern that this had all been a misunderstanding, but Page's explanation made perfect sense. Ivankov and Flack had betrayed him, and they had to be brought down at all costs. He had to destroy them, even if that meant cooperating with the authorities. It was then that he remembered Mr Sykes, Ivankov's accountant and the hotel he was staying in. If they could find him, he would surely have evidence that would bury those bastards. Page gobbled up the information greedily and he knew exactly who to call to extract the information.

Tony Sykes pulled the duvet over his shoulders and burrowed deeper into the luxury mattress in his hotel penthouse. He was determined to sleep for most of the morning. The perks of being Ivankov's accountant were beyond his wildest dreams. He had wealth, status and women on call at any time of the day. Christ, he even had a personal bodyguard that were responsible for his safety and escorted him to his appointments. He felt like a celebrity and all he had to do to maintain this lifestyle was to manage Ivankov's money.

Sykes was a financial wizard who coordinated Ivankov's vast wealth with the aplomb of an expert pianist. He moved Ivankov's money into accounts all over the world, set up shell companies in his client's name and laundered dirty money into legitimate enterprises. These skills made him an invaluable asset for Ivankov, and his rewards were lavish and generous. Of course, he had to be at Ivankov's beck and call whenever his services were desired, but that was a price that Sykes was happy to pay.

Sykes had risen to prominence in Ivankov's organisation when he helped spearhead a massive tax fraud of an American energy company, in which he forged documents that raised the company's stock price two thousand percent. Eager investors had poured money into the company only to find that they been fooled and subsequently lost most of their money.

As a key part of Ivankov's entourage, Sykes rubbed shoulders with the highest echelons of society. He attended parties that were hosted by billionaire businessmen and royal dignitaries. He snorted cocaine with rock stars and partied with glamour models. It was all a façade. Sykes was under no illusion. Everyone knew he was with Ivankov and they treated him well in the hope that this would curry favour with the Russian. Sykes didn't care in the slightest. He had spent last night in one of London's most cosmopolitan clubs in the VIP area, without having to buy a single drink. He had left in the early hours of the morning with two models who had been told by the club owner to "give Sykes a good time."

Sykes had heard the girls leave just as the sun was coming up. He felt his manhood stiffen at the thought of their lithe bodies writhing upon the bed. They had put on a lesbian performance for his pleasure, before taking it in turns to give him oral sex. Life was good.

All of a sudden, he felt a sharp sensation pressing down firmly at the base of his pelvis that jolted him to his senses. His first instinct was that one of the girls had returned for more fornication but as he opened his eyes and the room came into focus, he saw two large men with dark hair and chiselled jaw lines towering over him. It only took him a few seconds to realise that they were identical twins. One of them was sat at the foot of the bed with an impassive face, whilst the other was stood directly over him with a wicked grin and a knife pressed firmly against Sykes' penis.

"Good morning, Mr Sykes," said Kane cheerfully. There was a malevolent glint in his grey eyes.

Sykes squirmed and tried to push the man off him, but he was too strong. "Who the fuck are you?" he squealed.

Kane put his finger to his lips. "Be quiet, or I'll slice off your dick. You don't want to wake those Russian goons in the next room." Kane sliced the knife slowly across Sykes' abdomen to emphasise his point, drawing a thin trickle of blood that oozed to the surface of his skin.

Sykes felt a very real wave of fear wash over him, but he steeled himself to remain calm. "Do you have any idea who I work for you stupid motherfucker?" he hissed.

This time it was the other twin who spoke. He flashed his police identification badge. "We know all about you and Sergei Ivankov, Mr Sykes."

Sykes looked incredulously at the two men. "What the fuck? Is this a police operation? We own the police. There's nothing—"

Before Sykes could finish his sentence, Kane slapped him hard across the face and pressed the point of the knife into his eye socket. "Now you listen to me, you maggot dick motherfucker. Your boss is going down and you're going to give us everything we want, or I swear to God, I'll kill you right now and feed your body to the crabs in the Thames."

Sykes froze and suddenly lost control of his bodily functions. A brown stain appeared on the duvet and a revolting smell permeated the room.

Nicholls stood up and curled his nose in disgust. "I'm afraid my brother isn't known for his subtilty Mr Sykes. However, I do have to insist that you cooperate with us. Please can you get your laptop, and we'll tell you want we need."

The task force met later that day in a small, inconspicuous townhouse near the centre of the city. Seated around a large oak table in the living room were Jimmy Nicholls, John Kane, Holly Kane, Kevin Page, Martin Bromwich, an analyst in the National Crime Agency, and the leader of the Conservative party, Darren Healy.

Everyone looked tired, except John Kane and Darren Healey. The leader of the Conservatives looked a world away from the gaunt, fragile figure that had appeared on television in recent weeks. Today he looked resolute and implacable.

Kane had finally briefed his brother after they had torched McGovern's lap dancing club. Nicholls now knew that Healey's illness had all been a ruse as part of the operation to bring down Flack, Kilbride and McGovern. A movie make-up artist had been hired to give his skin an unhealthy pallor and add angry blemishes and veins, giving the appearance of illness. Healey was in charge of the task force, and it was he who called the shots and coordinated the operation. Kane and Page were working under his command. Healey was wearing a white shirt with a grey tie and black trousers, and his auburn hair was stylishly gelled. Everyone in the task force were dressed much more casually in jeans and sweatshirts.

Healey turned to Nicholls who was sitting to the side of him. "It is good to finally meet you, Jimmy," he said cordially. "I am sure your brother has brought you up to speed, but I would also like you to hear it from me too."

Nicholls nodded respectfully.

"I met your brother some years ago when I was his special forces commander in the army. He was a raw, angry young man back then, but we trained him and helped hone his skills to mould him into one of the bravest and most remarkable people I have ever met in my life." Nicholls looked at his brother in admiration at the compliment, but Kane pretended to ignore him.

"When John became aware of his tragic family situation, he came to me, and I promised that I would help him get justice for his mother's murder. Of course, by that time I had left the army and I was in politics, but a promise is a promise." Healey splayed his hands wide to emphasise his point.

"To cut a long story short, it didn't take much digging to discover that John's claims about police corruption and links to organised crime, actually held a lot of weight. When I presented the evidence to the PM, he asked me to lead a taskforce in collaboration with the National Crime Agency to uncover the true scale of corruption and bring it down using whatever means necessary.

Of course, this is a clandestine investigation. Everything you hear today is top secret. Kev, here represents the legal part of our investigation." Healey gestured to Page. "He has done everything by the book, using authorised investigative techniques that we can present to the courts if there are any questions asked. John on the other hand, is our ace in the hole. He has been authorised to use whatever means necessary to uncover the truth. As you can imagine, his methods are not entirely legal, so his involvement is completely off the record. We erased his identity so officially he does not exist. It was his idea to bring Holly into the operation and she has helped turn McGovern to our side." Healey acknowledged Holly with a warm smile.

"And gradually piece by piece, the team were able to uncover the shocking scale of how organised crime and corrupt police officers control the city. For Christ's sake, we've got police units running drugs to dealers around the city. Those sons of bitches are worse than the criminals themselves. They swore an oath to protect the public." Healey's anger was conspicuously beginning to rise, and spittle bubbled venomously on his lips. "And it soon became clear that the puppet masters of this evil empire were Flack and McGovern. Through a mixture of bribery and blackmail, these bastards have operated for years with complete impunity because they think they are untouchable. We quickly realised that bringing them down was not going to be easy, because they are too powerful and too well insulated to take down publicly, through legal means."

Healey paused. He took another long sip of his coffee to pacify his rising temper.

"Their power is based on bribery and blackmail. Anyone who can't be bought is blackmailed. The most common technique is to get targets drunk when the opportunity presents itself, ply them with prostitutes and film their sexual encounters. It's how they ensnared the wealthy industrial Doug White and got him to hand over his business site for pittance. He's a self-professed family man with too much to lose if videos surfaced of him having sex with younger girls.

We had to find out who Flack, and McGovern controlled," said Healey slamming his fist into the palm of his hand. "As you know, my illness was just a ruse. We needed to bring our enemies into the open and get them to make a move, so we could see what we were up against. It's allowed us to find out what they were planning and by Jesus, it's frightening. They think they can place that son of a bitch Kilbride in power and build a prison system of Soviet style gulags, up and down the country for their own personal profit."

Healey glared intensely at each person around the table. "Well not on our fucking watch." He held his stare at Nicholls for longer than the others which made him fidget uncomfortably.

"Holly's done an amazing job to turn McGovern onto our side and the information he has given us, is priceless. We know precisely how his criminal organisation works and who's dirty. There's evidence to send people to jail for the rest of their lives—"

"Are we going to arrest them?" interrupted Nicholls.

Healey grimaced. "I spoke at length with the PM this morning. The list of corrupt police officers, politicians and businessman goes on and on and on. We both agree that public prosecutions are not in the best interests of the country at the moment. It is just too incendiary for the public to hear. Imagine if people find out that the institutions that are supposed to protect them have been corrupted and perverted by criminals to suit their own needs. They'll be anarchy on the streets of England if any of this comes out. Our mandate is to protect the country from itself as well. Besides If we went after all of these bastards individually it would take years and years to prosecute them, and that's after all the appeals and legal wranglings. Even then, there's no guarantee we'd get Flack. They will all get their just deserts. Of that I can assure you, Jimmy. Now is the time to complete the final stage of the operation."

"What about McGovern, sir?" asked Kane eagerly.

"As far as I'm concerned that bastard has served his purpose. Does everyone agree." Healey scanned the room quickly and registered the nods. Even Nicholls found himself nodding, although he couldn't explain why. It was against everything he stood for to approve of vigilante styled justice.

"Good," said Healey curtly, looking at Kane as he spoke. "He is yours and Hollys to deal with." Nicholls saw a smile flicker briefly on the face of his sister.

"For now, our priority is Ivankov. He is someone who represents a very real threat to our investigation. Make no mistake, this bastard has an insatiable appetite, which has been well and truly whetted by Flack's proposal. He is one of the most powerful and dangerous mobsters in the world and he has the support of the Kremlin to contend with as well. The PM is very concerned about his involvement. It could jeopardise everything."

Healey fidgeted in his seat as if he had an itch that he couldn't quite reach. He turned to the slim looking man who was sitting next to him. "Mr Bromwich here has been through his accounts with a toothcomb, and he's found out some interesting information. Martin, can you debrief us of your findings?"

Martin Bromwich was a small, nervous looking man who had been a data analyst in the National Crime Agency for the last ten years. He had a receding hairline and an unremarkable face that was shielded by an oversized pair of reading glasses. "Early this morning, my team gained access to the laptop of Tony Sykes, who is Sergei Ivankov's chief accountant," he said tentatively. "What we found on there is actually quite remarkable and could prove very useful to our investigation. As we expected, Ivankov's accounts show that he is the kingpin in a vast money laundering system called the laundromat. Ivankov receives vast sums of money, and I'm talking billions of pounds, from an array of Russian companies owned by Russian oligarchs and politicians. The money is pumped into offshore shell companies allowing these individuals to clean their money, so to speak. They can then withdraw funds to use in bogus trade deals that can be invested in property all over the world but especially in London. Ivankov's name and passport details appear in nearly all the bank documents for these offshore shell companies, so he is clearly the lynchpin in this operation."

Page coughed loudly. "But Russian money laundering has been going on for years. There's not much we can do about it and it's notoriously difficult to prove. Ivankov can deny everything, and his diplomatic status protects him from prosecution."

Bromwich smiled. "It's not quite that simple, John," he said triumphantly. "We did some burrowing and we found out that Ivankov is actually siphoning off some of the funds into a secret Cyprus account. The account is owned by a Dimitri Vusilev, but the passport details on the banking documents are Ivankovs', which means it's definitely his account."

"What does that mean?" asked Page.

"It means that Ivankov is being a naughty boy," chirped Bromwich. "He's stealing from his investors. It's only a tiny amount of money each time, but if you add it all up, there's over half a billion pounds there in total. I don't think his investors will be happy to hear that he's skimming from them even if they are billionaires themselves."

"That's excellent work from you and your team, Martin," said Healey.

"And that's not all," replied Bromwich hurriedly and with real gusto. "We found a lot more incriminating evidence we could use against Ivankov. There are forged papers that prove he deliberately inflated stock prices to con investors in several American companies. There are emails between Ivankov and terrorist groups confirming the sale of missiles, shot guns and all manner of illegal explosives. We've found social media posts on the platform Reddit which prove the Russians interfered with the last US election and attempted to influence public opinion. We even found a bill of sale for five airplanes, clearly illustrating flight routes from Colombia to America, which also comes with a handy memo on how to avoid detection by the US coast guard and Drug Enforcement Agency. And last but not least, there was also a comprehensive video library of some rather distasteful pornographic material involving various unattractive young men and women and a collection of farm animals. Now, we could probably attribute most of this material to Sykes to be fair. But if all else fails, there is a good chance we could get a criminal conviction for possessing indecent images as well."

Everybody around the table laughed.

"Jesus Christ!" said Kane excitedly. "It's like the American scientist who lost the schematics for the nuclear bomb on a commuter train. How could Ivankov be so careless?"

"He thinks he's untouchable," replied Healey triumphantly. "He's got close friends in the Kremlin and rumour has it, he even goes shooting with the Russian President at his summer retreat. He thinks they'll protect him, whatever sins he commits in other countries. I'm going to pass this information on to the PM straight after this meeting. We can hopefully use this evidence as collateral for the next phase of the operation. Martin, can you draw up a brief report summarising these findings that I can use in my meeting with the PM?"

"Of course, sir," responded Bromwich obediently.

"There is just one more thing," said Healey, turning ominously towards Nicholls. "I do not believe in coincidences young man. I find it very strange that Flack has taken such a keen interest in your career all these years. The son of the woman he had murdered all those years ago. It doesn't make any sense to me, as yet, but I'm sure Flack has got something planned for you. It is important you stay vigilant Jimmy and update us if he tries to contact you. His time is running out and I'll bet you a bottom dollar that the son of a bitch has an escape plan in mind."

Before Nicholls could answer, Kane slapped him hard on the back. "He doesn't need to worry, sir. Me and Holly have got his back."

Met Commissioner Daniel Flack patted his foot surreptitiously on the floor mat of his car. It was an involuntary spasm caused by anxiety. There was no one else with him, but Flack instinctively tried to disguise the movements. He reached into his jacket pocket and pulled out another cigarette. The ashtray was already crammed with the crushed remains of a packet of twenty that he had bought earlier in the morning. He lit the final cigarette and glanced distastefully at his nicotine-stained fingers.

The last twenty-four hours had drained him of all of his usual composure and filled him with a sense of utter dread. He had only learned about McGovern's disappearance on the news, just before a meeting with station chiefs. It had felt as if someone had punched him hard in the stomach, causing his whole body to tremble. His legs had literally given way and the only way he could stand unaided was to tense every muscle in his body and drive his legs into the ground. Flack's union with McGovern had helped the pair of them dominate power and control the city for decades. Their future plans depended on this alliance. McGovern's political clout and his relationship with Ivankov were essential if they were going to consolidate their ambitions for Secure8. His mind flashed with incessant questions and theories about what had happened to McGovern and his club. Who could have taken it down? Was McGovern dead and by whose hand? Was he next? The news reports were scarce and sketchy, which only served to fuel his irascibility and anxiety.

Flack was furious that the National Crime Agency had taken charge of the case and were being so tight lipped about their investigation. They would not confirm if McGovern was dead or alive. Flack had telephoned the Home Secretary and the Mayor of London for answers, but his concerns had been unanimously brushed aside. He had been told that the National Crime Agency had been given complete jurisdiction and the case was confidential. There was nothing more to be said.

Flack knew he was being blindsided, but he couldn't explain why. It was highly unusual for the National Crime Agency to work on any substantial investigation without cooperation from the police. In the pit of his stomach, he feared that this might mean that the Met was under investigation too, but it was too early to jump to conclusions. If this was the case, he would find out sooner rather than later and he would have to have faith in his contingency plans. A more pressing matter was dealing with a volatile Russian, who was demanding answers that Flack simply didn't have at the moment.

Flack glanced at his watch. It was nearly one o'clock in the afternoon. He had arranged to meet Ivankov on a stretch of wasteland next to an overground railway line. As always, he had turned up early. The contrast between the dilapidated brick railway on his right and modern skyscrapers standing imperiously in the distance, couldn't have been starker. The arches of the brick structures were overgrown with dense foliage that partially concealed rusting fridges, washing machines and cookers that had been unceremoniously discarded by callous owners.

Flack finished his final cigarette and flicked it into a metal drum that was mottled with rust. He took a deep breath to compose himself and fought away a gnawing feeling that he was being watched. Flack heard the rumble of Ivankov's Mercedes-Benz-G-Class long before the vehicle came into view. The monstrous black car gleamed in the light and Flack had to shield his eyes as it pulled alongside him. The window opened and he heard Ivankov's voice.

"Get in Mr Flack. We have urgent business to discuss."

Flack steeled himself and opened the door.

Ivankov was sprawled out on the back seat, wearing a thick cashmere coat. His eyes were disguised by a huge pair of cartier sunglasses, so Flack was unable to read his expression. He sat beside him and waited.

"Well, Mr Flack. The last twenty-four hours have certainly been eventful," he said quietly although there was something threatening and sinister about his voice. "I would be very grateful if you could tell me what the fuck has happened to my friend Patrick McGovern?"

Flack took a deep breath. Ivankov was a massive man, and his hands were hanging ominously at his side, like huge frankfurters that were poised to strangle the life out of the Met Commissioner if he failed to give satisfactory answers to his questions.

Flack instinctively knew that it was pointless lying or even trying to stall Ivankov. Instead, he answered honestly. "Sergei, at this moment, I just don't know."

Silence.

Ivankov absorbed the answer like a cloud of radiation. He spluttered with incredulity and banged his hand against the passenger door with such force that the blow resonated throughout the whole car. "What do you mean you don't know?" he growled. "You're supposed to be the chief of police. What kind of a fucked-up country is this?" Flack noticed that his accent seemed to have totally disappeared as his animalistic rage boiled to the surface.

Ivankov pulled off his sunglasses and threw them hard into the back of the driver's seat. There was a faint crack as the glass splintered. His face was the colour of beetroot, and the eyes were like burning embers of coal. "Now, you listen to me, Mr Flack." Ivankov leaned over so his face was millimetres away from Flack and the Met Commissioner could almost taste the vodka radiating from his pores. "Last week, I went back to Russia, and I spoke to some very important people in the Kremlin about your proposals for Secure8 and do you know what? They fucking loved them. So much so, that we have already started to make plans for buying into this prison idea."

Ivankov paused to light a cigar from his jacket pocket. He didn't offer one to Flack. "And now this week, one of my partners in this proposal is missing, his business has been attacked and no-one knows what has happened? Already I am being bombarded with phone calls and messages from back home, demanding answers and I have nothing for them. Do you know how stupid this makes me look?"

Flack had not achieved his position in life by shirking from challenges. He stared back at the Russian as calmly as he could. "Sergei, of course you are correct. This is not an ideal situation. I do not know what has happened to Patrick. I have tried to make enquiries, but no-one is prepared to tell me anything at the moment."

Ivankov took a deep puff of his cigar and sat back in the comfortable leather seat. "Does this mean that all our plans are in jeopardy, Mr Flack?" As his voice quietened, his Russian accent seemed to return in abundance.

"Not at all, Sergei," replied Flack firmly. "If Patrick is dead, then we have lost a partner and a friend. Of course, that is a setback, but it is not an insurmountable problem. If Patrick has been apprehended by the authorities, then again that is a challenge we can overcome. We both know that Patrick would cut his own throat, rather than cooperate with the police."

"Why are you being kept out of the loop, Mr Flack?"

Flack leaned forward. "Again Sergei. I do not know. It could be nothing or it could be that the Met is under investigation too."

"That is a very concerning development, Mr Flack."

"Yes, it is," replied Flack. "But I have always been careful. They will not find anything incriminating that ties me with his organisation if they are looking in my dirty laundry."

"But is that a risk we are prepared to take at the moment? England is certainly a curious country. In Russia, the people in law enforcement all share the same values and they work together. I do not understand why this not the case over here?" Ivankov's brow furrowed as he considered their options. "Perhaps it is best to involve some of my people to help resolve the situation?"

"No," replied Flack, a little more assertively than he had meant to. "I have it under control Sergei. You have to trust me. We just need to play for time for the moment. That is all."

Ivankov sighed tiredly. "Please could you elaborate, Mr Flack?"

"In a couple of months, the general election would have taken place," said Flack with a wry smile. "You do not need to be psychic to be able to predict the result. Labour are finished. The Conservatives are already too far ahead in the polls to be defeated. Their leader is conspicuous by his absence on the campaign trail. Already the media are getting suspicious and making suggestions about his health. A few newspapers are already touting Kilbride as his successor. Once he is in power, all our problems will be over. The case against Patrick and myself will be dropped and we can begin our profitable era of mass incarceration."

Ivankov's mouth did not move but his eyes flickered like a serpent. "I must confess," he said rubbing his chin fastidiously. "That does sound like a sensible option, for now. But do please tell me, what are your plans to stall this investigation, Mr Flack?"

"The investigation is after bent coppers, Sergei. It is time to give them one," said Flack. "I may need to borrow some of your men, my friend. I'm not sure who is watching me at the moment."

Chapter 9
The Noose

Patrick McGovern shivered under his blanket as the orderly, manoeuvred the wheelchair down the corridor. The doctors had said he was well enough to be discharged but the stabbing pain resonating in his abdomen, showed no signs of abating and he still felt delirious and groggy.

His physical weakness was exacerbated by the nagging stain on his soul from cooperating with the authorities. He felt hollow and numb as the power he once held, had suddenly evaporated like the setting sun. He was a spent force. An old warship on his way to be dismantled. The only consolation on the horizon was that he would spend his twilight years with Elena. She was his salvation. The only light left in his world. Her love would be enough for him to endure the ignominy of a life now devoid of purpose.

The wheelchair stopped outside a lift. McGovern shuddered as he caught sight of his reflection in the metal panel. It was as if his muscles had withered away like a plant in the desert. He was a shadow of the man he used to be, since his near-death experience. The orderly pushed McGovern through the doors as they opened, and they both waited patiently for the lift to descend. Conscious of his vulnerability, the crime boss was wearing a plain beige dressing gown that was pulled up to his jaw line and a grey baseball cap with a long peak that cast a shadow over his face when he ducked his head.

McGovern thought disconsolately about his two sons. They were not strong enough or ruthless enough to take control of his criminal empire. He imagined them being brushed aside or even killed in the power struggle that would follow his departure. He prayed it would be the former and that they would be able to find themselves a purpose in life of their own accord. Perhaps in a few years, he would be able to come out of hiding and renew his relationship with them—although in his heart of hearts, he knew this was unlikely. The Russians would never forget him. He would be executed like a dog if he ever resurfaced on the streets.

The plan was for him and Elena to go into witness protection for the short term and let the dust die down. When it was safe, he and Elena would disappear to the costa del sol and build a new life together. He already owned property out there, albeit under a different name. In a year or two, he could buy a club or a restaurant to keep the finances flowing. That would have to suffice for the immediate future.

The lift seemed to take an eternity to descend to the ground floor. He shifted uncomfortably in the wheelchair, willing the doors to open. When they finally did, his eyes nervously scanned the foyer for signs of life. His gaze narrowed in on a black range rover that was tucked away behind a bollard. The door opened and Elena jumped out. McGovern felt a rush of relief. She looked as beautiful as ever. She was wearing blue jeans and a denim jacket, and her mousey brown hair cascaded from an American baseball cap, as she ran over to him.

She smiled when she saw him although there was something cold and distant in her eyes. Perhaps she was tired, McGovern thought. The last few days must have been emotionally draining for her. Elena gave him a hug and a kiss on the cheek, which helped to revitalise his soul. Once he had recovered and regained his strength, everything would be alright. He would ensure she didn't regret the life that she had chosen with him.

It was then that McGovern noticed the driver. He looked oddly familiar. McGovern was sure that he had seen him before, but he couldn't quite place his face. He was tall and muscular with hair as dark as a raven's wing. There was a scar that stretched down the side of his face. He looked as if he could handle himself, that was for sure. McGovern felt relieved that they had assigned someone formidable to protect them in witness protection. Much better than an inexperienced new recruit fresh out of training and covered in pimples.

The driver smiled grimly and opened the passenger door, which activated a ramp. He gruffly took hold of McGovern's wheelchair and thrust him into the range rover with such force that McGovern thought his whole body would topple over.

"Watch it you bastard," he croaked. His throat still felt like he was gargling razor blades and it was a colossal effort to expel any words. The driver looked at him and glared intently but said nothing. To McGovern's surprise, Elena totally ignored him and sat in the passenger door on the driver's side. It was the orderly who fastened McGovern to the seat and secured his seat belt who said a few words to check if he was alright. No-one else seemed to care in the slightest. McGovern couldn't understand what was going on. For the first time in his life, he felt scared and vulnerable.

The vehicle drove out of the car park and into the daylight. McGovern was almost blinded by the dazzling light, and he had to shield his eyes from the dazzling glare of the sun. He felt nauseous and dizzy as the car hurtled though the streets, jolting him back and forth like a rag doll. It was as if the driver was deliberately trying to make the ride as uncomfortable as possible for him. He tried to call out, but no words would form in his mouth, which seemed as dry as a desert. The range rover turned sharply around a corner which provoked a sharp, stabbing sensation in the pit of his stomach. He spewed up over the window. No one moved or made any attempt to help him.

After what seemed like an eternity, the light was suddenly consumed by darkness, and they came to a stop. McGovern assumed they had gone underground again, but it was difficult to tell as his nearest window was covered in vomit. The range rover meandered slowly on for about another one hundred metres, until it came to a stop and McGovern heard the driver yank up the handbrake and open his door.

McGovern started to sweat profusely. He felt lifeless and devoid of any energy. The back door opened, and Elena's face was suddenly next to his. Her eyes were as feral as a wild beast. She looked at him with barely contained disgust.

"I have been waiting for this moment all my life, Patrick," she hissed, spraying spittle over McGovern's face. Her Eastern accent had suddenly vanished, and there was a very conspicuous cockney undertone in her voice. "Did you honestly think that I could ever have feelings for you? You destroyed my family you son of a bitch. Now it is time to take my vengeance."

McGovern couldn't speak. His heart felt like it was in a vice, and it was slowly being crushed. He had no idea what was going on.

The huge driver barged in and yanked the wheelchair out of the vehicle, with such force that it crashed against the floor and toppled over. McGovern smashed his head on the concrete floor and his body spilled out of the wheelchair. The driver laughed cruelly and picked up the crime boss by the collar. With one arm, he raised him into the air and lowered him back onto the wheelchair like a hydraulic lorry loader.

"I promised my sister that I'd let her deal with you, McGovern," he said quietly with a broad Scottish accent. "I must admit, I would have enjoyed making you suffer, but a promise is a promise." The driver smiled sadistically and grabbed a large, grubby bag from within the car that he slung effortlessly over his shoulder. He turned away from McGovern, and as he walked, the bag expelled a clanging sound as it rocked back and forth against his shoulder.

Panic gnawed at McGovern, and he felt paralysed in his wheelchair as he glanced around at his surroundings. He was in a dimly lit car park, beneath a large building that was constricted by concrete pillars wedged in the corners. It was deserted. They were the only ones there. He contemplated calling out, but no-one would hear him in here.

All of a sudden, he was tipped back roughly, and he smelt Elena's perfume. She was tantalisingly close to him.

"I have waited all my life for this you son of a bitch," she said softly. Her words were like molten sulphur on his cheek.

McGovern tried to answer her, but his jaw was locked solid, and the words wouldn't form in his mouth. "Who are you?" he spluttered after what seemed like an eternity.

Elena laughed wickedly. Was that even her name? McGovern chastised himself for his naivety. Of course, it wasn't. He had been played. That much was obvious but for what purpose. He knew that he had too many sins to remember everyone who sought revenge upon him.

"You have destroyed too many lives to mention, Patrick," she said vengefully. "I doubt you would remember my mother, even if I told you her name." The wheelchair came to an abrupt halt, and she flicked an arm out. In her hand was a photo of a pretty girl with a milky complexion and long auburn hair. McGovern instantly recognised her, but he couldn't picture a name.

"This is my mother. Her name was Julia Kane."

McGovern's memory flickered into life and suddenly, everything became clear to him. Of course, he remembered her. It had been around a quarter of a century ago the last time he saw her, but for some reason he remembered it like it was yesterday.

It had all been Flack's idea to ensnare Kilbride and blackmail his billionaire father. Kilbride had been barely out of his teens at the time, but he was a regular visitor at McGovern's whore house when Flack had first noticed him. Flack had paid a Romanian girl to start goading him about his manhood during a visit, in the hope that Kilbride would do something stupid. The plan had worked out better than either of them could have anticipated. Kilbride had lost his temper and struck the girl so violently, that she had died from her injuries. Flack and McGovern had then burst in on the scene like wolves. Kilbride had been blubbering like a child as the enormity of his actions had suddenly hit home. While McGovern feigned rage and threatened to have Kilbride shot, Flack had consoled the youngster and made a discreet call to his father. It was the prefect set up. Kilbride's father would do whatever it took to keep his son out of prison. His business empire and contacts were slowly absorbed, and Kilbride was channelled into politics. Both of them were under no illusions what would happen if they didn't play ball. Flack had enough evidence from the murder to put Kilbride away for a long time.

Julia Kane had been working in the next room when the Romanian girl was killed. She had heard the noise and burst in on the scene to defend the call girl, only to find out it was too late. Julia had even tried to attack Kilbride for what he had done. She had to be held back by some of McGovern's men as Kilbride wept like a baby in the corner of the room.

McGovern pictured her implacable face as she demanded that he call the police to arrest Kilbride. The silly bitch wouldn't leave it alone, even when he warned her to keep quiet. It had taken three of McGovern's men to pull her away and drive her home, but it was abundantly clear she was not going to let it go. The next day, it was decided that she had to die. Flack arranged for Daniel Bircham, one of his police officers that Julia trusted to pick her up. He had driven her to an abandoned warehouse where McGovern and Baldock were waiting. As Julia exited the car, McGovern shot her in the back of the head. McGovern told Baldock and Bircham to deal with the body and he had spent the rest of the afternoon in the pub.

McGovern's focus fizzed back to reality. These were obviously Julia's children but how had they uncovered the truth? It didn't take him long to figure it out, the gorge slowly rising in his throat—Baldock. They got to Baldock and cut it out of him. That's how they knew what happened. And this was the next part of their revenge.

"You do remember her don't you, Patrick?" said the Scottish voice sanctimoniously, jolting the wheelchair forcefully across the dimly lit foyer.

McGovern didn't answer. Instinctively, his mind was frantically scrambling for something that he could use to bargain for his life. The bitter realisation was that he had nothing left to sell. The fear was visceral now. He could feel his entire body trembling and his insides seemed about to implode.

"Please," he begged. "It was all Flack. If you let me live, I will help you get him." McGovern knew he sounded pathetic.

Holly laughed callously behind him. "It is too late for that, Patrick, but don't worry. That bastard Flack is next on the list. You're not going to be lonely in hell, you son of a bitch."

They stopped outside a set of steel double doors. They were padlocked. The huge Scottish man fished a key from his pocket and briskly unlocked them. He hurled the chain nonchalantly to the side. McGovern tried to turn to speak to the pair, but he was thrust violently through the entrance. He had no time to raise his hands, so his head crashed painfully against the metal.

The force of the impact disorientated McGovern and it took him a while for his vision to become accustomed to the new room. It was well lit and spacious. On the far side was a long table with people sitting round. As McGovern drew closer, he could see that they were all young women. They all stopped talking to stare as he approached. McGovern couldn't be sure, but he sensed a seething hatred in the faces of some of the women.

The wheelchair abruptly stopped about ten metres from the table. McGovern felt himself rock back before he was propelled forward on to the floor by a forceful thrust from his captor. His body smacked hard against the concrete floor.

He felt a strong hand clamp down on his neck and a warm breath on his ear.

"My name is Holly Kane, and this is my brother, John," the voice hissed. "I want you to know that every second I was with you, I was dreaming of this moment, Patrick." She squeezed tightly, lacerating the skin with her fingernails.

"The women you see in front of you are all victims of your evil sex trafficking operation. No doubt they would have spent the rest of their lives in abject misery, if you had anything to do about it."

McGovern stared at the women. Some of them had already begun to move tentatively towards him.

"The good news for them is that they are on their way home," said Holly triumphantly. "But not before we have arranged a little bit of payback."

As she spoke, her brother stepped forward and tossed the bag he was carrying at the foot of the table. It spilled open to reveal a maelstrom of rust tinted knives.

"Now Patrick, nothing would give me or my brother greater pleasure than to send you to hell personally," laughed Holly. "But we agreed that we would let the other victims go first." She stooped over him. A knife flashed and she tore away his dressing gown with a swoop of her hand, exposing his nakedness. She moved over to the table and started to speak to the woman in another language.

Her brother grabbed under McGovern's armpit and lifted him to his feet. "Not all the girls are Russian, Patrick, but most are capable of understanding the language," he said quietly. "She's telling them all that you are the man who made them into sex slaves." He looked at McGovern with unfathomable eyes.

"She does have a way with words, my sister. I'll give her that," he said smiling cruelly. "She's saying that you are an evil man who has profited from the misery of others of years." McGovern saw Holly point conspicuously at the bag of knives. "She says that now is the time for them to claim their vengeance and take back what you stole from them." He paused briefly to suppress his expanding grin. "I don't think they'll need much encouragement, by the way. They don't seem to like you very much."

Kane slammed McGovern so hard into the table that it skidded along the floor. McGovern managed to catch himself on the edge, but he barely had enough strength to keep himself upright. The room seemed to spin, and he spewed up what remained of his breakfast pitifully upon the table.

One of the braver girls started to edge cautiously over to the bag of knives, which was a few feet away from McGovern's foot. She had short brown hair and possessed a steely, malevolent look in her emerald eyes. She stooped and fished out a large rusty knife with a serrated edge. There was a brief moment of wonderment in her eyes as she stared at the rusty blade, before she turned her attention to McGovern. Her actions seemed to galvanise a few of the other girls, who followed in her wake and helped themselves to knives from the bag.

McGovern realised with an icy dread that dripped down his spine, that he was now the prey. He tried to back away, but all of his remaining strength had deserted his muscles. He raised his hands in supplication and tried to beg for his life, but no words would form in his mouth, save a pitiful choking sound. The brown-haired girl was now only a couple of steps away from him. He could see flecks of grey in her hair and hear her breathing get quicker and shallower. She very calmy and very slowly turned the point of her knife towards him. The knuckles on her hand turned white as she gripped the blade tightly.

McGovern was so terrified that he lost control of his bladder and a stream of urine trickled down his leg and on to the floor. The women barely registered the acrid smell that filled their nostrils, so intent were they on taking their vengeance.

They moved closer to surround McGovern like a pack of wolves cutting off any possibility of escape.

McGovern glanced around desperately. The large Scottish man and his sister were watching intently, with an imperious grin on their faces, as if they were Romans in the colosseum awaiting a blood-soaked spectacle. The women were edging closer to him, their knives glinting from the fluorescent factory light above them.

McGovern wasn't sure if he was imagining it, but the women's' faces looked almost feral. They had been transformed into the faces of wild beasts, driven by an animalistic desire for vengeance. Were they possessed by demons?

The brunette was now within an arm reach of him. For a brief moment, they caught each other's gaze. Her eyes were wild and lucid, and spittle was frothing at her mouth. Time seemed to slow down. McGovern could almost feel the burning hatred, that seeped like lava from her pores. She raised her knife above her head.

"Please, no," spluttered McGovern incoherently.

The woman paused temporarily as if his words had suddenly brought her out of her savage trance. She looked at him and then very slowly, a cruel smile spread across her face. Her knife slashed down. For a second, McGovern thought that she had missed him, but then he was hit by a throbbing pain in his chest, and a bitterly cold wind seemed to sweep through his body. He looked down at his chest and blood erupted from a gaping wound by his nipple.

McGovern tried to stem the bleeding by clamping his hand upon the wound, but rivers of blood poured through his fingers, and on to the floor. Emboldened by her attack, the woman stepped closer and plunged the knife into his side. This time, the pain came immediately.

McGovern felt any strength he still had wash away with each pulse of blood. His vison began to blur. There was a whirl of movement in front of him and then he felt as if he was being pierced by a frenzy of ice-cold lightning bolts throughout his body.

His legs gave way, and his vison was enveloped by a suffocating blackness. The next thing he knew, he was lying on the floor. The pain was radiating out through his entire body as his life blood seeped out to create a crimson puddle on the concrete floor. McGovern was consumed by a terrifying fear that gnawed away at his soul like a carnivorous beast.

He tried to curl into a ball to shield himself from his attackers, but his legs

172

and arms wouldn't respond to the commands of his nervous system. In desperation, he blinked frantically, and his sight slowly returned, but he almost wished that it hadn't. Crowded around him were a collection of demonic, beast like creatures with ragged horns and sharp, protruding fangs that dripped saliva and blood on to the floor. McGovern screamed in terror and tried to fend them off, but they just howled with laughter and dragged him across the floor with clawed hands, that lacerated his skin. He tried to grip the floor, but his fingernails were torn away by the futile effort.

All of a sudden there was a deafening grunting sound and the demonic beasts howled and released him. An enormous shape, bristling with muscles barged the beasts away and grabbed hold of McGovern's neck. He closed his eyes and smelt a foul stench of rotten meat that pervaded his nostrils. When he eventually opened his eyes, the demonic beasts were gone, and the Scottish man and his sister were standing in front of him. The woman was holding a knife. She took out a picture of her mother with her other hand. The auburn hair and milky complexion brought McGovern's memories flooding back.

"I wanted my mother's face to be the last thing you ever saw," she said venomously.

The man laughed as she stepped over and swung her arm wildly.

McGovern screamed in agony as Holly took her bloody revenge.

Chapter 10
Checkmate

8 Hours Earlier...

Jimmy Nicholls fidgeted uncomfortably on the dilapidated sofa in Kane's caravan. He was spending more and more time here, only going home to pick up new clothes and to use the washing machine. There was something liberating about spending time with his brother. It wasn't that long ago, he felt isolated and alone. It was good to be part of a family.

He felt the phone vibrate in his pocket, briefly before he heard the monotonous ring tone. He had been expecting the call since the previous evening. Kane had told him what to do. He couldn't quite believe how he had been duped for so long. The pain was like a raw wound, that festered and throbbed as he contemplated his betrayal.

McGovern saw the name of the caller flash on the phone. He had to stifle his emotions. There was still an important part that he had to play. He couldn't let anyone down now. He took a deep breath and swallowed the bile that had erupted in his throat.

"Good morning, Jenny," he said cautiously. Kane had advised him to be nondescript. "What can I do for you?"

There was a pronounced silence. Nicholls contemplated hanging up. "Jimmy is that you?" came the timid reply. "I wasn't sure if ringing you was a good idea. I just…" Another pause.

"Jenny, what do you want?" he said tiredly. "It was you that made the decision to move out, not me."

"I know, I know," she said with a hint of barely disguised desperation in her tone. "But the last few days I haven't been able to stop thinking about you." Another long pause. "I was wondering if I had made a big mistake."

Nicholls gritted his teeth. "What do you want to me to say Jenny?" His voice

174

rising. "I love you," he growled begrudgingly. "I didn't stop loving you because you walked out on me."

"I love you too," she screamed. Nicholls could hear her crying on the other end of the line. He waited, letting the tension build.

"So, what do we do next?"

"I need to see you," she said, a little too quickly. "Today. Can you come home this morning?"

So, this was how she would get him, thought Nicholls. He pinched the bridge of his nose to suppress the sharp pain that had suddenly developed in his head. "I'm off work at the moment, so I'll pop by around nine or ten?" he said. "Can you meet me there?"

"Ooh, that's amazing darling," she said, patently ignoring his question. "I can't wait to see you. Where are you now?"

"Listen. I can't really talk at the moment," he bristled. "I will see you later and we can try and work out where we go from here." He hung up, before she had time to respond.

Nicholls reached out for the opaque bottle of spirits that was sat invitingly on the side table. He took a swig from the bottle and then grimaced as the fiery whisky within burned the back of his throat. It was time for him to play his part. He just hoped that Kane was right about what he had told him, because if he wasn't, Nicholls might never be coming back.

The drive to Nicholls' home seemed to take him no time at all, as his mind was pre-occupied about what was going to happen next. As he pulled into his estate, he saw Jenny's shiny, black Audi parked imperiously on the kerb by his house. He pulled up beside her and firmly yanked up the handbrake, as if he was trying to dispel some of his nervous energy. He trudged up the path and opened the door cautiously.

"Jenny?" he called out.

"I'm in the living room," came the reply. He took off his coat and hung it on the rack by the front door. He took a few steps down the corridor and stepped into the living room. He saw Jenny, sitting seductively on the leather couch. She had a sad, glazed look in her eyes. He was about to say something, when a strong arm clamped down around his neck and a foul-smelling cloth was thrust over his mouth and nose. The acrid smell burned his nostrils. The room started to spin. Then there was blackness.

When Nicholls came to, he was tied to a wooden chair in the centre of the room. Jenny was sitting in the same place, quietly sobbing into a handkerchief. Detective Superintendent Daniel Bircham was standing in front of him, frantically puffing on a cigarette, as if it was his last ever one. There were two formidable looking men either side of him in immaculate grey suits. One had a flattened nose and a muscular jaw line, and the other was bald and had one of the thickest necks that Nicholls had ever seen. These were clearly Ivankov's men thought Nicholls ominously.

Nicholls was stunned at how much Bircham had aged in the brief period that he had been absent from the force. The man's wavy hair was greasy and flushed with silver streaks and his rotund face was peppered with spidery veins that sprawled over his sallow skin like purple cobwebs. He looked nervous and agitated at the two Russian behemoths beside him.

Bircham was the first to notice that Nicholls had regained consciousness and he hastily stubbed out his cigarette into a cup on the nearest table. Nicholls noticed a strange looking contraption next to the mug. It was composed of a sheet of metal that had been folded into a cylindrical brace. There was a metal rod that extended from the brace which was attached to a leather strap at the bottom. Both the metal brace and the strap were connected to two small iron rings.

"Aahh, Jimmy," said Bircham sadly. He looked genuinely forlorn to see his work colleague in this position. "I want you to know that all of this is nothing personal. I always liked you."

Nicholls instinctively felt a pulse of blood surge through his body, and he strained to break free, but the cable ties that secured him to the chair, held fast. "What the fuck are you talking about? What is going on here?" he growled.

"You are my boy, what we call, collateral damage," replied Bircham callously. "The Met is currently being investigated and they are looking for dirty cops. Unfortunately, you are going to have to be our scapegoat I'm afraid, Jimmy and take all the flack."

"Sir, I don't understand what you mean. Why am I tied up?" replied Nicholls bullishly.

Bircham sighed, as if he felt compelled to reveal everything. The jowls on his jawline wobbled like jelly. "You have been very blind to everything that has been going on, I'm afraid, Jimmy."

"Are you telling me that it's you who is the bent copper?" Nicholls' voice was dripping with venom.

"You are in no position to judge me, Jimmy," responded Bircham defensively. "When I first joined the force, I was barely paid enough to provide for my family. It was disgraceful what they paid us. I had to top up earnings any way I could. I wasn't going to let my kids starve."

"Are you trying to make excuses for your actions then, sir? You certainly haven't gone short of food in your time" said Nicholls sarcastically. He jostled in the chair, but the cable ties were scratching the surface of his skin and causing him to bleed.

Bircham raised his hands defensively. "At the time, everyone was doing it. We accepted bribes to turn a blind eye, here and there. It was no big thing. But once you start, I soon discovered that there was no going back." Bircham paused to take out another cigarette and he lit it slowly and methodically, as he considered how much more of his illegal activities, he was prepared to divulge to Nicholls. It didn't really matter what he said as Nicholls was going to die anyway.

"It made sense for us to ally ourselves with organised criminals. We were never going to stop the drug trade anyway. We might as well take a bite out of the pie for ourselves."

Nicholls looked icily at Jenny, who couldn't meet his gaze. "And you were using me all the time, I suppose. Fucking bitch."

Jenny seemed to be galvanised by the insult. She choked back on her tears and swept her long, brown hair out of her eyes. "I'm sorry, Jimmy," she said. "I didn't know it would turn out like this."

"But you had no problems setting me up though and getting me here on false pretences? Was any of it real?"

"I became very fond of you, Jimmy. I'm sorry it had to end like this. Perhaps in another lifetime—"

"Fuck off, you bitch," yelled Nicholls. He spat a mouthful of phlegm in her direction, but it didn't land anywhere near her. "Don't speak to me again. It was your father that set us up together. I take it he's involved in all of this?" Nicholls looked Jenny squarely in the eyes, but his question was clearly directed to Bircham.

"But of course, Jimmy," laughed Bircham cruelly. "Her father is the architect of this all. He's the criminal kingpin of the entire country. He's set you up like a kipper from day one." He paused to take a long puff on his cigarette and then blew the smoke in Nicholls' direction.

"We needed an insurance policy if things turned sour and unfortunately that's got to be you, my son." Bircham pointed a flabby finger at Jenny. "She may look all innocent that one, but she dances to the tune her father plays, that's for sure. She's planted enough evidence on you to make you look like Pablo Escobar. I bet you didn't know that she's set up an offshore bank account for you in the Bahamas, to make it look like you're the bent copper receiving money from illegal crime. I think, you've got a couple of million stored away, here and there. It's just too bad you won't ever see a penny of it." Bircham sneered callously at Nicholls.

"Of course, Flack has already set up an anti-corruption task force to investigate. It's just a pity they will be too late to arrest you." Bircham reached into his pocket and fished out a piece of paper, that he waved triumphantly above his head. "This is the real coup de grace though. A letter written by you, admitting all of your crimes. All the evidence we need to close out the case. I must say, I take my hat off to your good lady for forging it. I'm told by handwriting experts that the likeness to your writing style is perfect." He smiled and made a mocking clapping gesture in Jenny's direction. She responded by burying her head in her hands and started to cry again.

Nicholls was momentarily stunned by the Machiavellian nature of his betrayal, but he quickly regained his senses. Not long now, he told himself repeatedly. "You're not going to get away with this you bastard," he growled.

"But we will, Jimmy, my boy," said Bircham gleefully. "Flack has already got his hooks into a big wig politician. When the Tories win the general election, Jason Kilbride will be the next prime minister. When that happens, we'll all be untouchable. We're just playing for time at the moment."

"Kilbride?" said Nicholls quietly, feigning ignorance.

"He's the deputy leader of the Tories. Darren Healey has cancer. From what I've been told, he's gravely ill. It's only a matter of time before Kilbride takes over." Bircham's eyes narrowed. "You and he have a bit of a personal connection from a long time ago."

When Nicholls didn't respond, Bircham stepped closer to him and kneeled down so their faces were almost touching. "He got your mother killed," he said quietly.

Don't ruin it now, Nicholls told himself as he felt the rage inside him boiling and bubbling, like a volcano on the precipice of an eruption. They don't know you know.

"What do you mean you son of a bitch?" he growled, doing his best to supress his visceral anger.

"Many years ago, Kilbride killed a prostitute who worked in McGovern's brothel. Flack told her to make fun of him. I think she laughed at the size of his prick, if I recall correctly. Well, it certainly hit a raw nerve. Kilbride beat her so badly, that she died. It couldn't have worked out any better for us. We had the son of a bitch on toast after that. Unfortunately, your mother wouldn't leave it alone. She wasn't going to let it lie. That was then Flack and McGovern decided that she had to die as well."

There was something sadistic and cruel about Bircham's tone. Nicholls wondered about how he had missed it before. Perhaps some people were good at masking their true selves. Bircham had been his superior officer for years. He had always considered him a decent but incompetent man. How wrong he had been.

"Anyway, I thought I owed you that, Jimmy," said Bircham rising to his feet. "You can go to your grave now, knowing the truth. He saw the flicker of fear in Nicholls eyes and pointed at the strange contraption on the table.

"Unfortunately for you, this is the end of the road though. We need our bent copper dead and out of the picture so there's no awkward questions." He gestured to the two men sitting behind him. "These guys are some of our Russian friends that we do business with. By all accounts they are experts at the faked suicide. We need you to conveniently blow your own brains out to make it look like you're guilty. The suicide note will explain everything, of course. You're sorry for everything, blah, blah, blah, blah, blah and that you couldn't face prison.

They're going to use this rigged suicide machine to do it, would you believe? That way, the results of the post-mortem will conclusively show that you pulled the trigger, and the verdict will be classed as suicide so the case will be closed pretty quickly. Anyway Jimmy, that's more than enough from me. It's time for the mother and son reunion you've been waiting for." Bircham nodded to the two Russians who rose impeccably in unison at his signal and moved steadily towards Nicholls.

"Wait," shouted Nicholls, fidgeting frantically in his chair. "You don't need to do this."

The two Russian juggernauts ignored his pleas. Their faces were as implacable and unyielding as the sea. One of them went behind him and sliced through the cable ties, freeing Nicholls' hands and the other slammed a strait jacket over his head, which was fitted with a heavy steel frame at the collar. The weight of the metal was almost suffocating, and Nicholls had to use all his strength to keep himself upright.

The bald Russian then deftly released a panel in the strait jacket and pulled out Nicholls' right arm. He then fed the limb into the cylindrical brace on the table and screwed it shut. Nicholls felt an intense pressure biting down on his upper arm, as if he was being consumed by a metal beast. The other Russian placed a gun in Nicholls' hand and fixed it in with a leather strap. He then attached a small chain from the tip of the barrel to a hook on the collar of the strait jacket. Finally, he put his hand underneath Nicholls' elbow and slowly forced it upwards.

Nicholls felt his arm bend and slowly out of the corner of his eye, he saw the gun moving inexorably towards his temple. "Jesus, Fucking Christ," he screamed in terror. "Please stop. You can't do this."

The Russians didn't acknowledge him. They were experienced executioners who had heard it all before. The gun was now so close to his eyes that it had begun to blur, and the muzzle looked like a cannon. Nicholls felt the hands of one of the men press down on the grip of the gun, forcing his own finger on to the trigger.

"**WAIT**," shouted Nicholls, as loud as he could, remembering what his brother had told him. "I know everything. I know about Secure8, the deal with Flack and Ivankov. I know everything. Let me out. For Christ's sake, please let me out." He was almost in tears at this point.

The two Russians stopped in their tracks and looked hesitantly at each other. They released their grip and stepped back. Nicholls tried to drop the gun but the strap around his hand was secure, and it was still attached to the metal collar around his neck.

The bald Russian stepped closer towards him. Nicholls could see the acne scars on his cheeks and smell the cigarette smoke on his breath.

"What did you say?" he growled coldly, in heavily accented English.

Nicholls took a deep breath. He had rehearsed what he had been told to say, but the thought of impending death had made his mind go blank. "Look in my jacket pocket," he squealed in desperation. "I've got a photo of Flack and Ivankov together. I know everything about what they've been up to."

The Russian unclipped the metal collar around Nicholls' neck and tossed it nonchalantly aside. He pulled off the strait jacket and reached into his jacket pocket. There was a brown envelope inside. He pulled it out and pushed Nicholls out of the way.

Nicholls felt like he had just run a marathon. He watched as the man ripped open the envelope and pulled out a black and white photograph. It was the one that had been pinned to the notice board in Kane's caravan.

Bircham snatched the photograph out of the Russian man's hands and waved it in the face of Nicholls.

"What the fuck is this, Jimmy? How did you get hold of it?"

Nicholls felt galvanised by the uncertainty in the room. "Did you honestly think I didn't know about what was going on, you son of a bitch?"

Bircham looked momentarily stunned. His flabby jawline began to wobble as he considered what to say. He was clearly unsure what to do next and glanced anxiously at the two Russians for guidance.

Nicholls capitalised on the uncertainty. "I wasn't just going to do nothing about my mother's death now was I?" He felt the raw, vitriolic rage surge through his body. "When you put me on gardening leave, I tried to uncover the truth for myself. I'm a cop for Christ's sake! What did you expect me to do?"

Bircham steadied himself and snatched the photo from the Russian. It was clearly Ivankov and Flack. Any fool could see that. It didn't look good. That was for sure. How on earth could the Met commissioner explain why he was meeting up with one of the most notorious crime lords in the Russian mafia? He needed to find out more. "You don't know shit, Nicholls. You're just bluffing." The high-pitched tone of his voice though betrayed his anxiety.

Nicholls laughed contemptuously. "I didn't need to be Serpico to get to the truth, you worthless piece of shit." He stared venomously at the detective chief inspector. "I tracked down my mother's neighbours and low and behold, one of them used to be her best friend. Tell me Daniel, do you remember Marie?"

Bircham visibly recoiled at the mention of her name and Nicholls enjoyed watching her face register in his mind. He was quite conspicuously afraid now. That was abundantly clear for everyone in the room to see.

"You do remember her, don't you?" he said triumphantly. "She told me everything about how you and Flack were bent coppers, in bed with McGovern." Nicholls couldn't resist a sly smile. "She was there when you drove my mother away to her death, Daniel. Oh yes, I do know everything you son of a bitch and I promise you that you are going to suffer for all of your crimes."

Bircham's face went a sickly grey colour. The pallor reminded Nicholls of a mouldy slab of concrete. His chin wobbled as he tried to form the words in his mouth to respond to Nicholls. Even Jenny had stopped fiddling with her phone as she sensed the change in momentum in the room.

"Do you mean you were playing us all along?" stuttered Bircham eventually. The words were jumbled and disjointed in his mouth. "Why the fuck would you do that?"

Nicholls stared at Bircham as if there was no-one else in the room. His heart was pounding furiously through his rib cage. "I wanted to get your confession on table, you stupid son of a bitch." He laughed manically and the relief poured out of him in a cathartic tidal wave. Nicholl pulled on his shirt with his partially imprisoned left hand to reveal a wire that was taped just below his nipple.

Time seemed to stand still. Bircham rocked unsteadily on his feet as if there were tremors shooting through the floor. The Russians started to move over towards him, but then they froze in their tracks as if Nicholls had his hand on a detonator.

"What the fuck have you done?" screamed Bircham, steadying himself on the nearest armchair. "You've set us up you bastard!"

Nicholls laughed again. He had never felt so powerful. He ignored the caterwauling of the fat police chief and stared menacingly at Jenny. Their eyes met. "My advice to you my love is to run while you still can." She looked scared at the threat but didn't move.

The bald Russian suddenly seized the initiative and ripped away the rest of Nicholls' shirt to expose the rest of the wire. He causally pulled it off and tossed it away. "Who is listening to us?"

Nicholls laughed again. "Relax my friend. It is not the police. No-one will be kicking down the doors anytime soon, if that's what you're worried about."

"Then who is it you fuck?" hissed Bircham. His face was suddenly right next to Nicholls, and he could smell the sourness of his breath.

Nicholls ignored him and looked at the two Russians. "I need to see your boss, gents. Take me there now and I will reveal everything."

The bald Russian nodded obediently and disappeared into the kitchen. He spoke quietly but everyone could hear the agitated response from the other side of the phone. When he returned the room was deathly silent in anticipation.

"Sasha wants to see you right now," he said emotionlessly. "We will take you right away." The two Russians started to disassemble the suicide machine and free Nicholls from his straps.

"No," shouted Bircham angrily as he realised what was about to happen. "We have orders to kill him right now. We can't let him leave here alive." He moved aggressively as if he intended to stop the Russians from releasing Nicholls, but one angry glance from the bald man, neutralised his objections.

"The situation has changed," said the bald man. "Sasha wants to see him. There is nothing that can change that now."

Chapter 11
The Kessel

Nicholls had his hands tied together with cables before he was bundled unceremoniously out of the house and forced into the back of a transit van that was parked opposite his car. There was no attempt by the Russians to disguise what they were doing as they manhandled him roughly across the pavement. A few curtains twitched in the neighbouring houses, but no one came out to see what was going on.

The transit van had two seats on each side that were covered in a mildew infested sheet. Nicholls was pushed on to the nearest one by the Russian with the flattened nose, who sat opposite him with Bircham.

The police chief had regained much of his composure, although a silky sheen of sweat still glistened on his forehead. "You might as well tell us who it is you're working with, Jimmy," he said with feigned confidence. "If it's that dumb bitch Marie, then it's only a matter of time before we find her. If you give her up now, I promise she won't suffer."

Nicholls looked at Bircham and smiled coldly. "My mother trusted you, Daniel. I trusted you. You're a spineless piece of shit. I have nothing more to say to you."

"Do you think you can negotiate with Ivankov?" he said incredulously. "I'm doing you a favour. That snake will cut the information out of you piece by piece."

Nicholls clenched his jaw and turned away.

The drive was relatively short. Nicholls guessed that Ivankov had been holed up in a luxury hotel in the city centre and they would meet somewhere halfway. After a while, the background traffic noises began to slowly subside, and they drove for about ten minutes in relative silence.

The van suddenly came to an abrupt stop, propelling Bircham off the seat and on to his knees. The doors sprung open, and the bald Russian grunted something incomprehensible to his compatriot before Nicholls was dragged into the open.

Nicholls could see that they were in the courtyard of a large industrial complex that was surrounded on all sides by a box of derelict old factories. He noticed a huge black Mercedes parked in front of them. Ivankov was already here, he thought ominously.

"Last chance, Jimmy boy," said Bircham. "Tell me who you're working with and no one else has to suffer. Ivankov will make it very personal if you upset him. Think about the parents that adopted you. You wouldn't want anything to happen to them now, would you?"

Nicholls ignored him and let himself be led into the nearest building. There was a huge orange skip by the front entrance that was piled high with scrap metal. The side of the building was open and supported by rusty metal supports. The space within was cloaked in darkness, even though it was the middle of the day and water dripped stubbornly from the ceiling to make sporadic puddles on the concrete below.

The ground floor was littered with old and decrepit industrial machinery that had long since been abandoned and exposed to the elements. In the centre was a fearsome looking metal contraption which was connected to an old-fashioned conveyor belt. Nicholls imagined a line of disinterested employers assembling parts in the factory's hay day.

Just above his eyeline, Nicholls saw a second level with a perforated metal rail that circumvented the entire floor. At various points along the rail, there were an array of chain pulleys that allowed ground floor employers to lift heavy objects around the factory.

The bald Russian grunted and nodded to a set of stairs on the far side of the room. Nicholls could see an industrial light flickering noisily on the wall which illuminated several human shadows above them.

Nicholls was led up the stairs by the two Russians. There was only enough space for one person to ascend at a time, so the bald Russian took the lead and the one with the flattened nose fell in behind the policeman. As they stepped out on to the second level, Nicholls saw a huge figure sitting in a black leather chair that looked incongruously out of touch with the dilapidated surroundings. He was flanked on each side by a row of large men wearing matching grey suits. Ivankov.

As they drew closer, Nicholls could see that Ivankov was an absolute bear of a man. He was perched dangerously on the front of the chair with his huge elbows resting on his knees and his hands pressed together in the shape of a dagger. It looked like he was poised to strike at any moment. He was wearing a long, black trench coat that almost reached down to his ankles and his face was an indignant red to reflect his angry mood. His lips were pursed, and his eyes were dark and malevolent. Sitting next to him, like an obedient lap dog was his accountant, Tony Sykes. His eyes widened in terror as he recognised Nicholls.

"Ahh, Detective Inspector Nicholls," said Ivankov in near perfect English. "I wish I could say that it was nice to meet you, but unfortunately you have interrupted my lunch at the Ritz with two beautiful brunettes." His face was expressionless, but his voice was dripping with malice.

One of the Russians pulled on Nicholls' shirt to get him to stop. He could feel the eyes of Ivankov's bodyguards, bearing down on him as he straightened up.

"Mr Ivankov. It is good of you to accommodate me," he said respectfully.

"Be that as it may, Mr Nicholls. You should be dead by now. The only reason that you're not, is because you have a rather compromising photo of me with the commissioner of the Met police force."

"That is correct," said Nicholls.

"Would you mind informing me where you got it?"

Nicholls felt oddly powerful. He had no doubt that all the men in the room were trained killers, but he was not afraid in the slightest. "My mother was murdered," he said stoically. "I followed the men that killed her, and it led me to you and Flack."

McGovern sighed and recoiled in his chair. "Fine police work, I must say young man. Perhaps my colleague here, Mr Bircham has underestimated you." Nicholls glanced quickly at the detective. He looked nervous and bowed his head to avoid making eye contact.

"But that doesn't explain how you know so much about our plans with Secure8." His tone was slowly becoming more menacing. He opened his mouth wider to smile and his gold tooth glinted in the light.

"Your accountant told me," he said quietly.

Sykes jumped out of the chair as if he had been electrocuted. "It's a lie," he hissed venomously. "Kill the bastard now."

Nicholls laughed. "Come on now, Tony. There's no need to be like that. You told us about all of Sergei's secret accounts and offshore companies."

Ivankov grimaced and his jaw clenched tightly. He looked like he was about to explode. The mask is about to come off thought Nicholls ominously.

"Thanks to Sykes, we've now got a list of all your money laundering accounts in Cyprus, Sergei."

An explosion of movement. "Enough," thundered Ivankov, rising to his feet. He pointed a huge finger at Sykes. "What have you done?" he growled angrily. The unexpected noise caused a flock of pigeons to flutter nervously above them.

Tony Sykes looked petrified. His head darted across the landing as he scanned quickly for an escape route. Ivankov took a step towards him and one of his bodyguards closed the space behind Sykes to cut him off. The accountant's face drained of colour, and he went as white as a sheet. Nicholls could see him shaking with fear as if an electric current was resonating through his body.

Sykes cowered in front of the colossal figure of Ivankov and he held out his hands nervously in supplication. "They had a gun at my head, Sergei," he screamed.

"You work for me, you gutless bastard," boomed Ivankov. The force of his words seemed to propel Sykes backward against the metal rail.

"I'm sorry, Sergei," he whined pathetically. "It won't happen again. I should have told you straight away."

Ivankov stopped a few inches away from the accountant and grabbed hold of the lapels of his suit. Sykes was almost on his knees at this point, so Ivankov had to stoop to get a good grip. It looked oddly comical. The enormous Russian bent over the diminutive accountant like he was nothing more than a rag doll.

"All I asked for was for a bit of loyalty, Tony." Ivankov lifted him up and patted his cheek like a parent affectionately admonishing a small child.

Sykes sensed a reprieve. "Of course, Sergei," he said obediently. "I'm your man. I swear it."

"Now if anyone puts a gun to your head again and asks you to betray me, what do you think you should do, Tony?"

Sykes looked puzzled. "I'm not sure what you—" Sergei smacked him hard across the face, before he had time to answer.

"You tell them to pull the fucking trigger, arsehole. That's what you say, because you're better off dead, than betraying me."

Ivankov took hold of both lapels with each hand and raised the screaming accountant into the air.

"**NO, PLEASE,**" yelped Sykes pitifully.

Ivankov shook his head callously and threw the accountant powerfully over the rail. Sykes frantically tried to grasp at something to hold, but his hands could only clutch at thin air. Nicholls was blindsided so he didn't see him fall, but he heard a cacophony of high-pitched yelping sounds that were soon silenced by a sickening thud, as his body crashed on to the concrete floor below.

Ivankov wiped his hands together and peered over the rail. He grunted with approval at the sight below, before turning his attention back to Nicholls.

"I must thank you, Mr Nicholls. I am always keen to find out about the loyalty of the people who work for me. It is a shame Mr Sykes was not a braver man because he was a damn good accountant." Ivankov sighed. "He will be difficult to replace."

Nicholls didn't respond. Ivankov's anger seemed to have dissipated as quickly as it had appeared. He was very similar to his brother in that respect.

"Now, you must tell me, who you are working with and where I can find this recording you have made together?"

Nicholls shook his head stubbornly.

Ivankov smiled. "I can see you are brave Mr Nicholls. I admire that. Perhaps if you tell me, I will not kill you or your accomplice."

Nicholls sensed movement to the side of him and he saw Bircham straighten uncomfortably. Keeping Nicholls alive was clearly not part of his orders, but there was no way he could counteract whatever Ivankov planned.

"Come now, Mr Nicholls. I could use a man with your integrity to come and work for me. It is just business. You can make a new life for yourself in another country away from all this unpleasantness. How does America sound?" Ivankov opened his huge hands as if he was the CEO of international company with a legitimate offer for Nicholls to consider.

"I'm not going to betray my family," replied Nicholls.

Ivankov shook his head and his face feigned sadness. "That is unfortunate, Mr Nicholls. I was hoping it wouldn't have to come to this, you know."

Ivankov swept his arm in the direction of his bodyguards. "If you do not talk, then I will reluctantly have to ask my men to loosen your tongue." He moved over to a small table beside his chair, that Nicholls hadn't noticed before. It had a grubby sheet on top that Ivankov pulled off to reveal a collection of knives and rusty tools underneath.

"Believe me when I say that my men are very good at making people talk,

Mr Nicholls," said Ivankov casually. "Of course, some people talk sooner than others, but the end result is always the same."

Nicholls looked up into the darkness above him and took a long, slow breath of air. He could feel the adrenaline pulsating through his veins, but he wasn't afraid in the slightest. Ivankov was one of the most notorious and ferocious gangsters in the world, and he was just about to have him tortured. He should have been terrified, but he wasn't.

"Sergei, I'm afraid to say that you have a bit of a problem," said Nicholls slowly and clearly.

Ivankov picked up a huge knife and raised his eyebrow with mock curiosity, before running his finger playfully over the edge. "Oh, do I Mr Nicholls? Would you care to elaborate?"

"Sykes's laptop and briefcase actually revealed quite a lot more than we thought it would."

Ivankov hesitated. His eyes narrowed and his brow furrowed. I've hit a nerve thought Nicholls.

"We found evidence of your culpability in a number of offences including fraud, terrorism, election rigging and drug smuggling—just to name but a few."

Ivankov's face turned pale and there was a real glint of visceral hatred directed at Nicholls, before his lips curled into a massive grin and he started to laugh. It was a booming laugh that seemed to reverberate around the entire factory.

"So what, Mr Nicholls? I have never claimed to be a boy scout." The tone was thick with derision. "Do you intend to try and blackmail me now?"

Nicholls shook his head firmly. "Of course not. We both know that you have diplomatic status in this country which absolves you from criminal prosecutions here."

Ivankov looked impatient. "Then get to your point."

"You were protected by the Kremlin, Sergei," said Nicholls slowly and deliberately. "However, that all changed when we communicated with Moscow to inform them of some of your other transgressions."

Ivankov shot a withering look at Nicholls. "What other transgressions?"

"The fact that you were siphoning off funds from some of your Russian investors into a secret account that is owned by one Dimitri Vusilev."

Ivankov suddenly looked shell shocked at the mention of the name, and he rocked back slightly as if he had been hit by an invisible force.

"Documentation in the briefcase proves that you are Vusilev, Sergei."

"I have many accounts, Mr Nicholls. Sykes was in charge of my finances. I didn't know about them all," he said hurriedly.

"Unfortunately, Moscow didn't agree with that claim. They came to the same conclusion as us." Nicholls paused to let his words hit home. "You were stealing from them."

Ivankov shuffled backwards and leant back on his armchair for support. His face was conspicuous with worry.

Nicholls moved over to the disconsolate Russian. No-one tried to stop him. "They've thrown you to the wolves, Sergei," he whispered. "Your diplomatic status has been revoked and you are now facing criminal charges back home."

Ivankov punched the table next to him so hard that many of the torture instruments jumped into the air like they were performing puppets.

Nicholls sensed his weakness and moved in for the coup de grace. "Unfortunately, you won't be going home, Sergei. The British Home Office yesterday made a deal with the Americans to extradite you to the US to face charges over there, ranging from drug smuggling to terrorism."

Ivankov laughed half-heartedly and waved a finger. "You're bluffing you bastard. You think that I can be arrested like a common criminal?"

Nicholls shook his head defiantly. "Afraid not, Sergei."

Ivankov's face went a beetroot red, and spittle began to bubble on his lips. "Kill this son of a bitch," he growled to his nearest bodyguard.

The man next to him was squat and muscular with half of his right ear lobe missing. He didn't move. Ivankov grabbed him by the collar of his suit. "Did you not hear me?" he shouted desperately.

"They don't work for you anymore, Sergei," said Nicholls triumphantly. "They've been told to assist the authorities with your apprehension. It's over for you, I'm afraid."

All of a sudden there was a rumbling sound outside as a tidal wave of roaring engines came to a screeching halt. Doors hurriedly opened and then slammed shut as a crescendo of footsteps hammered on the worn tarmac like a heavy rainstorm.

Ivankov pushed his bodyguard away and stared disbelievingly at the entrance of the factory, as a pack of masked men poured through the opening and pointed their firearms at the balcony above them. Nicholls glanced at Bircham and smiled. His eyes were wide with fear. I hope the bastard shits himself, thought

Nicholls.

Kevin Page strode confidently through the flanks of armed men. He was wearing a bullet proof vest that was emblazoned with the initials of the National Crime Agency. He had a battered megaphone pressed against his mouth.

"Sergei Ivankov," he said calmly and clearly. The words reverberated around the factory. "You are under arrest. We are here to take you into custody."

Ivankov shook his head. His face had turned grey, like the scales of a dying fish. "No, no, no," he said hesitantly. "I am a foreign diplomat. You have no right to arrest me."

Page stepped forward. "I'm afraid your diplomatic status has been revoked. You are facing criminal charges. Come down now please, sir. There is no way for you to escape."

Ivankov growled and his head sank slowly in resignation until it came to a rest on the top bar of the railing. He was gripping the metal that tightly that his hands had bleached white, and the entire railing was shaking.

He looked up at Nicholls. There was a savage ferocity in his eyes. "You set me up, you bastard," he hissed. "I'll cut your eyes out." He grabbed a rusty knife from the table and pointed it at the policeman.

Nicholls instinctively stepped backwards as Ivankov lurched forwards. In an instant, the bodyguard with half an ear had grabbed Ivankov's wrist and another one skilfully threw the Russian onto the floor, so the weapon spilled from his grip. Before he even had time to comprehend what was going on, two men leaped forward and dropped on to Ivankov's back with their knees and tied up his hands, so he was trussed up like a turkey on Christmas day.

Ivankov was then bundled unceremoniously down the steps towards the officers. Nicholls motioned for Bircham to follow, and he obediently bowed his head and shuffled reluctantly behind the Russian. The two bodyguards lifted their former boss onto his knees to face the diminutive Page, as if he was a prisoner awaiting the executioner's block.

Page brushed a strand of whispery grey hair into a clump of matted gel at the top of his hairline and puffed out his chest. "You are going to America, Sergei to face charges over there," he said sternly. Ivankov didn't respond but stared defiantly at Page.

"We are taking you to the airport, where we will be met by US army personnel. They will put you on a plane. As soon as you set foot on US soil, you'll be formally arrested and taken to prison where you will stay, until your trial."

Ivankov bristled. "You have no idea, who the fuck you're dealing with. When I get out, I will track you down and make you pay for this."

Page smiled, which seemed to infuriate Ivankov even more. "I'm sure in the past that threat would've have carried a lot of weight. But I'm afraid that is no longer the case anymore. You're done, Sergei." He nodded towards some of the officers that were nearest to him, who lifted the Russian up and started to drag him out of the factory.

"No, please," begged Ivankov pitifully. "Do not take me to America. I will come and work for you. I have information that you can use for leverage against the Russian government."

Page looked at Ivankov coldly. "The decision has already been made, Sergei. I'm afraid it is beyond my pay grade to reverse that now. Take him away."

Ivankov screamed as he was dragged away and thrown into the back of a truck.

Page turned his attention towards Bircham, who was trembling in the corner like a leaf. "Ahh, detective Bircham," he said gleefully. "Thank you very much for the information you've given us on police corruption in the Met. Taped conversations can be very persuasive in court."

Bircham didn't say anything, but his face turned even whiter as he processed the ramifications of what was happening. Conspiracy to murder. Drug Dealing. Fraud. Corruption in a public office. He would be going to prison for the rest of his life, unless he could cut a deal.

Page looked over at one of the masked men. "Anyway Daniel, while you are stewing about your fate, there is someone I do need to introduce to you."

Right on cue, the masked man stood up and secured his firearm. He slowly made his way over to Bircham. The man got to within a metre of the cowering policeman, before he bent down and whipped off his mask.

"**BOO!**" Kane shouted forcing his face into the policeman's eye line. Bircham flinched as if he had been punched and he buried his head in his hands.

"Do you not recognise me, you piece of shit?" laughed Kane.

Bircham squinted. He knew the face in front of him, but it didn't make sense. It was the face of Nicholls, yet he was standing conspicuously next to him.

Kane stood up and moved next to his brother. "You killed our mother," he hissed. "It's time for you to pay for your sins."

Bircham stared at the two men. They were the mirror image of each other. It took him a few breaths to figure it out and then the thunderbolt that struck, left him dumfounded in a mixture of disbelief and terror. A flashback of two small twin brothers crying as he drove their mother away to her murderers, appeared in his mind's eye. All of those years ago and now they were back together. He felt the strength in his muscles evaporate, and he was violently sick just before he passed out.

"I must say Jimmy, your performance was worthy of an Oscar," said Page slapping Nicholls playfully on the back. Nicholls looked at his brother and there was a huge smile on his face. The three men had moved away from the main group of agency officers to talk.

"Are you kidding me?" yelped Nicholls. "I nearly crapped myself when those Russian goons put my arm in that suicide machine. I thought I was dead for sure."

"It was all an act," laughed Page. "They had been told by Moscow to do whatever we wanted them to do. They set up Bircham and Jenny like kippers in our little stage play. We've got Bircham's confession on tape and we were able to trap Ivankov here like a rat, out of public view."

"It was just a shame we couldn't get Flack here as well," said Kane quietly. "Then we could have finished it once and for all."

"He's finished now Ivankov's been arrested," replied Page grimly. "His base of support has gone. You can end it all tonight and finally take back what he stole from you."

Kane nodded. "We will head over to meet him when this mess has been cleaned up."

Page nodded. "Remember, it must look natural," he said warningly. "There can't be any suspicions of foul play."

"Don't worry about that. I've got it all planned." Kane looked insulted. He plucked out a syringe from his jacket pocket. "I got this little bad boy from the Russians," he said proudly. "It's a nerve agent. Once I inject this into him, it will make him feel like he's been boiled alive. It will take him several minutes to die, but by the next morning, all traces of the poison will have disappeared. The coroner will think the bastard has just had a heart attack."

Nicholls grimaced. The thought of killing Flack in such a manner was unpalatable but he certainly deserved to suffer for everything he had done. Of that there was no doubt, but whether the old man's death would bring the family closure, was another matter altogether.

"What about Bircham?" he asked Page, looking at the overweight policeman who was still sprawled on the floor.

"We have no further use for that son of a bitch," said Page. "He is the bent copper that the authorities are after. His taped confession is all the evidence we need to pin everything on his shoulders. He's yours to dispose with as you please."

Kane didn't need a second invitation. As soon as Page had finished speaking, he retrieved a bucket by the wall that was filled with foul smelling water and hurled it over Bircham. The policeman stirred slightly, which prompted Kane to kick him hard in his ample midriff. The blow forced Bircham to come spluttering to his knees.

Bircham held out an arm in supplication and coughed up some phlegm as he staggered unsteadily to his feet.

"Alright, you've got me," he wheezed. "I admit everything. If you cut me a deal, I'll tell you everything you want to know." Bircham seemed unsure who to direct his request to, and his gaze flitted from Kane to Nicholls and then to Page.

"I can help you nail Flack and all the other bent coppers in the Met." There was a hint of desperation in his voice. "I want witness protection for me and my family mind…"

"We know everything already, Detective," interrupted Kane, who was seemingly preoccupied with a rusty metal chain that was attached to the wall via a pulley system. "What else can you possibly offer us?

Bircham looked almost offended. "But I know everything about Flack's criminal empire and how it works. I would be the star witness in your case."

Kane moved slowly around the overweight policeman like a shark circling his prey. "Where would the justice be in that? You get to live the rest of your life in comfort with your family. That doesn't seem to be a fair trade in my mind."

"That is how the criminal justice system works," pleaded Bircham. "I was just following Flack's orders. He is the kingpin you need to bring down and I can help you do that."

"I'm afraid there is nothing left of your soul to sell, you bastard," laughed Kane. His arms flashed quickly, and he wrapped part of the chain tightly around Bircham's neck. As the policeman desperately struggled to remove the metallic noose, Kane pulled the other end of the chain deftly, causing Bircham to rise to his tiptoes.

"Please, Jimmy," gasped Bircham as the chain slowly constricted his air supply. He turned frantically towards Nicholls. His face was beginning to turn a livid blue colour and his eyes were bulging and twitching uncontrollably.

Nicholls looked Bircham squarely in the eyes and registered the horror that had consumed him as he realised his life was about to end. "Did my mother beg for her life too?"

"No, Jimmy. Please don't…" Kane yanked hard on the chain, cutting off the words on Bircham's tongue. He then grasped the chain with both hands and yanked down forcefully, causing Bircham to lift slowly into the air. He was grotesquely obese and must have weighed a lot, but Kane made the exertion look almost effortless.

"Time to dance, fat boy," jeered Kane as he wrapped the chain deftly around a hook on the wall. Bircham's legs twitched as if he was trying to climb an invisible ladder and his choking sounds became more guttural. All of a sudden, there was a splashing sound that was quickly followed by a nauseating smell. Bircham had lost control of his anal sphincter.

Nicholls turned away in disgust. He had seen enough. He walked out of the factory and into the fading afternoon light. It was some time before Kane and Page appeared. Presumably, they had disposed of the body.

"One more to go, Jimmy boy," said Kane, patting his brother on the back.

Chapter 12
The Scorpion's Sting

Daniel Flack reclined on his cashmere sofa and stared thoughtfully at the many paintings that adorned the walls in his lounge. It was to all extents and purposes a traditional living room that was decorated with two imposing chandeliers, tufted settees and heavy swag curtains. Flack was an avid reader of literature and either side of the enormous fireplace, were two impressive oak bookcases that climbed majestically all the way to the top of the ceiling.

It was one o'clock in the morning, but Flack was still wearing the royal blue suit that he had worn all day. Sleep was not a pre-requisite for him to function effectively. Sometimes he would drift off on his armchair for a couple of hours and that was quite sufficient for him to cope with the demands of the day ahead. He did not like to waste any more time than was absolutely necessary, in his bed.

On the small wooden table, next to the arm rest, was a leather satchel and a tumbler that was half full of brandy. The decanter beside the glass was nearly empty of the amber liquid.

"I know you're there," he said loudly in the direction of the open door that led to the corridor. "I have hidden cameras at the back of my garden. You activated the motion sensors when you came through about an hour ago."

There was no reply.

"Oh, come on," he growled angrily. "I am an old man. I am no threat to you now. I just want to talk."

There was some hesitant shuffling coming from the corridor. Flack stood up as if he was about to greet a guest. Almost on cue, Nicholls and Kane walked sheepishly into the lounge. They were both wearing a dark jumper, combat trousers and boots. Kane looked furious that Flack had somehow pre-empted their arrival.

If Flack was surprised to see the two brothers in his house at this ungodly hour, he certainly didn't show it. His face retained the mask of affability that he had used all his life. There was even an ironic smile forming at the corner of his mouth.

"Ah, Jimmy and John. Re-united at long last. I must say this is a sight to warm the cockles of your heart," he said cheerfully. "Please come and have a seat and enjoy a drink with me."

Kane bristled with conspicuous annoyance. "We'd rather stand, thank you."

Flack shrugged his shoulders. "Suit yourself. I'm afraid though that I'm going to have sit down. Arthritis in my knees you see." He pointed sadly at his legs to illustrate his point.

"You said you were expecting us?" enquired Nicholls.

"I wasn't expecting YOU per se," laughed Flack. "I knew the government would send someone out to deal with me. It is a pleasant surprise to find that death is wearing a familiar face though."

"How did you know we were coming?"

"I could sense it, my boy," said Flack calmly. "When the NCA took over the McGovern case, I knew something was wrong. Now, I can't get hold of Ivankov, or Bircham either. I do not believe in coincidence, I'm afraid. It means my time is coming up very shortly."

"It's no more than you deserve, you son of a bitch," growled Kane.

Flack pursed his lips to make him look regretful. "I don't deny it, John. I deserve to die a thousand times over for what I did to you and your family. There are dozens of others as well that would gratefully take their vengeance for what I have done to them. I know the government can't afford to have me arrested and have a public trial. Think of the outrage. The Commissioner of the Met being tried for corruption, murder and drug dealing. The scandal would be too much for the country to take."

He drained the last of the brandy and wiped his face with a napkin from his jacket pocket. "No, I knew they would try and dispose of me quietly, without any fuss. That is what I would have done if I was in their place."

Kane reached into his pocket and pulled out the syringe containing the nerve agent. "You are very astute. This is what we are going to use to finish the job. It will give you the agonising death that you truly deserve you bastard."

Flack nodded his head in acknowledgment and an exaggerated expression of disgust appeared on his face. "Before you do me in, please humour me and tell me how you found each other."

"John found me," said Nicholls forcefully. "He told me about your criminal empire with McGovern and how you had my mother killed because she threatened to expose you. I can't believe I trusted you and looked up to you. You deserve to rot in jail for everything you've done'." Nicholls felt the bile rising in his throat as he struggled to contain his emotions.

"It's all true I'm afraid, Jimmy. I won't make any excuses. I wanted wealth and power and I wasn't at all bothered about how I got them."

Nicholls felt the anger rising within him. "Then tell me why you groomed me to be a police officer?" He shouted. "You must have known who I was. Christ, you even set me up with your daughter." Nicholls was almost incandescent with rage and Kane placed a hand on his shoulder to try and calm him.

"I liked your mother a lot," said Flack quietly. "I genuinely did. It broke my heart when McGovern decided to kill her. She was a clever woman. I think she knew what was going to happen to her. That's why she told me that I was your father."

The words exploded in the room like a grenade. Nicholls took an instinctive step back and looked at Kane. Neither of them knew what to say. The surprise on Kane's face was evidence enough that even he had been overwhelmed by the incredible revelation too.

Flack looked at the men and began to chuckle. "Don't worry. I can see the shock on your faces. It is not true. I think your mother told me that in the hope that it would save her life. I ignored her and pushed the thought to the back of my mind. However, it just wouldn't stay there. As the years went by, I just had to find out whether she was telling the truth.

That's why I found you, Jimmy. I needed to know whether you were my son or not." He looked at Kane. "I kept tracks of you too, John, right up until you joined the army"

Flack sighed. "Jimmy, you were a really bright kid. I must admit that I liked you. I got hold of your hairbrush when you were a teenager, and I got a DNA test done. I was disappointed when the results came back, and they showed that we weren't related. Nonetheless I still had a half-baked idea to mould you into my protégé. Can you believe that?" Flack started to laugh.

"Of course, I realised pretty quickly that you were far too principled and good to ever do anything dishonest, so that was never going to work."

"Yet you were still prepared to set me up and have me murdered as a scapegoat for your crimes," said Nicholls venomously.

"You were my insurance policy," Jimmy. You can't win a game of chess without sacrificing a few pieces along the way. It was purely business my boy. It doesn't mean I didn't like you."

"You're psychotic," growled Nicholls angrily. "You've betrayed everything the police stand for."

"Like I said, you have every right to want revenge. Why don't you take it now?" Flack held his arms aloft and spread them wide to emphasise his vulnerability. "You had a sister too, didn't you? What ever happened to her?"

Kane sneered. "She killed McGovern. He pissed himself just before he died. I wonder if you'll do the same?"

Flack ignored the threat. "And Ivankov?"

Kane laughed. "A deal was made with the Russians to give him up. He's currently on his way to spend the rest of his life in an American prison."

Flack smiled and clapped his hands. "Bravo. I must say, well played." The ageing commissioner took a few moments to digest the information. He looked thoughtful and scratched his silvery beard. "Now, I spoke to Bircham and Ivankov only this afternoon so you must have only just made your move? I presume Bircham is in prison or maybe even dead too?

"The latter," said Kane cheerfully.

"Well, that means that I am the final piece to the jigsaw. Once I am dead, then your revenge is complete." There was a hint of condescension in his tone. He even sounded strangely confident despite the threat of his imminent murder.

Flack sat down and looked at the empty decanter with conspicuous annoyance. "I can't even have a final drink," he said sadly. Kane seemed to take the comment as an invitation to make his move. He took a step towards the commissioner, like a shark slowly circling its prey. He waved the syringe sadistically at the old man, trying to scare him. "If you have any final words, now is the time to say them you evil bastard."

For a few moments, Flack sat as still as a statute as if he was resigned to his fate. He seemed determined not to show any fear at Kane's approach. Nicholls held his breath. He felt compelled to watch out of a sense of morbid curiosity, in the way that most people can't tear their eyes away from a car crash, no matter how gory. Kane was almost upon him when Flack stubbornly held out his hand like a policeman stopping traffic on a busy roadway. It was as if he had suddenly remembered something that might save his life.

"Now, there is just one thing John," he said confidently. Kane stopped in his tracks. "Now why don't you just sit down on the seat over there. I need to explain something to you. After that you can make a decision to kill me if you still wish to."

Kane stared at Flack coldly. For a second, Nicholls thought he was going to ignore him and plunge the syringe into the commissioner's unguarded neck. Instead, he briefly contemplated the request and decided there was nothing to lose in hearing Flack out. Kane shrugged his shoulders in barely concealed annoyance and sat down on the nearest armchair. "You've got five minutes," he said, pointedly looking at his wristwatch to emphasise the point.

Flack smiled like a bad poker player who couldn't hide his unbeatable hand. "Unfortunately for you, I do have an ace up my sleeve that I'm going to play."

"You need more than that you fucking bastard," scoffed Kane.

The grin on Flack's face grew, making Kane scowl.

"Some years ago, McGovern set up an army general with one of his prostitutes." Flack winked at Nicholls playfully. "As you know, these sexual encounters were filmed so they could be used to blackmail the participants. Now, this particular army general was into some pretty kinky stuff I can tell you. I won't go into the gory details, but he particularly enjoyed being whipped and having dildos shoved up his arse."

"What's this got to do with us?" snapped Kane impatiently.

"As you can imagine, the dumb fool was mortified when he saw the video. He came from quite an aristocratic family with a distinguished history, and he was terrified of the damage we could do to his reputation if we leaked the video." Flack paused to take a cigar out of his jacket pocket. He looked at Kane. "Do you mind if I have a smoke?"

When Kane didn't respond, Flack plucked out a lighter and lit the cigar. He took a deep draw and blew out a slivery whisp of smoke that matched his hair colour. "That's better," he said. "Now where were we? Ah yes, the army general. Anyway, how this chap was able to get into such a prominent position in charge of our country's defences was beyond me. Totally incompetent. We were only looking to try and secure a military contract for a private business friend but when I applied a bit of pressure, this guy spilled everything, and I mean everything."

"What do you mean everything?" asked Kane.

"He was so scared about the video being leaked that he gave up some rather compromising secrets about our involvement with the war in the Middle East," said Flack accusingly.

"What secrets are these?" interrupted Nicholls.

Flack raised his hand. "Patience, Jimmy. I will get to it in a minute. All I can say is that it is a bloody good thing that this general was not around during the Second World War. If he was, then my guess is that we'd all be speaking German now…"

"Enough," snarled Nicholls, rising to his feet angrily. Even though he was only a few metres away, his imposing figure still towered over Flack. "Stop your games now. What secrets are you talking about?"

"Temper, Jonathan," said Flack calmy. "I am getting to that." He took another long drag of the cigar as if to deliberately provoke Kane further. "Firstly, he gave up a transcript of a conversation between then then prime minister and the US secretary of state, in which they both discussed quite openly that there were never any weapons of mass destruction in Iraq and that the war in the middle east was purely about helping western oil companies to set up shop there."

Flack waited a few moments to let the enormity of the news sink in. The look of shock on the brothers' faces, said it all. This was sensational. The war in the middle east had polarised British society at the time and had been justified on the pretext that Iraq had weapons of mass destruction that could be used against the west, at any time.

"Are you serious?" asked Nicholls.

"I'm as serious as cancer," said Flack. "It's all in my briefcase." He pointed to the satchel on the table next to him. "And not only that, but I've also got proof of British war crimes in the middle east too. Wilful killing, torture, rape and the deliberate targeting of civilians during bombing raids." He tapped each finger to illustrate his point.

"You're lying," said Nicholls. "There's no way the government would be that stupid."

Flack shrugged his shoulders and tossed the briefcase to Nicholls, who held on to the satchel. like it contained a bomb. "Take it. I've got plenty of copies," he said casually.

Nicholls looked at his brother, who was still eyeing Flack malevolently. They were both clearly unsure what to do next.

"I'm not a politician," continued Flack, "but if the media were to get hold of these documents, it would provide them with the ammunition for one on the most explosive news stories in modern times. Who knows how the people in this country will react when they find out they've been lied to? What will happen in the middle east? Anything from open rebellion to a huge increase in terrorist activity, would be my guess. Anyway, there's no doubt that our soldiers out there would be in the firing line with huge targets painted on their back."

"Do you think you can blackmail us with this?" growled Kane.

"Oh, come on John," snapped Flack tiredly. "This goes above your own petty revenge mission. Did you honestly think I would not have taken measures to ensure my own protection? Ring up whichever government bigwig is in charge of this little operation and let them know about my deal?"

"Your deal?"

"I just want to retire," said Flack with a smile on his face. "I know the gig is up for me as Met Commissioner, but I want to live out the rest of my days on a nice little Caribbean island somewhere, without having to constantly look over my shoulder for government assassins coming to finish me off." He looked at Nicholls. "This deal would obviously have to apply to Jenny, as well. She's not to blame for my crimes."

"And if we say no?" said Kane, trying hard to suppress his rage.

"You can take your revenge right now, John." Flack's eyes narrowed and he met Kane's stare. "But if you do, then you need to know that I have left explicit instructions for my contacts in the media to publish these stories immediately. Can you imagine the shitstorm that would create?"

Kane laughed. "Do you think this is going to save you from your crimes?"

"Oh, you'd best believe I do," laughed Flack. "The life of one old man is not worth the threat to national security if this news leaks out. If you let me retire in peace, then I promise I will keep it all to myself."

"Your promises are worth nothing to us," replied Kane.

"That doesn't concern me. This is above your pay grade. Run along like a good little assassin and let your bosses know that I have the weapons of mass destruction now, and my finger is resting on the trigger." Flack turned away and dropped his cigar into the brandy glass.

Kane grimaced in impotent fury. He snatched the briefcase from his brother. "Don't let that bastard out of your sight," he hissed.

Kane swiftly disappeared out the door. Within moments, Nicholls and Flack could hear him speaking angrily on the phone.

"It sounds like your superiors are coming round to my point of view," laughed Flack arrogantly.

Nicholls felt something snap inside him "I trusted you," he said icily. "I looked up to you. Everything you said to me was a lie. You're nothing more than an inhuman monster. My brother will find a way to make you pay for your crimes."

"I doubt that, Jimmy," scoffed Flack. "The mistake that McGovern and Ivankov made was that they thought that they were indestructible. I made sure that I had a cast iron insurance policy if things went wrong."

"You're just a bent copper that got lucky," hissed Nicholls. "I don't know how you can live with yourself. I went to the Ritz with my brother. I saw some of the girls that had been trafficked to work in the sex trade. You made a deal with the devil, and I swear you'll have to answer for your crimes, soon enough."

"Wow, you really are naïve Jimmy," laughed Flack. "Sometimes a deal with the devil is better than no deal at all. I mean, look at me. I'm the Met commissioner. I had it all, power, status and wealth. Now I'm going to enjoy the fruits of my labour on a tropical island, sipping cocktails on the beach. Life has given me everything that I ever wanted."

"You became rich on the misery of others—"

"Now you listen to me, you sanctimonious little prick," interrupted Flack angrily. "There are only two types of people in this world, sheep and wolves. Most people are sheep. They're too scared to break the rules and they end up living miserable lives, devoid of any real worth. Wolves make the rules. They run where they want, they do what they want and they eat the fucking sheep, Jimmy. I'd rather be a wolf for a day than spend a lifetime as a sheep. What are you, son? You're a brilliant policeman. There's no denying that. But you'll always be a follower. You're not ruthless enough to make the rules and seize the day."

Nicholls turned away from Flack with a look of disgust etched on his face. "I would never ever want to be anything like you, you evil bastard. If you're a wolf, then I'm a sheep dog. My job is to protect people from predators like you. That's why I became a policeman."

Flack gave Nicholls a round of mock applause. "Beautifully said. Perhaps they should put that on your gravestone. I knew I was right about you all along. Perhaps I made the wrong decision on which brother to send away. Your brother has a bit of the devil inside him. He would've made a good wolf under my tutelage."

"He's nothing like you either," said Nicholls defensively. "He's got demons inside him. I'll give you that, but he knows how to chain them up. When John's demons are unshackled, nothing can stop him."

Flack gave a derisory smile and looked away. Nicholls looked at the doorway to see his brother standing there. He wasn't sure how long he'd been there. There was a look of unrestrained ferocity on his face and his eyes were glazed and distant. He was battling his demons thought Nicholls and the struggle to curb his natural instincts was taking a lot out of him.

There was a long silence. Flack's confidence seemed to drain away as he sensed the presence of something very raw and visceral, permeating the room. After what seemed like an eternity, Kane spoke.

"You need to stand down as commissioner for the Met immediately," said Kane coldly. "Then you need to disappear. No press conferences, no interviews. Just fuck off."

Flack chuckled and clapped his hands. "I knew it. My resignation letter is already in the briefcase. You don't have to worry about me. I've already booked my plane ticket to the Caribbean."

Kane marched over aggressively to the old man, which made Flack flinch instinctively. "This isn't over, you son of a bitch."

Flack remained in his seat and looked disinterested by the threat. He gently patted Kane's cheek with the palm of his hand. "Oh yes, it is, Johnny boy. You had your chance, and you blew it." He reached into his jacket pocket and pulled out a phone, which he pressed into Kane's hand. "This is a gesture of my good faith. We can't leave any loose ends now, can we?"

"What the fuck is this?" said Kane in disgust.

"Why it's my burner phone, Johnny. Something that every good bent copper needs."

"Why do we need it?" said Kane dismissively. "You have your deal."

"You can get in contact with all the corrupt policeman in our operation." There was a sly look in his eyes. "Perhaps you could pretend to be me and contact them on my profile. I'm sure you could get them all together and arrange a leaving party for me if you wanted to?"

Kane stood up slowly and quickly digested the information. "How will they know they're not being set up?"

"We use a software package that sends encrypted messages. Your analysts will be able to find it easily enough. My password is viper. Once you're on the platform, you can see how we coordinate our operations."

"Kilbride?" asked Nicholls.

"Yeah, he's on there too. I changed his name on my contacts so you can find that bastard easily. Say hello from me when you take him down, will you?"

Kane put the phone in his pocket. "This changes nothing. We will meet again Commissioner. You can count on it."

Flack shook his head. "I doubt that John. It was good to see you both again though. Send me your addresses and I'll forward you a postcard sometime."

Nicholls felt a terrible sense of injustice and anger surge through his body. They couldn't do anything to Flack, and he clearly knew it. "You're a monster of a human being," he said calmy. "I'm going to make it my personal mission to bring you down, so don't get too comfortable."

Nicholls didn't wait for a response. He grabbed his brother by the arm and they both walked out the front door, without looking back.

Jason Kilbride had an uneasy feeling in the pit of his stomach that he couldn't explain. He should've been feeling on top of the world. The polls showed that the conservatives were miles ahead in the election race and his star was continuing to rise. He had performed with aplomb in a televised debate that week and wherever he went, the public seemed to shower him with affection. But something was wrong. The leader of the party, Darren Healey who had privately named him as his successor had been decidedly cold and distant with him for a number of weeks. Kilbride got the impression that Healey was avoiding him for some reason. He put it down to his chemotherapy and the toll that the treatment must have been taking on his body, but something didn't feel right. He was being blindsided, but he couldn't for the life of him explain why.

And then there was the bizarre message that he had received that day from Flack, asking him to meet up urgently. Usually, they communicated by exchanging text messages on their encrypted phones but to actually meet up face to face was highly unusual and in Kilbride's mind, extremely risky. Why would they want to meet up when they were so close to achieving their goals and potentially jeopardise their plans? The obvious answer that kept jumping up in Kilbride's mind was that something had gone wrong, and it needed sorting urgently.

He checked his phone again. The tone of the message was short and curt, which was typical of the Met commissioner. He certainly didn't like to give much away. **Need to meet asap to discuss action plan. Come to WDCN 5EU at 1100. Knock three times on warehouse door. Code word is VIPER.**

Perhaps he was overthinking things. The meeting was inconvenient, and it meant he had to reschedule a number of tasks, but it didn't necessarily mean that something was wrong. With a bit of luck, it would be concluded quite quickly, and he could still meet up later that evening with the gorgeous redhead he was seeing at the moment. The thought of her waiting naked in his bed gave him a thrill and he instantly became aroused.

He was sitting in his silver Mercedes in a service station car park. It was half past four. The sky was a brilliant blue and the glow of the sun dispensed warm yellow waves that wafted in through the tinted windows. He was wearing sunglasses and a baseball hat, so people wouldn't recognise him. The sooner this meeting was over the better. He started the car, typed the postcode into the sat nav and pulled slowly onto the parkway.

"Where the fuck's Darnell?" the man said aggressively.

"He's been off sick," came the reply.

"That fucker is never sick. What's wrong with him, Smithy?"

"Dunno. I heard he needed an operation so won't be back for a while."

"Jesus! When are we doing our next job? I'm skint at the moment."

There was a hint of irritation in the older man's voice. "I'd imagine we're going to find out soon. Just relax, Clifford."

"I know, but my girlfriend's bleeding me dry. I need a payday like you wouldn't believe."

The older man, Smithy sighed. "You know the score. We were told to keep a low profile for a while. The boss wants to meet us here, so it looks like we'll be up and running again soon."

"I don't trust that fat bastard," the man scowled.

"It's not him that wants to meet us. It's the top man."

The younger man looked impressed. "Jesus Christ. If I'd known it was him coming, I would've shaved my arse!"

"It's definitely prettier than your face," laughed the older man.

The younger man smiled and punched the older man playfully in the arm. He took out a cigarette and sat down with the rest of his colleagues on the dust coated chairs in the back room.

The men were all part of the Special Command Firearms unit in the Met. Most of them were grizzled veterans who were all relaxed in each other's company. They conducted operations with a ruthless efficiency and were renowned throughout all of law enforcement for their no-nonsense approach. It would have come as a massive surprise to many that the unit was also totally corrupt. Operating under Flack's command they acted as a death squad to eliminate McGovern's criminal enemies and helped transport his lucrative drug shipments throughout the city. Each one of the men that was sitting in the old garage workshop had blood on their hands, and it didn't bother them in the slightest.

In a corner of the room, on an oil-soaked table a group of the officers played cards, whilst the rest of the men were quite content to sit on their own and entertain themselves. They had been told to wait and that was just what they would do.

All of a sudden there was a tentative knocking on the door. Instinctively, all of the men became alert and stopped what they were doing. Clifford, the most senior officer who had taken unofficial control of the unit as a result of Darnell's unexpected absence, stood up and walked over to the door to see who was there. The front entrance of the garage had a peeled hangar which was operated by a roller shutter. When it was unlocked it allowed the unit's large convey trucks to drive through, where they would be loaded with McGovern's drugs. Most of the time, just like it was now, the hangar was locked and the only way to access the garage was through a discreet wooden door on the side of the building.

"Who is it?" shouted Clifford.

"I've been told to come here," came the voice. "Password is viper."

"Ahh, the politician," said Clifford with more enthusiasm. "We were told to expect you."

He opened the door to see Kilbride standing nervously in front of him.

"Come in man," said Clifford impatiently, tugging on Kilbride's shirt.

Kilbride didn't need a second invitation. He felt exposed and vulnerable on the street. He walked through the door and took off his sunglasses. When the officers saw it was Kilbride, they went back to their own business. No-one acknowledged him.

"What's this all about?" asked Kilbride.

"Beat's me," said Clifford. "The guvnor told us to meet here and that's what we're doing."

Kilbride sighed. "I suppose we'll find out soon enough." He was just about to sit down, when the sound of an engine echoed around the room as a vehicle pulled up outside. Again, the men went into alert mode as someone turned off the engine and jumped out of the vehicle. The footsteps outside got louder, before they suddenly stopped behind the hangar.

Silence.

A loud, banging sound made Kilbride almost jump out of his skin and a couple of the officers reached for their firearms. Whoever was outside was kicking the hangar door hard.

"Hello. Anyone there?" came a loud voice with a distinctive Scottish accent.

"Who is it?" shouted Clifford.

"I've got a delivery for a D. Bircham," replied the voice. "Is he here?"

Clifford thought about his answer briefly. "Yeah, he's here. I can sign for it if you want?"

"Fantastic. Can you let me in?" said the courier.

"There's a door on the side of the building. Go over there and I'll open it for you," said Clifford.

Clifford put his gun away and opened the side door. He was slightly taken back by the size of the courier. He was a huge man with a chiselled jaw and raven black hair that was partially tucked under a baseball cap. His muscles protruded and bulged through the drab beige unform he wore.

"What is it? asked Clifford.

"No idea," laughed the courier brandishing a large parcel. "They don't tell us that. If you ask me, it feels like something mechanical. Could be for the garage, I suppose?

Clifford snatched the parcel impatiently and made an ambiguous scribble on the courier's electronic device. "That sounds about right. He's always ordering stuff without letting us know."

The courier smiled. "No problem, sir. Have a nice day." He turned away and climbed back into the transit van that was parked on the garage forecourt.

Clifford closed the door and went back into the room. No one seemed particularly interested in the delivery. Kilbride was sitting in the manager's office, looking at something on his phone. He stared to tear away at the tape on the front of the parcel. The cardboard flaps slowly popped open, and Clifford put his hand into the box. He felt something coarse and greasy. At first, he thought it was a hat but as he pulled the object out, he realised he was clutching human hair.

"Oh, my fucking god," screamed Clifford in abject horror, dropping the parcel.

The men in his unit jumped up in alarm. "What is it?" called out Smithy.

Clifford could barely speak. His face had drained of colour, and he was pointing a shaking finger at the parcel.

The younger man, Smithy took the initiative and approached the box. He reached inside and pulled out the object. "Jesus Christ. It's Bircham."

He slowly pulled out the policeman's head and held it aloft for all to see. His skin was covered in dark purple blotches and his tongue lolled out of his mouth. The eyes were a muddy brown colour, like an old, rotten apple and they had rolled to the back of the sockets. The ragged flesh at the base of his neck was dotted with clumps of dark, clotted blood where the head had been hacked off.

Kilbride stared at the head in disbelief. His stomach started to cramp, and he vomited over another officer's shoes.

Clifford slowly began to regain his senses. He looked around at the men in his unit. Their faces were pale and twisted with shock and disgust. He checked the parcel, but there was nothing else in there.

"There's something in his mouth," shouted one of the men.

Clifford moved over to Smithy to inspect the head. It was true. There was something there.

"I don't believe it," said Clifford. "It's a phone."

Almost as soon as the words had left his mouth, the phone started ringing. Smithy almost dropped the head in alarm.

"Take it out," he screamed.

"For fuck's sake man," shouted Clifford. "Hold still." He reached into Bircham's mouth and yanked out the phone, which had been secured with some kind of adhesive, so he also ripped away part of the man's lip as well.

He answered it. Silence.

"Who's this?" he said loudly, but his shaky voice betrayed his fear.

"Paul Clifford," replied the voice with the distinctive Scottish accent that they had heard just a few minutes ago.

"This is the courier, isn't it?" replied Clifford tentatively. "Who are you?"

"I am the punishment of God," said Kane loudly. "If you had not committed great sins, God would not have sent a punishment like me upon you."

"What the fuck are you talking about?"

Kane sneered. "You're all a bunch of bent coppers. For too long, you have gotten rich on the misery of others. Today is the day that you must face the consequences for the crimes you have committed."

"Listen here," stuttered Clifford. "Do not judge us by whatever Bircham has done. We're police officers doing our job."

Kane laughed. "Liars and murderers, the lot of you. You're the worst of all because you took an oath to protect people. In ancient Persia the punishment for corrupt officials was being skinned alive. I just wish that I could see the look on your faces, when you reap your rewards."

"Listen here you son of a bitch," shouted Clifford, as he finally managed to summon up some courage. "You have no idea who you're dealing with. You're a dead man. Can you hear me?"

"There is no force on earth that can save you now," replied Kane. "Kilbride. Can you hear me?"

Kilbride had edged himself towards the corner of the room. Upon hearing his name, he stopped dead in his tracks. He shook his head in disbelief.

"Jason Kilbride. I know you're there," said Kane assuredly. "Answer me, you bastard"

"What do you want with me?" said Kilbride timidly.

"You think you're going to be the next prime minister, don't you?"

"I'm not going to discuss politics with you."

Kane started to laugh again. "I wanted to be the one to tell you that that will never every happen. You've been played you son of a bitch."

Kilbride, flushed with anger. "What the hell are you talking about?"

"Healey's illness has all been a ruse. It was a ploy to bring the real criminals out into the open so we could find out what they were planning and bring them down."

"I have no idea what you're talking about?" said Kilbride defensively.

"Yes, you do," replied Kane. "You're just a puppet for McGovern and Flack, you stupid bastard. When you murdered that prostitute all those years ago, they made you work for them. They thought they could make you the prime minister, didn't they?"

"You're making some very serious allegations," said Kilbride. "I hope you have some proof to back it up."

"Oh, I have plenty of proof, Jason. Don't you worry about that. Do you want to see it?"

Kilbride stared at the other officers for support. They stood as still as statues, unwilling to meet his gaze. He shook his head, unsure how to respond. "Go on then. Show me what you've got."

"Do you see the black tool-box in the corner of the room?"

Kilbride looked up. He saw the toolbox immediately. "Yeah. What of it?"

"Go over to it and open the bottom compartment," came the instruction.

Kilbride reluctantly moved towards the toolbox. The bottom compartment was stiff, but he managed to prise it open. In front of him were two framed photographs. One of them was of a pretty, twenty something lady with auburn hair and milky skin. The other was of a young man with a youthful complexion and hopeful eyes.

"Who are these people? Am I supposed to know them?" asked Kilbride.

"The woman is my mother," said Kane bitterly. "She was murdered by McGovern because she wanted you to face justice over the death of the prostitute."

Kilbride felt as if someone had just stabbed him in the stomach. "Jesus Christ. Who gave you this information?"

Kane ignored him. "The man is—"

"Fucking hell," interrupted Clifford, looking over Kilbride's shoulder. He had gone as white as a sheet. "That's Jack Marsden."

"Their blood is on your hands," said Kane. "All of the victims of your crimes are here to see justice being served."

"What do you mean?" replied Kilbride.

"Look behind the photos," said Kane softly.

Kilbride did as he was asked. His eyes were drawn to the flashing numbers on the small plastic device that was wedged tightly at the base of the drawer. For a split second he didn't know what it was.

He glanced quickly at Clifford. His mouth was agape, and it looked like he was screaming, but there was no sound. A group of officers were frantically trying to pull open the door, but it was locked from the outside.

He picked up the photograph of the young woman. He knew the face but for the life of him, he couldn't remember her name.

There was a flash of intense light, and then nothing more.

Six Months Later

Sitting around the table in the discreet but luxurious townhouse on the outskirts of the city were Jimmy Nicholls, John Kane, Holly Kane and Kevin Page. The table in front of them contained the remains of a Chinese takeaway that had been almost totally devoured by the group. Kane and Nicholls were both drinking bottles of beer, whilst Holly and Page had chosen Coca-Cola as their preferred beverage.

No-one spoke. Nicholls noted how they all seemed to look exhausted—that was everyone apart from his brother, who always seemed to radiate an aura of insatiable energy. They all had their eyes glued on the television screen that was fixed above their heads. The new prime minister, Darren Healey, was coming on to give a hotly anticipated press conference.

The news reporter on the screen suddenly pressed his fingers to his ears as he received confirmation that the PM was ready, and he excitedly announced his arrival as Healey calmly walked on to the modest wooden platform in the Downing Street press office.

Healey looked as strong as a bullock. The rumours about his ailing health that had been whispered around political circles before the election, had now all evaporated like the early morning mist on a summer's day. As expected, the conservatives had won in a landslide, and Healey had become the next prime minister. In the first few months of his term, he announced some sweeping reforms to revolutionise welfare and education provision in deprived areas, which gained considerable public approval and alarmed a lot of the staunch conservatives in his party.

Over the next few months, parliament was rocked to the core as many notable politicians resigned unexpectedly. Rumour had it that most of these individuals had met with Healey only the day before they penned their resignation letter. Healey was adamant that these MPs had done so on their own volition, but he was unable to stop the rumours circulating that they had been pushed out.

As a consequence of these upheavals, parliament was decidedly disjointed for a period as new faces came in to replace the leaving MPs. Healey soon gained the nickname 'the tinkerman' by the media as he seemed to constantly be reshuffling and appointing new ministers in his government.

Healey was dressed immaculately in a black, Brioni suit with a white shirt and a navy-blue tie. He had a sombre look on his face as he faced the cameras.

"It is difficult to believe that it is over half a year since the explosion that killed Jason Kilbride and an entire unit of brave policemen, while they were on an operation to bring down an organised criminal syndicate." Kilbride's voice seemed to crackle with emotion, and he paused to wipe a tear from his eye with a grey handkerchief from his top pocket.

"He's a good actor," said Kane with a smirk on his face.

"Jason was my friend, and he would have been an excellent Home Secretary for the country," continued Healey.

"We must honour him and the others that sacrificed their lives in the line of duty by continuing to fight for our streets." Healey clenched his hand into a fist and shook it at the cameras. "We cannot and must not let the criminals win," he shouted passionately.

"We must be tough on crime and tough on the causes of crime if we are going to repair our country and take it back from the criminal gangs. It is imperative that we show criminals that crime does not pay and there are consequences for their actions."

There was a quiet ripple of applause from a number of journalists as Healey spoke. He looked up and gave them a grim nod.

"But we also must do more to make the country more equal by giving people in deprived areas goals and dreams for the future. My government promises here and now to spend more money on closing the educational gap between rich and poor and provide more opportunities for young people to get on the career ladder and learn a trade. And if a young person does make the wrong choices, then we will not throw that young person on the scrapheap for the rest of their life and consign them to a career of crime. Prisons will get more funding for rehabilitation. There will be opportunities for every prisoner to get clean of drugs and alcohol and gain qualifications to allow them to get a job when they get out."

Healey paused to take a drink of water. The ripples of applause were slowly becoming louder.

"In the short term, I am going to increase funding to the police. In sixth months, there will be over twenty thousand new police officers on our streets. But these new recruits will be trained differently to other police officers. Tackling crime is a responsibility for the whole community. For too long, relationships between police officers and the communities they serve, has been too strained. Police forces and their officers need to be trained to build better relationships with their communities, if they are to receive their support. That is what Jason would have wanted and these policies will be his legacy."

Healey looked beyond the stage and smiled. "I would now like to invite the Home Secretary to come up and outline these proposals in more detail. You've heard quite enough from me for the time being."

Healey welcomed the Home Secretary with a warm handshake before he quickly left the podium to a loud round of applause.

"I must say," said Kane swigging greedily from his bottle of beer. "He's a charismatic old devil. You have to give that."

Page nodded his head in agreement. "And a damn fine politician too. He knows what the public wants."

For the first time in a long while, Nicholls felt at ease. They had all done what they had set out to do, even though there was a gnawing anger that Flack had evaded justice. They had almost single-handedly destroyed the organised crime network in the capital and dealt a hammer blow to police corruption in the Met. It was an incredible achievement—something to be really proud of.

Nicholls was quite content to let Page and Kane talk. He held Holly's hand tenderly under the table. That was enough for him.

In next to no time at all, there was a loud knock on the door and in walked the prime minister. Nicholls looked at his watch. The press conference had been live. He had certainly wasted no time in getting here. His driver must have seriously put their foot down.

"Have you scoundrels left any beers for me?" he said with a smile on his face.

Kane casually reached into the crate under the table and tossed a bottle to the prime minister.

Healy took a look at the TV and scowled. His press conference was being dissected by the news media, who had a picture of Kilbride on the screen.

"Please turn that off," he said. "The sight of that bastard makes me feel quite ill."

Page and Kane nodded in agreement. "It was a sound move politically to turn him into a martyr, but that son of a bitch shouldn't be remembered as a hero."

Healey sat down on the chair next to Nicholls and crossed his legs. "It irks me too like you wouldn't believe, but we used his death to galvanise our campaign. The damage would have been catastrophic if the truth had come out. We just have to hope he is getting his just deserts in hell, I'm afraid."

Healey took a long drink from the beer. "Let's forget about them all and look forward to the future."

"Here, here," said Page.

"You all have done an amazing job for your country," said Healey. "When John came and told me about what had happened to him and his family, I could scarcely believe it. We quickly learned how organised criminals and corrupt police officers were pulling all the strings." Healey shook his head with disgust. "But against all the odds, you brought down the bastards." He smiled and bowed his head respectfully to them all individually, in acknowledgment of their efforts.

"We have a new chance to build a stronger society. Of course, it will not be easy, but you have given us a real opportunity to do that. No-one but a select few, will ever know about what you have done and for that I am sorry."

"There are victories whose glories lie in the fact that they are known only to those that win them," said Kane softly.

"Ahh, Nelson Mandela, if I am not mistaken," replied Healey. "He used his battles against the Afrikaan guards on Robben island to maintain his resolve."

"You are very wise, sir," laughed Kane.

"And you never cease to surprise me either, John," said Healey with a smile on his face. "Of course, none of this would have been possible without the support of the ex-prime minister. He is a good man. I am planning to bring him into my cabinet very soon. He will be an invaluable asset to help rebuild the country."

"Jesus Christ," said Page. "Has that ever happened before? An ex-prime minister swapping parties?"

"Not that I know of," replied Healey curtly. "There is always a first time for everything. Anyway, we are desperately short of good politicians. I've had to unload of rotten apples recently as I'm sure you've seen."

"How did you do it, sir?" asked Page.

"I saw them all one by one. I showed them all the evidence that we had against them from McGovern's treasure trove. Then I looked them in the eye and told them to quit or they would face criminal charges for corruption. Needless to say, they all jumped at the chance."

"There's still a lot of corrupt police officers to deal with, sir," said Nicholls.

"Yes, I know, Jimmy," he said tiredly. "It will be your job to pick them off one by one."

Nicholls looked puzzled. "What do you mean, sir?"

Healey grinned and held out his hands playfully. "Not that I mean you have to start straight away, son. Take a holiday with your brother and your sister first. You all deserve a break."

"You've lost me sir?"

"I want you to head the Met's anti-corruption unit. I think you'd be perfect for the role."

Nicholls was lost for words. "I don't know what to say, sir."

"You don't need to say anything. Holiday first and then we'll talk when you get back" Healey winked sardonically at Nicholls. "I hear you've got quite a bit of money in your account these days. You have my blessing to spend it however you want. My feeling is that you've all earned it."

"We could all go to the Caribbean?" said Kane coyly, nudging his brother in the ribs.

Healey's eyes narrowed. "Flack?"

"We've got some good news."

"You've found his informant in the press?" said Healey excitedly.

Kane grinned. "Not me. Jimmy tracked him down by cross examining Flack's accounts and phone records. We then lured him out into the open."

"The evidence?"

"We've got it all," said Kane proudly. "Flack's leverage has gone."

Healey took a few seconds to compose himself as he absorbed the incredible news. He took a deep breath and smiled. "Well, I've heard the Caribbean is beautiful at this time of the year." He stood up abruptly and helped himself to another beer. "I must go to another meeting. Please do say hello to the commissioner for me."

Nicholls watched the prime minster leave in awed silence. He didn't know where his life was going, but he knew he wouldn't be alone, and that made him glad.